THE
PALACE
OF
EROS

ALSO BY CARO DE ROBERTIS

The President and the Frog

Cantoras

Radical Hope (ed.)

The Gods of Tango

Perla

The Invisible Mountain

AS TRANSLATOR

The Divine Boys, by Laura Restrepo

Surrender, by Ray Loriga

Against the Inquisition, by Marcos Aguinis

The Neruda Case, by Roberto Ampuero

Bonsai, by Alejandro Zambra

THE
PALACE
OF
EROS

CARO DE ROBERTIS

PRIMERO
SUEÑO PRESS
———
ATRIA

New York London Toronto Sydney New Delhi

An Imprint of Simon & Schuster, LLC
1230 Avenue of the Americas
New York, NY 10020

First Primero Sueño Press hardcover edition August 2024

PRIMERO SUEÑO PRESS **/ ATRIA** BOOKS and colophon are trademarks of Simon & Schuster, LLC

Simon & Schuster: Celebrating 100 Years of Publishing in 2024

For information about special discounts for bulk purchases, please contact Simon & Schuster Special Sales at 1-866-506-1949 or business@simonandschuster.com.

The Simon & Schuster Speakers Bureau can bring authors to your live event. For more information or to book an event, contact the Simon & Schuster Speakers Bureau at 1-866-248-3049 or visit our website at www.simonspeakers.com.

Interior design by Jill Putorti

Manufactured in the United States of America

1 3 5 7 9 10 8 6 4 2

Library of Congress Cataloging-in-Publication Data

Names: De Robertis, Carolina, author.
Title: The palace of Eros / by Caro de Robertis.
Description: First Atria Books hardcover edition. |
New York : Atria Books, 2024.
Identifiers: LCCN 2023043251 (print) | LCCN 2023043252 (ebook) |
ISBN 9781668035238 (hardcover) | ISBN 9781668035245 (trade paperback) |
ISBN9781668035252 (ebook)
Subjects: LCSH: Psyche (Greek deity)—Fiction. | Eros (Greek deity)—Fiction. | LCGFT: Mythological fiction. | Novels.
Classification: LCC PS3604.E129 P35 2024 (print) | LCC PS3604.E129 (ebook) | DDC 813/.6—dc23/eng/20231116
LC record available at https://lccn.loc.gov/2023043251
LC ebook record available at https://lccn.loc.gov/2023043252

ISBN 978-1-6680-3523-8
ISBN 978-1-6680-3525-2 (ebook)

for queer folks, all of us, far and wide and throughout time

they remember what their god whispered

into their ribs: *Wake up and ache for your life.*
—NATALIE DIAZ, "POSTCOLONIAL LOVE POEM"

Of course, women so empowered are dangerous.
—AUDRE LORDE, "USES OF THE EROTIC: THE EROTIC AS POWER"

All of time collapses in the immediacy of desire. Eros has known this since before the world began.

Perhaps because of that, she should have predicted how loving a mortal woman could topple her. How what happened in that palace with Psyche would shake her, transmute her, bring her to her knees, forever change the way her arrows glittered as they soared.

But she didn't predict it. Did not see it coming.

Eros knew all about ecstasy, and passion, and transgression. As the goddess of desire, she harnessed these forces, and for centuries she'd watched them level the lives of men and gods alike.

But this.

This.

The question she'd burn with later, when forced to see the cost of her defiance: Why? Why do it, why risk everything?

Did I do it for her?

Or did I do it to be true?

PART ONE

Earth

1

I arrived at her palace by soaring from a rock where I'd been left for dead. How I came to be on that rock is not the core of my story, but it's where I'll begin—for all stories have roots, as plants do, as people do. As legends do. In the case of legends, too much distance from the root can twist the tale into a lie. Think of the hordes who want it that way, who obscure on purpose. You've seen it, haven't you? The way they balk at a story with too many sharp edges or unfamiliar colors? How bards and gossips warp a tale to their will? I know why they do it, the allure of audience delight. The trouble comes when feeding that delight means flattening out what gives a story life and power, its wilder shapes, the jagged or the billowed, the spike and fall of songs usually buried under silence. There are truths that some don't want to hear. Without those truths, stories lose their teeth. Limbs. Bones. It's safer that way, for gossips and bards. Which is why I don't trust them when it comes to my story with Eros, the story of Eros and me.

I wouldn't trust them either if I were you.

Sit closer. Let me give you my telling, starting at the root.

*   *   *

According to my mother, I arrived in the last hour before sunrise, so fast the village healer didn't come in time and instead I fell into the trembling hands of a kitchen maid. You burned, my mother said, like an arrow made of sunlight, as if you could shoot through me, as if you'd turned my flesh to air, that's how you flew into the world. Insistent, you were. You wept that night as if you missed the motion. You were not quiet like your sisters when they were born. This frightened me, so I sang you an old song about the earth, to help you land here, my love, my dear Psyche. To blunt the longing. Girls need that.

"To be close to the earth?" I asked.

"To stop dreaming of flight."

I was five then and entranced by the rare thrill of a walk alone with my mother as we carried the washing from the river. The story landed in me like a welcome stone, forming ripples I was still too young to understand.

Later I'd know.

About flight, and girls, and dreaming. How a body can be arrow, can be air, can burn.

When the men came, my world shattered—but before that, I was un-afraid, and I knew joy. I will tell that, too, for I want you to have the whole story, a story as whole as I can weave in language not made to hold these truths, not made for me, or you. Perhaps you'll know the feel-ing, and the limitations of my speaking won't matter, you'll understand. Perhaps you too recall a time when you were small and the days gleamed with secret light, as if the walls and bowls and stones and river and leaves each caught the sun inside them and shivered with the glow of their own being. I was completely alive inside. I was still free. Joy hid everywhere.

In the scent of grass and dirt when I lay on the ground. In the feel of heat on my skin on summer days, and the whip of cold in winter. In the rush of the river around me when I bathed there, a living aqueous body surrounding mine. In the way a tree could subsume me, swallow my shadow into its own like water poured to water, blending dark with dark, a recognition and a coming home. In the ease of sinking my body into the cool scope of a tree, oak or olive, fig or pine, blended into them, until I felt my roots deep in the earth below and my head green with leaves reaching greedily up to the sun. In the rich murmur of rain against our roof, spilling tales from the heavens, a wet weeping and laughter of secrets I longed to translate or swim into with my human mind. I could stay up all night listening to the language of the rain. I dreamed I could be rain, sky, river, tree. I dreamed I could be melted by my love for the world. Poured and blended. Lost, remade.

These were silent journeys, utterly private. I never spoke of them to anyone. When I was very small, I thought everyone lived this way inside, in a constant connection to infinity. Including my sisters. Though in the end, it was my sisters who showed me how wrong I was to imagine that everyone was like me. Theirs was a different way of moving through the world. It was often my sisters who called me back from the dream-space, into the task at hand. *Psyche, what are you doing, you're distracted again, what's the matter with you, hurry up, the dark is coming soon!*

They were ever-present as the air itself, my sisters, Iantha and Coronis, Coronis and Iantha. Elegant and limber as the saplings that rise at the river's shore. They towered over me; they interrupted my reveries but also brought shape and life to my days. These two tall girls who knew things I did not, who were older than me. I watched them in a kind of enchanted awe.

Iantha was the eldest, sharp-witted, always the first to know things: when a goat was about to give birth, which river rocks made the best stepping stones, how to stitch fast without stabbing your own fingers, when the traveling merchants had arrived in the village with ribbons and spices and thread. She had a laugh capable of reducing a person to the size of a mushroom, or warming the hardest stone. I feared that laugh and pined to hear it. Her presence woke me and yet dwarfed me, all at once. I wanted to be near her; I was nurtured by her shadow.

Coronis was the middle sister, the most fair. Her hair was the color of threshed wheat, though she preferred to hear it called the color of the sun. She could not match our elder sister in wits, but made up for it in charm, for she moved with a dancing grace even when picking figs or scrubbing pots, and when we were small it was she who had the reputation as a beauty bound to steal the hearts of men and earn her a place beside a king.

The two of them often kept their thoughts to themselves or to the tightly sealed container of their bond. With a quick glance they could enact a whole conversation that was impossible for me to decipher. They were inseparable even when they quarreled, even when they would not direct a word to each other. They'd learned to read each other's thoughts before I was born; they saw no need to slow down their secret language so I could understand. I had the constant feeling that my older sisters held—in their palms, their thoughts, their voices—the keys to the world. I wanted to see or hear the glint of what they knew, what they shared with each other.

I'd follow them around as they played their games and did their spinning and weaving, or washed their clothes at the river. I often struggled to keep up with them on my shorter legs, and well they knew it, for they laughed at the sight of me loping out of breath to catch up with them in the forest, though at other times they'd help me through brambles or across the stream with its stepping stones. I was always determined to stay close and hear every word they exchanged, no matter the subject, as they whispered or chatted or howled: what they thought about this or that boy they'd glimpsed at a distance in the village; the meaning of a tale they'd heard the servants murmur at the fire; how to oil their hair so it shone as if lit from within.

When they oiled their hair, I watched them studiously, then snuck some of the unguent to try, hoping it might seep into my scalp and unlock some special powers in my mind, though all it got me was a scolding when I was discovered. *Psyche! You're too small for that! Look at the mess you've made!* And only then did I see the slick puddle on the floor. I'd been so eager to reach for the bottle, entranced by olive oil, the way it made my fingers gleam and slide against each other, that I hadn't noticed the spill. Messy Psyche. Wild, impulsive Psyche. As my sisters braided their hair—as well as mine, with calm, steady hands whose touch I relished—they talked their future husbands into being. My hair was the darkest among the three, a deep black punctuated by slender strands the shade of fertile soil. Secretly, I loved my hair, the only part of me that inspired a private—what? Not vanity, exactly, so much as a sumptuousness, a sensual joy in my own self, though of course I knew better than to breathe a word of it to anyone, how I liked to run my fingers through its richness when no one was looking, how the swing of braids against my body pleased me, how I loved that my hair took after our mother's own black curls.

For I was dark like my mother, like the people of this valley before the Greek ships came. My mother's mother was born three years before the Greeks arrived, with their spears and swords and insistence on claiming the land. They claimed the women, too, and the girls, especially the girls. I know little about my grandmother. I've pieced together her story from scraps of telling, dropped by my mother in the women's room on long afternoons in a voice so quiet you had to lean in close to catch the words. I know my grandmother remembered her own mother weeping in the corner of the kitchen, curled into a ball behind a curtain of her loose black hair, because her husband had disappeared. The disappearance was never explained to my three-year-old grandmother beyond the words *he is gone*, which her mother repeated like a hymn or curse. There was no body, no blood, no funeral pyre, no tracks to where he might have fled, no speaking of his story or his name. Only an absence, soon filled by a Greek merchant who took my great-grandmother as his wife. She bore him more children. The children from before, like my grandmother, grew up careful to serve and obey and stay in their stepfather's good graces, for their fate was now in his hands.

When my grandmother was fourteen, she was married off to a much older man who'd recently come from Greece. This was Iloneus, my grandfather. He established a farm across the mountains that ring our valley, happy to finally claim his own patch of earth, a far more fertile place than the rocky crags from which he'd sailed on his ship of hungry men, or so he told his children. My mother was among those children, listening quietly as she refilled his wine. She grew up speaking only Greek, for her father, Iloneus, forbade the old language from the home. It came to her only in music. Her mother hummed as she wove, sang softly in the night, soothed children with tunes when no one else could hear. Those are the songs my mother gave us when we were small, which enfolded my sisters and me, like the one she crooned when I was born. Old songs. In the old language, the language of the land, she sometimes called it. The melodies flowed like a stream over dark stones. Sounds unmade of meaning, unclasped from thought or time. Sounds that carried what could not be spoken, soul to throat to ear to soul. I didn't learn the songs, but they settled in me, deep inside me and yet absent at the same time.

My mother was both Greek and something else, and the something else carried on in my olive skin and thick black hair. Not all the Greeks were pale and fair-haired, but our father was, and Coronis took after him, while Iantha was a blend of the two, her hair a medium brown, her skin tone somewhere between Coronis's and mine. Both of my sisters took pride in their lighter locks and the rarity of their hazel eyes. They believed this would give them an advantage in the future, especially fair Coronis. It was not only vanity that made them think so, for everyone believed it, including my mother, who was the most beautiful woman I could ever have imagined yet who believed the daughters who were lighter than her stood the stronger chance with suitors. Nobody saw the future coming. Not one of us could have glimpsed it even in a dream.

"They will fall on their knees for us," Iantha would say, tugging slightly too hard on a rope of my hair, braiding with efficient flicks.

Coronis smirked. "Especially for me."

"Hmmf! Perhaps." Iantha sounded grudging. "But I'll make up for it with my wit; I'll charm them with my stories. Sit still, Psyche."

"Sorry." I stopped my fidgeting so their talk would carry on.

"Ah, Iantha!" Coronis batted her playfully. "On what cloud are you? You think suitors want to hear a girl talk?"

They laughed, together. I laughed along, tentative, uncertain.

"What do you think is so funny?" Iantha said. "You can't possibly know what we're talking about."

I bit my lip in confusion; I knew there had been a joke, but its meaning hovered just outside my understanding. Why wouldn't suitors want to hear a girl talk? What was funny or ridiculous about that? If a man liked a girl and wanted her for a bride, wouldn't he want to know her thoughts? Especially if that girl was Iantha, whose stories and flights of fancy could have captivated the dullest rock. My favorite nights were those when Iantha agreed to tell us stories into the dark, inventing monsters and wondrous landscapes for our horror and delight. Coronis loved her stories too, though she was grudging about saying so. What were the other things the men would want, if not that? They made no sense, suitors. I couldn't fathom why my sisters held them in such high regard.

"I know enough."

"You don't," Coronis said. "And you shouldn't have to know yet. It's better that way."

"Don't rush into knowing," Iantha murmured in agreement, as she put the finishing touches on my braid. "In any case, you'll need to be a lot less wild and loud if you want suitors to take you seriously."

"Maybe I don't need them." I held my chin high with a bravado I did not feel.

"You see?" Coronis stroked her smooth hair. "She does not know."

It began the year after my first blood. My father had been calling on my sisters to sit in the presence of men who came to visit. Iantha and Coronis were to be silent and still as the men talked. I was also of marriageable age, but my father wanted to leave me out until he'd seen to the two elder girls. I was glad of this. I had no wish to join them, no wish to be betrothed; in fact, in that time, I spent my days studiously avoiding thoughts of the future, which seemed like a forest path that would grow narrower and more brambled with each step. Soon there would be nowhere to turn, no move that wouldn't leave me stabbed by thorns, and no way of turning back. I was old enough now to understand that marriage was inevitable, no matter how little I wanted it. I did not envy my sisters. I searched their faces when they returned from that hall in the evenings. Sometimes I glimpsed streaks of pride or worry, and other times there were reactions I couldn't decipher, hidden beneath a blankness I'd never seen in them before. I avoided the hall where my father received the strange men, devoting myself to helping the servants with the cooking, and to all the tasks of the women's room: sewing, spinning, and above all the loom, whenever my mother let me have her seat. I wove ferociously. I wove as if the motion could slow time and keep me there forever, keep me free.

One afternoon, my mother sent me into the hall with a platter of sliced pears and goat cheese, for the enjoyment of the guests. Later, I would wonder whether she came to regret that decision and wish she'd gone herself, sent a kitchen girl, or at least made me veil my face. But who could say whether any of that would have made a difference? Perhaps, if that hadn't been the day, the Fates would still have found a way to infiltrate my world with the venom-dipped thread of my destiny, for they say the threads of Fate will always find the human lives for which they were spun.

I felt the guest's gaze on me as soon as I entered the room. Keen weasel eyes in a face sagging with sweat. He stopped speaking in the middle of a sentence and watched me put the platter on a table to his side. My father, sensing a shift in the air but unsure of its source, launched into fast talk, something about goats and ravines, but the man did not seem to be paying attention.

"Tell me, Lelex, who is this?"

"My third daughter, Psyche." My father's voice stayed courteous, but I heard the stiffness in it. The dismissal, meant for me.

I felt the eyes of the suitor rove my body. My father's anger bright as flame. And my sisters' confusion, beaming from them, the hardest part to bear.

My cheeks burned as I left the room. I stung with more than I could name. Humiliation. Invasion. Inner chaos. What had I done? How had I brought my family shame?

The next day, we were at work in the women's room when a servant came to call the three daughters of the house into the main hall.

"What?" Iantha glanced at me. "Her too?"

"He said all three."

The air bristled around us as we walked to the main hall. I felt the heat of my sisters' thinking, but they did not say a word.

Three men sat with our father, one of them the suitor from the day before. My father gestured for us to sit along the wall, where three stools waited.

"There she is," the first man said.

They stared at me openly, all of them at once. It was too many eyes. Even then, with only three men, I felt diminished by their looking and struggled to keep my hands still in my lap.

"So," one finally crowed, "it was no lie."

"You've lost your wager, Horace."

"What wager?" said my father. "What's this?"

The men laughed. They were merchants, they said, and the night before they'd gathered at a camp between this village and the next, talking over the fire. That was where the two new suitors had heard tell of a maiden more beautiful than the goddess Aphrodite herself, and not only more beautiful but also interesting in a manner Aphrodite could not claim, with her golden hair and pale skin, which everyone had long agreed to be the height of beauty and perhaps it was, perhaps it had been, perhaps it even always would be, but there was a different kind of beauty distilled to perfection in the mortal maiden in question, a different flavor, a different taste. Dark beauty, lush as night. They hadn't believed the tales, but as the wine flowed they'd been drawn into the story, sparked by it, and ultimately moved to place their bets. Horace had bet against the existence of such a mortal girl, while the other man had bet in favor. Now they'd come to see with their own eyes.

The word *taste* dug into my skin like a splinter. I did not want to be tasted.

To either side of me I felt my sisters burn.

My father stroked his beard, a gesture he often used to hide bewilderment or inner turmoil, though those who didn't know him might well mistake it for a sign of contemplative thought. I wanted to beg him to send the men away, to let me go, I did not want any part of their wager, not the win or loss.

But my father was trapped by the laws of hospitality, and could not easily send away his guests. A good and wealthy man receives visitors gracefully, for if not, what is he hiding? And whom might he anger? Guests are sacred to Zeus himself and could one day be a god in disguise. Stories abounded of such visits, steeped in warning. Like the story of Baucis and Philemon, who'd watched all their neighbors drown in a flood for spurning gods as guests. These particular men did not seem godly, but still, it was foolish to risk divine vengeance.

There was more to it, too, for my father. He seemed torn between warring parts of himself. The men's intentions were murky, but their keenness appealed to his ambition. My father was a dreamer, susceptible to grand visions of what could be. Dreaming had driven his life, made him what he was. His great ambition was to secure his status as one of the most important landowners in our valley for he, Lelex, was also a Greek on new shores. He had set out alone from the land of his birth, having fought with his four older brothers for reasons he never spoke of but whose bitterness still lingered on his tongue. He'd sailed over the sea and traveled inland to find terrain where he could anchor a new life, in pursuit of dreams, manhood, prosperity. When he landed, he'd gone to the house of Iloneus, an older Greek who'd voyaged here some years before, and a farmer of some renown. There, while paying his respects, he'd found his bride, my mother, the prettiest of the girls despite her dark features, so he told it in later years to gatherings of men. She'd been young and well-formed, his bride; she should have given him sons. That she had failed to do so was the great curse of his life. In other ways, he'd prospered, raising fat and healthy sheep that supplied wool across the valley and beyond it, to coastal Poseidonia and the ships that launched out from its ports into the greater world. He had land and servants and well-stocked granaries. But his wife had failed him not once, not twice, but three times, saddling him with girls, and I, of course, like every daughter born in the wake of other daughters, was a surplus, a disappointment, a child who should not have been born.

I knew I was not supposed to exist long before I understood why.

Even so. Let my telling be complete. My father was not as cruel as he could have been, not as cruel as other fathers. When wine poured freely, he may have crowed about the curse of us, but sometimes he treated his misfortune as a joke. *Ah, well,* he'd say, raising his glass, *no use complaining, for what can be done about the Fates?*

Then he'd hold my mother's gaze until she smiled.

And now, here he was, facing unexpected suitors. A man burdened with three daughters could not take such a thing lightly. Three daughters, three deadweights—but also, three opportunities to marry girls off to his advantage. Merchants like these were not the goal, but their admiration might be a useful tool.

I saw these calculations pass over his face as he studied the men and let them stare at me.

The visit wore on.

Sun bore in through the single window.

I fought not to fidget on the hard stool. I wanted to get back to the loom, where threads awaited my eager hands. But anytime I shifted in my seat, as if to rise and go, my father's eyes flicked my way to remind me of my duty to spare him any hint of humiliation, strict, but also pleading, or at least I thought I saw a streak of pleading under the surface, and I could not bear to disappoint him. I kept my eyes down. This was expected of a modest girl, but also I couldn't stand their gazes, these men from some night fire down the valley. I'd never walked all the way to the midpoint between this village and the next; they knew more of the world than I did, these men, knew how the valley breathed in the dark, how it felt to stoke a fire beneath the hum of stars, to ride up the peaks that ringed us and down the other side, to follow paths out of villages and into the wild zones between them. I wanted these things they had, wanted to ask them about such journeys, what it was like, how the wind felt as they moved through its veils, but they gave no sign of interest in my thoughts.

Instead, their stares invaded me.

How did my father not see the grime of their looking, the way it slunk right under my skin?

I had never experienced such a thing before and could not grasp what they meant by it; I had no way of shielding myself or turning their attention into anything else. That one of them could ever become my husband—my stomach turned as though I'd swallowed rotten meat. That I'd be forced to obey one of these men for the rest of my life. It could happen, of course, to me as to any girl, but sitting still for these men's stares I felt I'd rather drown myself than succumb to such a fate.

Finally my father dismissed the three of us with a wave, and we returned to the women's room. As soon as we were out of sight of the main hall, Coronis strode fast in front of us, her back a hard wall of reproach. Iantha kept her gaze fixed ahead of her and did not wipe the tears from her face.

In the women's room, we set back to work. The air hung thick with heat, shared breath, unnamed thoughts. No one spoke. I took up the distaff and began to spin, while Iantha measured and coiled the strands. Coronis stood at the loom, where she wove and fumed, wove and fumed, eclipsed by her younger sister in the attentions of men, how could it be? She radiated disbelief, and I wanted to tell her that she could have those sweaty old men if she liked, she could take them all, but I didn't dare say a word.

I spun.

It was good wool, for which our household had earned some modest fame. Spinning calmed me, though it paled in comparison to the loom. Weaving was expansive, a looping and connecting that echoed the patterns of a river after rain, and while weaving I felt large, a roaming soul. I often lost myself deliciously in waking dreams, tempted to veer into designs of my own imagining, to weave visions into being instead of staying faithful to the pattern at hand. Pictures sprang into my mind and my fingers ached to shape them, but these were temptations I had to resist.

The loom was a place for serving the household, not for the fancies of some young girl, as my sisters had reminded me the few times I'd strayed. My mother had chided me more gently, *Daughter, if you chafe at what is needed from you it will only cause you suffering, for life requires doing things whether or not we want to.* I felt her eyes on me now, the warmth of their worry, but I would not meet her gaze. I spun and spun. The distaff heavy in my hand.

How much spinning lay ahead of me in this life and how much else?

I hoped the men would vanish. Prayed for it as I pulled the wool into thread to be measured, to be spooled, to be cut.

The next day, five men arrived: two from the day before, three new. They stayed long and late and drank too much of my father's wine. I sat silent before them, on display, dissolving from my skin.

My father's voice wove into theirs, talk and laughter, as he dutifully played the host—but he seemed unsettled. Shadows lengthened. Servants lit torches along the walls. The men had not risen to go. Finally, my father dismissed Iantha and Coronis with a wave of his hand, for it was clear that these men had no interest in their presence, and why waste an afternoon of women's work? Yet I remained.

The men talked, fell to silence, talked again, did what they wanted, looked where they wanted, gave off their scent, the sweltering, sharp sweat of them. Their rancid hunger on my breath, moving into my body against my will. Inhale. Exhale. I had no defenses against it. I longed to make it stop but didn't know how. My body was speared by them, no escape. Still. Ordered to be still. My mind rebelled and unlatched itself, roved elsewhere, to the curves of the river, yesterday's leaves, the boil of kitchen pots. Anything to separate me from the room where I sat. I did not look at them, but they didn't seem to care. They looked everywhere except my eyes, as if they assumed they'd find nothing there.

When they finally rose to go, my father gestured me away, and I walked down the hall in a body that felt changed, invaded, no longer my own.

The next day there were more, then more again. My father began to leave me with a servant to keep watch, for he could not waste his days overseeing crowds of suitors. For that was what they soon became: crowds. Each time men came, they took with them their stories of what they'd seen, a feat to boast about. They came from across the valley, and then, after a few weeks, from beyond it: men who'd traveled for days to lay eyes on the girl whose unusual beauty was said to rival that of the goddess Aphrodite herself.

Many rumors have flown about that time. Rumor moves faster than human legs, metamorphosing as she goes, all tongues and feathers and swift flight. In her restless hands, lies take the sheen of truth. So let me be clear, let me tell you as bluntly as I can: I never sought the attentions of those men. I did not want them to come see me, I did not revel in them, I longed for them to leave. I have been called arrogant, vain, greedy in my quest to beat Aphrodite on her own terrain. But none of it is true.

I was a beast in a cage, prowling.

Inside I paced and clawed and screeched.

Outside, I was forbidden to move or make a sound.

Eyes everywhere.

Sit, Psyche, sit still and be good.

Sit still and let them look at you.

Trapped by too many eyes.

They came in long trains and gawked through the windows uninvited.

They whispered in each other's ears and laughed.

They stared and stared and stared.

It became an infestation.

Droves of them, from far and wide.

Men everywhere, too much wine poured and food surrendered on trays.

My father couldn't keep up and grew haggard with the strain. Every night, he threatened to beat me if I embarrassed him the following day, if he heard even a word from the men that suggested his daughter had sullied his name, for his name had to be preserved above all else. Yet he did not dare beat me, for the cost to my face would be too great. Instead his blows landed on the servants or my mother. Any bruise I saw on them was the fault of my face.

I began to hate my face, to wish it gone.

I could feel the men's staring gradually scraping it away.

None of us knew what to do. Nothing like this had happened before, in the known history of our valley or beyond. There were no clear rules or traditions to guide the way. My sisters ceased speaking to me, as if I'd betrayed them. When I tried to talk to them, they turned away.

From day to day, my father swung between pride at his sudden fame and outrage at the invasion. He tried dismissing the men; they gathered outside the door in wait.

He positioned me at a window with wool to spin, a basket of it large enough to last the day. "Look at her from outside if you must!" he shouted through the window, ignoring the protests that pummeled his back as he strode from the room. I was relieved that I at least had something to occupy my hands.

Ignore them, I thought. Breathe. Keep your head down. Focus on something else.

Still, the men thickened like flies outside the house. Some left gifts in the grass; my father sent the servants out at the end of the day to collect them, and grudgingly sized them up. Fruit. Ceramics. The occasional textile. Not enough, he complained, to make up for the way

rippling with bitterness, men rippling with dreams, men alight with pain or rage or scorn, men desperate to prove themselves to other men, men brimming over with hopes they for some unfathomable reason seemed determined to pin on a young girl. My father let them all in, and though he grumbled that he had no choice because he couldn't stop the flood, he also seemed greedy for them, as if suitors were like coins: the more you had, the richer you'd be.

But suitors are nothing like coins. Not at all.

You can gather them endlessly and still find yourself with nothing.

A year passed. The crowds persisted. Men who claimed to be suitors packed the sheep enclosure. They came from across the mountains; they came from across the seas. My father, in a fit of optimism about my prospects, and drunk perhaps with newfound fame, built a new, larger corral for me to sit in, which at least was free of sheep droppings.

Rumor had it that the suitors had claimed a copse of trees down by the river, at the edge of my father's land, where, after staring at me, they went to rub themselves and spill their seed while I still shone fresh in their minds. Sometimes alone, sometimes together—so it was told by the old cook to one of the kitchen maids when they thought I couldn't hear.

"They mutter things to each other."

"What things?"

"About the girl Psyche, about this or that part of her, or whatever it is men mutter to each other in such copses of trees—you know."

"I most certainly do not know!" A giggle from the kitchen maid, of horror or glee. "How can you suggest I'd know anything of the sort?"

"Hmmf!"

I didn't know quite what they meant, but their laughter sank into my skin, haunted my nights.

My father heard this rumor, too. He was outraged. His daughter had been sullied and his own reputation bore the stain. For six days he refused to speak to me or look me in the eye, and I felt enfolded by the fog of my nebulous crime.

I learned from my sisters—their resentful whispers in the night, when they thought I was asleep—that news of these suitor visits had spread across the land. It had become so dramatic that it seemed Aphrodite herself was angry, for man after man had compared me favorably to the goddess, and even worse, the altar in her honor at the edge of our valley had grown neglected in my days of fame. Aphrodite was our patron goddess, this altar a main site of worship and requests for love, health, good crops, and other blessings. I had never seen it; I'd never traveled that far. But I'd heard about its beautiful stone table long as a house, carved into a cliff face, to which the devoted journeyed to offer gifts that now had stopped appearing. Her altar was bare. Spiderwebs bloomed in empty baskets. Flowers withered. Fruit rotted and yielded its flesh to crows and there was nobody to replace it. Panic flooded me at the news. It was terrible, dangerous, to anger the gods. I had done nothing, of course, but still, it was my name on wagging tongues. Would she, Aphrodite, all-seeing divine being, understand that I'd had no hand in spreading the stories of me, that I wanted no part of them? Or would I be punished for the acts of men?

"She won't like it," Coronis hissed. "The way Psyche is stealing from her."

"I'm not stealing," I whispered.

"Liar," said Coronis.

"Go to sleep," said Iantha.

But it was true, I was no thief. I tried to comfort myself: Aphrodite would see further than my sisters and give me reprieve. Surely she had more important things to do than worry about some peasant girl in a valley at the edge of the world. Why would she care? She was a goddess. She had altars everywhere, and grand temples in Greece, if my father's tales of his homeland were to be believed. Aphrodite had all the power. She could do anything, be anywhere, exist forever on the great Mount Olympus where the gods lived, where eternity yielded its sweet nectar, or so it was said.

I thought the gods had all the power, while I had none, for I spent all day doing what I was told. I did not yet understand all the curves and eddies of power, that you don't have to steal from the powerful to incur their wrath. You don't, in fact, have to do anything at all. You only need to be perceived as the cause of their discomfort. If the powerful feel something they do not want to feel, and they decide you are to blame, your fate is sealed.

And the gods, they feel things. That too I would one day learn. Some mortals believe the gods don't feel, that they transcend that inner realm somehow, but this I would come to see as one of the gravest mistakes a mortal can make.

2

Eros was not surprised when her mother summoned her to talk about that pesky mortal girl. Human rumors often veered into absurdity, but in this case they were right: Eros's mother, Aphrodite, the goddess of love and beauty, was jealous.

Her jealousy stormed through halls, withered grapes on the vine. It chafed and howled and turned the sky a sooty gray.

Eros watched the darkening through her bedroom window, from her own wing of the palace the two of them shared, and which was not supposed to be their primary home, first because they were Olympians and meant to share that great mountaintop palace with the other gods, and second because Aphrodite had a husband, Hephaestus, who was good and kind, and a good wife stays by her husband's side. But Aphrodite had no interest in being a good wife, or any sort of wife at all. Both she and Eros preferred to hive off to their separate palace, their mother-and-daughter haven, their glowing refuge from the noise and ways of other gods.

A refuge now full of Aphrodite's turbulence.

Sensing it, Eros shuddered, then shrugged. She was accustomed to the tide of her mother's moods. She rode them as smoothly as she rode the air. Whenever her mother seethed like this, it was best for Eros to keep to her own quarters and amusements until the spell wore off and all was calm again.

But this time, Aphrodite's mood did not subside. This time she had no interest in shaking off her own gloom. Instead, she called her daughter to her in a voice rippling with light: *Eros! Now! I need you, child.*

Eros found her at the colonnade that overlooked the orchard and the sea beyond. She stood tall, her white gown and long hair rippling in the wind. The splendor of Aphrodite. Glorious even in her brooding fury, even with the sky behind her dull as ash. "Yes, Mother?"

"You know about this mortal girl, this Psyche."

"Of course," Eros said, resisting the urge to add, *Everybody knows.*

"I can't have it. It cannot be allowed to stand. The balance of the cosmos has been disturbed."

It was absurd, an exaggeration, that this one mortal girl could have upset the entire balance of the cosmos, but Eros knew better than to contradict her mother when she was in such a mood.

"You're going to help me right the scales."

"Me?"

"You, Eros. Here's what you'll do. You'll go to this girl, this rude impostor, and make her fall in love with the ugliest, cruelest, most despicable man on earth."

"Sounds grim."

"It will be! For her. For us it will put things right again."

"Us?" Eros leaned against a marble pillar, gazing at her nails. Unable to resist goading her mother, the queen of poise.

"Of course, us," Aphrodite snapped. "My balance is your balance, and yours is mine! There's a crowd of men there every day. I'm sure you'll find one who'll do. Make sure he's horrible in both body and soul, then stab her with love for him—do it. You will ruin her for me, daughter."

Usually, Eros did her mother's bidding without a second thought, as if their wills were blended into one. But this day was different; she heard imperiousness in her mother's voice, and chafed at it. "Will I?"

"You will! I declare it! Don't test me, Eros."

"Oh, I wouldn't dream of it, Mother."

"I'm serious. Destroy her and I'll be happy, I will garland you with gifts."

"What gifts?" Eros said idly. She had no need of things.

"Whatever you want. A palace beneath the sea."

Eros dropped the pretense of distraction and took a good look at her mother. As always, she was pure beauty, and yet, there was something else in her face, a surprising tightness. This mortal had truly upset her—or perhaps it was the gossip of collective mortals that had done so. All that vast heavenly power her mother possessed, and still she needed worship to assert her domain, to feel the swell of her inner sails. How surprised humans would be at the vulnerability of their gods, Eros thought. Little do they know. They dream themselves as fragile and us as strong, rather than the way things are, each of us a blend of all things. It was strange to see her mother this way, and slightly disorienting, a shift in the delicate interplay between them. "And tell me, Mother, what would I do with that?"

"I don't know. Don't you want an extra palace?"

"In Poseidon's realm? Subject to his moody storms?"

"I thought you'd like it, given how you cavort with sea nymphs."

"I like wood nymphs, too, Mother."

"Fine, then! A palace on land."

"If I want a palace, I can make my own."

"I'll get you something else, anything."

"Hmmm."

"You'd be in my favor."

Here she had the upper hand, and they both knew it. Eros was free enough, these days, to fly where she wished, to love as she wished, all because her mother protected her from Zeus. Her mother kept Eros's secrets, served as her daughter's shield among the gods. And she needed a shield, given her past transgressions, what they'd cost her, what they could cost her even now if she didn't stay within certain lines. Though it wasn't so bad, was it? She did fine for herself. She didn't miss what she couldn't have, what she couldn't be. So she told herself, and in any case, there was plenty she could still do, within limits, and all she had to give in return was loyalty toward her mother, not so strenuous a thing, for her mother made few demands of her, engrossed as she was in her own pursuits. For this reason, it seemed a fair favor, not too much to ask, to shoot a single arrow into one human girl.

It would be easy, she told herself as she held her mother's gaze—and until she landed at Psyche's home, she even believed it.

3

Looking back, it's clear why the suitor visits failed. My fame wasn't about beauty at all. It was about possession, about who could boast that he'd laid eyes on a girl's dark features. Each suitor claimed his own small piece, as if they could each take a fistful, a shred of sheep's wool—shearing and shearing with no thought for the sheep. Everybody wanted to stare, but nobody wanted to marry a girl so many had claimed with their eyes. This girl whose face and body had been scraped raw by glances from across the land—they were afraid, perhaps, of not having her completely, for how can you own what the public has consumed?

My father's worries were many. During the second year of suitor visits, a drought set in over the land. The rains that usually nourished the earth before winter did not come. Instead, all the farmers in the valley watched the sky helplessly for clouds and feared for their harvests, as the cold steadily set in over bone-dry earth. My father took to pacing nervously, worried for the fate of his crops and livestock in the coming spring.

Also, for all his efforts, my father had failed to arrange a betrothal for the daughter at whom droves of men had gazed. Instead, it was my sisters who gained husbands, though not the ones they might have wished.

Among the suitors who'd come to see me, some were willing to consider the other eligible girls. My father seized his chance and made lucrative matches for them both. Iantha was betrothed to a nobleman from a land too rocky to bear fruit, but rich in livestock, while Coronis was given to the king of a small island known for its salted fish. Both men were as old as the father of their brides, Iantha's husband even older, a widower and a father of four, while Coronis's bore a scar across his cheek that according to servants' whispers had been earned, not in battle as the master claimed, but in a drunkards' brawl.

I tried and failed to read my sisters' expressions in those days after their betrothals. They would have palaces; they would be honored and served and would have fine clothing and food and wine. Those were good things. They meant survival. The men themselves were the price to be paid.

Still, while Iantha seemed more or less resigned, even relieved to have secured a wealthier match than might have been expected and to have avoided the jaws of an unwed life, Coronis brooded. I heard her crying in our bedchamber during the day, when she should have been in the women's room. My mother heard it too but did not go in, neither to comfort nor to insist she return to her duties, instead letting her daughter weep as she would. It was a gift to Coronis, not to force her back to work. Our mother was offering the only balm she could, for when a sorrow can't be stopped, there is solace in giving it room.

I looked over at my mother, bent over her wool as always, hands steady; only a tightness around her mouth betrayed her pain. So many times I'd seen that expression on her face, the fierce determination to turn it all inward and be as strong and hard as copper. I realized that, right now, my mother was hiding her pain so that Coronis didn't have to. All these silent sacrifices. I wondered what it had been like for her in the days preceding her own wedding, whether she had felt afraid, what she had dreamed for her life if she'd ever dared to do so, what had happened to those dreams once she became a wife. I'd never heard the full story of her betrothal, nor seen the village she came from, on the far slope of the mountains that hemmed our valley, closer to the sea than where we lived; her own mother had grown up even closer to the sea, so close that she'd known how it sounded and looked in a blanket of sun. My mother had not seen her childhood home since she was fifteen, when my father hoisted her and a sack full of her dowry onto a donkey that scaled the mountain and died just before reaching our valley, so that she not only traveled the rest of the way on foot but possibly received, from that inauspicious beginning, the curse that haunted her and kept her from producing male heirs. Once, only once, she'd told me that part, about the donkey and its death and the maybe-curse, and as she said it, her eyes never left the loom.

Now my mother worked quietly, not looking up no matter how many times my eyes darted her way. I tried to picture her, fifteen years old, younger than Iantha was now, riding that donkey toward a mountain peak with all her hopes and fears wrapped tight inside her, feeling the creature buckle under her thighs. Her husband, my father, was not a kind or easy man; did she already know that about him on the journey, or did her wedding night reveal it? What shape did that night take for her? I had so many questions, about her own wedding, about all weddings, about wedding nights and the nights that followed, about my sisters' futures and my own, but I didn't dare speak them. There are things that, once known, can't be erased from the mind.

The copse became hazardous. The servant girls tried to avoid the cluster of men on their way to fetch water or wood for the fire, but they could not always succeed, for the men grew bolder, roamed, prowled. They took the girls right there in the bushes, or dragged them to the copse to force them together and—I wish with all my soul that I had never overheard this fact, whispered in the kitchen, a stain I cannot scrub from my mind—as they did it they said my name. There were no more jokes about the copse in the kitchen, only weeping. A girl, a kitchen maid, her name was Melia, was so injured that she could not work for four days. My father was furious. The men had stolen from him, from the labor he was owed. And if she or any of the girls was now with child? How much labor lost, and to whose seed? He blamed me. He glared at me with such intensity that I kept my gaze down—on the floor, on my hands—whenever he was near. I feared that Melia might blame me too; this thought came to haunt my dreams and wake me in the night, cold with sweat. It was a terrible fear, but not unjustified. Once Melia returned to work, her face still bruised, she refused to look me in the eyes, which flooded me with shame. If it hadn't been for me, the poor girl would not have endured such torment. My very name a trapdoor into nightmares. I was tainted, cursed; I was the source of an unspeakable horror.

My father roved the house like a thunderstorm. "Enough! These suitors have bled me dry—no more."

The sheep filled both enclosures after that. My father locked me in a storage room that had no windows, no light, no way for me to be seen.

A new prison, with one cruel comfort: I was finally free from the men's eyes.

The storage room was dank and cold. It smelled of rotted apples and sadness. A grimy strip of light swelled and ebbed beneath the door as day wore into night. I took to crouching down to gulp air from the threshold where the door approached the ground, fresh air, a reprieve that made it worth fighting off rats to claim the space. I slept against a tall sack of grain, shivering under a single blanket, erect as a soldier on guard. I woke fitfully to the scurry of creatures for whom I was an intruder in their domain. Spider bites on my face. Good. Let them maim me, make me ugly so the world would leave me be. Twice a day, servants brought me plates of food and replaced the chamber pot. They did their work in a hurry and always came in twos, one of them standing in the doorway to bar my escape. My father's orders, no doubt. They could have saved their strength. I had no plans to run. What for? Where would I go?

I felt broken. I felt relieved. Maybe once my father's rage subsided and I was allowed out of this room, I could be free; with the suitors gone, I could start a new period of my life, couldn't I? A life of—what? I didn't know. Staying in my father's house forever? Perhaps. Perhaps I could survive it. Perhaps it would be best. Unbearable, but was it not better than marriage? What was worse, a father or a husband? I tried to picture it as the long hours wore on in that putrid dark: growing old as part of this household, a disappointment to my father and subject to whatever humiliations he dispensed, living proof of my family's misfortune, but still, free at least from the staring of crowds or whatever a husband would choose to do to me, and my mother would be here and I could weave alongside her on some days if I was lucky; I'd stay at this house I'd always known, where light slashed through air with all the magnificence of a royal mantle and most important of all, no more girls would be hurt in my name. Hope flickered in me. I dozed on the filthy floor, allowing dreams to circle me and sink into my skin, dreams in which I was a child again, dancing by the river as the night grew wings.

After five days—or perhaps it was six, for though I'd tried to count the days, they'd bled into each other and mixed their hues—my mother came to the room. She hovered in the doorway, looking at me for a long moment before she spoke.

"You can come out now," she said quietly.

"Is it thanks to you? Did you convince him?"

I knew the answer from the softening in her eyes. "That doesn't matter. Come, daughter, let's get you changed."

It was then I saw the fresh gown in her hands. I'd worn the same clothes all these days.

My eyes stung. I closed them, fought the tears. But when I felt her crouch beside me and pull me into her arms, I lost the fight.

I buried my face in her shoulder. "I'm scared." The scent of her. Violets and wool and the warmth of burning wood.

"My beloved child, my star, my light," she murmured, and a great tide of solace flooded me at the kindness in her voice—all will be well, I thought, it is over and my mother is here—until she finished her sentence: "So am I."

Things were not better, as I had hoped.

Rumor had continued to glide across the land, brushing every surface with her fingers.

Disaster propelled her movement, for the drought had lasted all of autumn and now winter descended on the land. The earth curled its fist around parched seeds. Bark split and cracked along branches. Vines collapsed from their trellises in defeat. The grass that fed the valley's sheep had withered beneath their hoofs. Cold pressed its great cloak over everything, and still no smattering of rain. Everyone knew, from the last drought before I was born, what would happen when the spring came, what the loss of an entire rainy season would mean. Sick, lethargic sheep. Lambs dying in the womb. Paltry crops and too little bread. People would go hungry and coffers would leak out their wealth. When I saw my father, I knew immediately from his haggard face that trouble was upon us, not only because of what the drought would do to our stores and livestock, but because of what it meant.

That the gods were angry.

That a goddess was angry.

At me.

A drought was coming, and the fault was mine because I'd offended Aphrodite. I feared her revenge, even though I hadn't stolen from her and didn't want what was hers. Beauty inspired violence. Look at Melia, the flatness in her eyes as she carried in the bread, the stiffness of her back as she avoided me. A pit of shame tore open inside me at the sight of her. What kind of life is that? I thought. Tell me, Aphrodite, what kind of life can that be? But what I thought didn't matter, as it could not remove the disgrace that clung to our family like grime.

The days wore on. Cold surrounded us, sank into our bones, chilled our dreams. We moved through the depths of winter in a house shrouded by silence.

My sisters seethed. In their eyes, I'd orchestrated this whole disaster to keep myself at the center of attention, just as they approached their wedding days, which would take place at the first hints of spring. Now, because of the panic about grain stores and dying crops, the feasts would be curtailed; the meat would be more meager, the bread less plentiful, all because their little sister had insisted on bringing a curse down on the land. The village still buzzed with talk about me, and though it was not kind talk, it bristled with insults, it was still my name on the people's tongues, not theirs.

"It's not fair," Coronis said one night, as I pretended to be asleep. "It's our time, and here she is again, usurping everything."

"I know," Iantha replied. "But at least we're finally getting married."

"So?"

"We have places to go. Good homes. Good matches."

"How do we know they're good?" Coronis sounded small, in a manner I'd never heard from her; she'd always been the brash one. I stayed very still, kept my breathing steady so they wouldn't know I was awake, so as not to disturb their private exchange.

"Calm down," Iantha said, not unkindly. "Our father made the matches."

"What does that prove?"

"It proves that they are good."

"You don't really believe that. You're not stupid."

"And all those times you called me stupid?"

I felt Coronis thinking in the dark. I thought she might launch into another thorny exchange; she always tried to compete with Iantha, could never admit her sister was excellent at a single thing. But maybe it was different now. Soon they'd be married, without each other for the first time, in a new house surrounded by strangers.

"You're intelligent, and you know it," Coronis said quietly. "Much too intelligent to believe our father is always right."

Now it was Iantha's turn to be quiet.

"And anyway," Coronis continued, "even if he were, he doesn't know our husbands well. Nor will he be there when they show us who they really are."

Iantha made a small sound into the dark, of reassurance or defeat. Silence stretched out between us, punctuated by the wail of an owl outside. "Sister, when you are married, you'll be cared for, you'll never be hungry a day in your life, you'll have everything you need. All will be well."

"You don't sound sure." Coronis's voice radiated pain. I ached for my sister, so full of life and spirit and sharp-tongued boldness that she would surely not fit easily into her role with that hard-faced man. I wasn't convinced that everything she needed would await her at her husband's home, and it was obvious that Coronis wasn't either. She saw too much. She already knew.

"You'll see," said Iantha.

"Will you see? Will you visit?"

"If I can."

"Promise me you'll visit. And that you'll invite me to come visit you, that we'll have days together, that we'll see each other again."

A tightening in my chest. They had not included me in this part of their dreaming. Already they were lost to me and I to them.

"I promise," Iantha said. "As long as our husbands give their blessing."

The sigh that came from Coronis was not a young girl's sound at all, but the sound of a woman, resigned to her shrunken life. "Of course."

How swiftly they were gone, my sisters. First one, then the other, as soon as the first buds broke through the dirt. The wildflowers were more sparse than I'd ever seen them, but still, they rose, all the more miraculous for their thirsty roots. Persephone was back in Olympus, at her mother Demeter's side—so the story went—and with the goddess of earth's fertility appeased by her daughter's return, the land began to warm. Time for weddings. I helped fill their bridal baths, warmed the water over fire. Clean water and petals for a fresh new life. A body prepared to be given away. Iantha was silent during her bath, and seemed to contemplate each ripple as if for prophecy, while Coronis, a week later, chattered nervously and made demands my mother and the servants and I did our best to indulge. More heat, fewer red petals, more red petals, honey dissolved to keep a bitter life at bay.

For each banquet, my father slaughtered a sheep, as despite the scarcity, at these two wedding feasts there would be meat for everyone. He told me to veil my face and stay in the kitchen as much as possible, helping the servants with the cooking and preparations. He wanted me out of sight, and I wanted the same. My gown became streaked with blood and my hair smelled of burning wood, and I was separated from my place among my family, but none of that mattered to me. Better to vanish from the crowd, the house, my own body. Though I did come to the door to watch my sisters play the bride, one after another, dancing to the drums and flutes and cymbals, Iantha with poised dignity and Coronis with damp eyes and a hesitant gait that spoke of inner turbulence, but only if you knew her, which her groom decidedly did not. He looked on her with satisfaction, the satisfaction of a man collecting good livestock at the market. He glanced over at me more than once, despite my veil, tracing the shape of my body beneath my bloodstained gown. I was relieved when he finally strode to the front door with my sister's wrist in his large hand, hoisted her onto a waiting donkey, and set off for his own kingdom with his newly acquired bride.

The loss of my sisters shook me. They were the only sisters I'd ever known, and there had been a time when we were whole together, despite the thorns of recent years. Even the teasing between us had sometimes felt like a dance that caught and held us, gave us anchor in this world. We had quarreled ceaselessly throughout my childhood, and yet, without them, the world felt colder. Without them there was no childhood left at all.

The very next night, my father announced what he would do.

We were at dinner, just the three of us now.

"Soon I will go see the Oracle."

My mother's jaw went tight, but she kept her voice soft. "The Oracle?"

"At Athena's temple, in Poseidonia, where the priestess can read the will of the gods."

"Please," my mother said. Her hair was braided into a crown around her head, which she held very still, spine straight, eyes fixed on my father. "Please, Lelex, I beg of you."

The air across the table prickled. My mother never pleaded with her husband, never defied him unless the circumstances were extreme. She was taking a risk for me. She remained poised, but I felt the undercurrent of her terror. The Oracle. A priestess who spoke the will of the gods. Any fate she pronounced must be carried out to the letter, no matter how grim. I stirred my stew, tried to understand the danger I was in.

"We have no choice," my father said, though he didn't sound angry, only tired, a burdened man. "This has been the worst drought in living memory. The people blame us. They say we're cursed by Aphrodite. They say the coming years will be just as dry if we don't heed the gods.

We have to know, have to face the curse and find out how to lift it from our heads."

I kept my eyes pinned to the table, searching the grooves in the wood for reprieve. If my father had reached this point, he was ready to risk everything, even me. I couldn't bring myself to eat any more. My insides twisted at the prospect of what the Oracle would say. Stop it, Psyche. Enough. I tried and failed to scold myself into a calmer state.

Was my father trying to save me, or punish me?

Or was he not thinking of me at all?

I scanned my mother for clues, but she'd grown silent as a vine.

Perhaps it'll be all right, I thought. Perhaps divine forces will rule in my favor: Athena or another goddess or god speaking through her priestess will take pity on me and open a path to a bearable life.

It seemed possible, though even then I sensed that was too much for a woman to expect from the world.

Athena's temple stood high on a hill overlooking Poseidonia, a town the Greeks had built when they first arrived. It was four days' travel from home. My father was gone for nine days, during which my mother and I worked quietly together, both at the loom, or I at the loom and she spinning wool, or she spinning wool and I measuring and cutting; she let me weave as often as I wanted, even let me stray from the patterns without reprimand, and I knew without her saying a word that this was a kindness, the greatest one she could think to offer, moments of freedom with color and thread. How well she knew me. I allowed myself to sink into my weaving, to stay in the moment with shape and warp and hue and keep my mind from venturing too far into the future.

At first it seemed too quiet without my sisters, even with the murmur and bustle of servants in the women's room, for we had spent years now spinning together and weaving from what we spun. The servants seemed to sense the shift and let their chatter fall into longer and longer lulls. Gradually, the silence between my mother and me blossomed, as rich as late afternoon sun. It gilded the floors and walls, gilded my skin. I could spend my life this way, I thought, in quiet rooms with my mother; perhaps the Oracle would allow it, even demand it, who knew what an Oracle might say and where the visions came from, but wouldn't that be the best possible decree, to be told never to marry? It was outlandish, too good to be real.

Only this is real, the moment, the loom, the light. Don't think about the future, don't think about what's next. You are here. Later I would wish I'd used that time not only to luxuriate in a shared silence but also to talk more with my mother, to ask her questions, about her youth, her childhood, her own mother, her family's ways before the Greeks came to these lands, the songs they sang and foods they cooked and gods they loved or feared, the whole scope of those past generations and what had been lost; I would wish that I'd filled in my knowledge of her stories and the stories at the root of her that were at the root of me as well; and also, I'd wish simply to have talked with her, to have heard her voice while I still could, to have pulled it into my skin like welcome ointment, her voice, her luminous voice, the voice of the only person who might have protected me if she'd had the power. Though of course she did not have it. My mother could do nothing but grieve in advance for a daughter who wove beside her, and this might have explained her silence. Or it might be that the silence was itself a conversation, a gift. It felt round and golden, surrounding us as the hours passed, offering comfort as I wove against the raw chaos of my mind.

When my father returned, on the tenth night, the look on his face sent my skin crawling. He would not meet my eyes.

I thought he'd send me away so he could speak to my mother, but instead he simply acted as if I were not there.

My mother glanced at me, and I understood her meaning. I should go. I retreated from the main hall but lingered outside the door, where I could still hear everything.

My father began to tell.

After four days, he'd arrived wearily at Athena's temple, which was so close to the sea that when he went to the markets of Poseidonia to buy a bull for sacrifice, he heard the croon of waves against the shore. He said that part with longing in his voice, and I imagined him there, in that coastal town, breathing the salty air and remembering his travel across that water years ago, to find his place in this valley. How did those waves sound? I'd never heard them for myself and did not know. A water-song. I tried to imagine it. My mother knew that sound. I wondered whether she too felt a longing for the sea. She said nothing, and my father went on. He'd led the sacrificial bull up the sloping path to Athena's temple, imposing and tall against the sky. He'd waited his turn. He'd performed ablutions. Blood was spilled and incense burned and prayers droned in all the correct ways. I promise no mistakes were made, he said. Everything was done properly, and still, despite all that, once it was all done and we waited for the Oracle to speak, she was silent for such a long time I thought she'd forgotten we were there, the priest and I, the petitioner and the one who would interpret what she spoke, both of us waiting for her word. When she began, it was not with words, not any I could recognize. She made sounds with an intensity I had not expected. The priest squinted for a moment before he began to translate her vision.

Her marriage . . . , he said.

I waited for the priest to go on, perfectly still, holding my breath.

Her marriage will be monstrous.

These words seemed to break the very air.

"Monstrous?" my mother repeated, cutting into her husband's telling. I heard the shudder in her voice, as if a biting night wind had just swept through the room, though it was a mild spring night and the windows were all covered. Caught in my father's story, I felt the tension that must have filled that temple hall. I could smell the incense, the bull's blood, the sweat and wax of dying candles. "What does that mean?"

"I asked that very question."

He went on.

For a long time, the priest only stared at him in silence, as if seeing him anew. He swayed a little as if he might lose his balance, maybe from the strength of the prophecy. The Oracle, meanwhile, kept her gaze focused on something far above his head. Her palms were lifted toward the heavens, and the expression on her face was like nothing my father had ever seen before. She was a young woman, younger than he'd thought he would find, younger than she'd seemed when he first entered and kneeled before her three-legged stool. She made more sounds, then paused again, seeming to hover in the altar smoke, other-worldly, aloft.

Some marriages, the priest told Psyche's father, *are an intrusion on nature. A crime. Monsters move among us, as we all know.*

My father asked, then, what kind of monster would be wedded to his daughter. As he recounted this, his voice went dull as ash. His question hung in the temple's cloistered air for a long time, until finally the Oracle spoke again.

A slither. The priest lit a candle. *A horror.* Two more candles. *A wrong.*

My father had stood silent, waiting. Surrounded by ghost-visions of fangs, scales, claws.

His words sliced into me. I wondered whether the Oracle had seen this monster, whether it had come to her in fragments or in one great burst, whether she knew more of its body and powers and hazards than she had chosen to tell, or whether she had told it and the male priest had conveyed less than he knew. The vision had passed through so many mouths before reaching me. I had a thousand questions for my father and for the priest and for the Oracle herself. I wished I could stride into that temple hall and talk to her directly, with no interpreters, get as close to the seeing of this monster as possible, for it was I and no one else who would be claimed by it and would have to face it if the Oracle's words were true. And why wouldn't they be? An Oracle sees farther than the rest of us and cannot be defied.

In the months that followed, I'd return to these words and wonder whether the Oracle had actually seen what was to come, the marriage that was to be my fate, whether she'd glimpsed my astounding future as it really was and chosen those words for it with eyes wide open. *A slither. A horror. A wrong.* Her words. Unless they were the words of the priest, who gathered the Oracle's sounds and turned them into prophecy. What space was there between what the Oracle had seen and what the priest put into language? How could they—how did anyone—give language to a thing beyond speaking? What if the word *monster* formed a kind of net with which to trawl the wide sea, gathering anything that didn't resemble the creatures deemed familiar and permitted in your world?

My father had waited for more detail on the monster; none came. Finally, he asked, *What can we do?*

Nothing.

There must be something!

The priest paused to listen to the Oracle one more time, then said, *Only this: give her to her fate.*

And the instructions rained down.

The bride was to be taken to a great cliff that loomed near her village and abandoned there strictly alone, lashed to a rock, left for the wind, left for her gruesome husband to take her to a wedding bed where, surely, given the monstrosity at the heart of this marriage, she would be torn to pieces. It had to be done for the gods to be appeased. Only then could the drought lift and balance be restored.

"It can't be," my mother said. "There must be some other way."

"There is not." My father went quiet, cowed by the force of destiny.

Silence swelled between them.

I crept to the room I used to share with my sisters and curled up on the floor. I lit no lamp. Numbness overtook me, as if shock had dulled my senses. I had shamed my father. He'd never forgive me. I would never have his protection again. He would do everything the Oracle had said, down to the tiniest detail, to save the crops and the sheep and the dignity of his name. My mother had no power to defy him, and she knew it. Bit by bit, sensation returned to my body. My chest ached, my spine burned. I wanted to fight against my fate, but my father had already bent to it.

A curse is not a quiet thing, nor a contained one. It has a way of seeping across barriers, like water through cloth, staining everything. I'd known of people who'd lost their parents' blessing and who'd sunk down past the viable margins of reality, never to be seen again, spoken of only in whispers. The shunning had no recourse. The exile had no end.

That night, in bed, my thoughts ran deeper than language, for language has not yet forged the necessary words. I cannot tell you the shape of what churned in me. I could not sleep. I longed to break out of myself, break out of my own skin.

Where else was there to run?

The stars outside my window shone hard and bright.

The sky vaulted, impossibly far.

I was trapped.

I tried not to imagine my monstrous future husband, but I could not stop my mind.

I thought of Coronis and Iantha, wondered how their wedding nights had gone and how they fared now.

I thought of hope and pain and futures unlived.

I prayed I'd find a way to accept the end of my conscious life.

I could not imagine, alone that night in our childhood room, that my true life in fact had not yet started, that at that very moment it was just beginning to gather into existence like the clouds of a formidable storm.

* * *

My mother insisted on a bridal bath, and I lacked the will or heart to fight her. I knew she meant it as a kindness, wanting to treat me like a real bride, and to offer me that rare luxurious gift of clean hot water for my body and my body alone. In normal times, we bathed in the river, or in the winter, in water we took turns stepping into and that grew more clouded after each use. As the youngest, I was usually the last person to bathe before the servants. But now my elder siblings were gone. And I was still my mother's child, and would be forever, as she seemed to remind me with the building of the fire, the warming of the water, the gentle pouring from a jug over my bare shoulders and chest. Clean water just for me.

She even oiled and braided my hair, humming one of her old songs, the one she'd once said had something to do with the underworld, the old ways of passing through the gates—how had she put it all those years ago? A winged spirit. A carrier of souls. Vanth. How had I remembered that name? The only name of the old gods I'd ever heard her speak. Sole shard of a broken jug once loved. Sharp-edged against my mind. It had been years since my mother told me of this spirit and explained this song to me, and yet I'd retained what she told me. With the help of Vanth, there was no need for Charon to take you across the River Styx, no need for coins to be placed under the tongues of the dead, for instead of paying for water-passage, our ancestors flew. Was my mother singing that song on purpose now? To guard me when I soon approached the underworld? A melody of death. A melody of grace. Not singing, just humming. No words, pure flowing sound, as my mother crooned and bathed me with infinitely tender hands.

There would be no wedding feast, since there was no groom to toast and honor. Only a bride to be sent away, mourned. Why lay out a banquet only for her? What was the point? I was not to be celebrated. I was to be taken to the great cliff and lashed there, left to my violent fate. Still, the people of the village knew of the plan, for my father had announced it to placate those who demanded appeasement of the gods. They had not been invited, nor had they been told to stay away. Naturally, by the time the sun had reached the center of the sky, most of the village had gathered outside our door. I heard them from the room where my mother draped me in jewelry. Bustling. Circling. Vultures, I thought. Eager for a glimpse of dead meat.

"So many are here." My mother placed the veil over my face, her hands as gentle as her tone.

"Of course they are. They wouldn't miss the rare chance to take a bride to be murdered."

"Psyche."

My eyes stung. "It's true, and you know it."

"Perhaps they want to wish you well."

"Well? Well?" So much more I ached to say. *They want me to die, they only care about the curse. They can't wait to see me go.*

"Here." My mother opened a cloth bundle and held up an amethyst necklace, her eyes pleading with me. "For you."

I stared at this treasure, one of the few things she had left of her own mother, whom she'd likely never see again. I was shocked she hadn't given it to Iantha or Coronis, that she wasn't keeping it for herself, knowing my fate. I saw myself torn to pieces, the scattered beads amidst bloodied limbs. I felt that I shouldn't accept such a gift, tried to tell her so, but when I opened my mouth to protest, she silenced me with a look so tender something broke inside me. Her arms encircled me to rest the necklace against my clavicle, and I smelled the violets of her scented oils, the sweet tang of her. She wiped tears from my face. "May it protect you."

The beads hung heavy on me as I walked into bleak sunshine. Through the veil I saw the crowd, their faces hazy and indistinct, though it seemed the whole village had come. My father stood in front of me and began to lead the way. A procession formed behind us, thick, lumbering. A bard struck up a marriage song, but it clashed with the grief-cries of old women and the stifled sobs of my mother, who no longer held back, so soon the bard's lyre turned to songs for burying the dead. What a sharp man he is, I thought, quick to adapt. I felt the people's stares on me, pity and disgust and also relief, for the monstrosity had been found and could be cut from the village like a sore.

Heat glared down on us.

The village paths gave way to rugged slopes.

The walk to the high cliff was long, and by the time we arrived I was gilded in sweat beneath my bridal gown.

One great rock stood overlooking the cliff, with the valley splayed below. The people moved in close; I smelled their sweat and eagerness to see what came next. They had known me, watched me grow up, greeted me in the plaza, extolled my beauty, been the faces of the only village I'd ever known. Faceless now, through the veil, for which I was grateful.

"Come here." My father pulled me by the arm and pressed my back against the great rock. He lashed me to it, as he'd been instructed to do. The looping of ropes seemed to take a long time. Nobody was singing now. Everybody watched. What for? What were these ropes meant to achieve? What had the Oracle been afraid of? That I might rebel and try to throw myself to my death in despair? That by dying before becoming a wife I'd ruin my family's chance to satisfy the gods? It wasn't such a great sacrifice for them, in the end—a girl, an unmarriageable girl. I thought of the old tale of the king who'd wanted the wind to fill the sails of his ships so he could wage war and win gold. Agamemnon. He'd sacrificed his own daughter to do it, let her throat be cut or slashed it himself, perhaps, wielded the knife at the altar, a girl-child killed to placate the gods. In that story, the girl had been innocent and good, but even so, the loss of her was nothing compared to what a man could gain. I felt neither good nor innocent—I'd caused violence against other girls—and so I was a smaller thing to lose. My father checked his handiwork, meticulous, almost delicate in his fingering of the knots. I tried to catch his gaze for a final moment, but he wouldn't meet my eye.

"Remember to obey him," he said. "So the curse can be lifted."

I didn't answer.

"Psyche." A warning in his tone.

I tried to look at him, but he seemed keen to find some lost speck in the void beyond the cliff. He looked tired and old. Worn down by time. I thought of the tales of him on that ship from Greece, scanning the horizon for his wide dreams. It should not have mattered to me, his refusal to meet my eye, his firm pull on the ropes as if securing a bundle of threshed wheat, but something tore open deep in my body, a great claw of grief. I wondered what to say, in this last moment with my father. I found no words in the hot fog of my mind. He kept his eyes on the ravine, and I thought he was preparing to say something else—to scold, admonish, or bid farewell—but he only sighed and turned to walk back down the mountain. My mother had been watching with a tear-streaked face, just behind him. I hadn't seen her. She met my gaze; I was the one who turned away first, overwhelmed by what I found in her eyes.

The crowd gradually turned and followed my father down the path, one by one, my mother among the last of them, and they no longer sang nor sobbed, a trudging silence like the silence of a tomb. They snaked down the slope, around the curve, and out of sight.

I took a gulp of raw air.

I was alone.

I strained against the ropes that held me. I slumped against them, strained again. Waited. I burned with too many thoughts and no thought at all. I writhed against the cords as if to free myself, though I could not, and even if I did, where would I go? Nowhere, I was nowhere, I was nothing, my future a blind terror.

Time passed, minutes, hours, I don't know.

In that time a flooding of my mind.

I closed my eyes, succumbed to dreams.

Ropes against the hot blue sky. Whipping, as if the heavens roared with horses driven to a gallop. Looping, as if to catch a mare. Taut against hungry clouds.

I lost my hold on time, there was no time;

at the lip of death there was no time;

and then they were coming undone, the ropes—not the feverish ones of my dreaming, but the real ones against my skin. Knot, curve, tether. Opening as if by some invisible, agile hand. Had the wind grown fingers? Had the monster—or his servant—come to collect me? I didn't dare open my eyes.

Perhaps it was Zephyrus, the great wind, known for his limber tricks.

I stood untied, exposed to swirling air.

Lean, said the breeze in my ears,

and in that moment I forgot to be afraid.

Instead, I stayed dead—pure spirit tipping out of life into whatever lay beyond.

I leaned forward. Eyes squeezed shut.

Yes   lean

A gust arose and wrapped me in its wings, and then—

We flew

4

It was all ready now.

The girl at the rock. The destination.

What a ploy, what a beautiful scheme.

She'd done it because she had to.

How buoyant Eros had felt that day before she reached Psyche's house, flying over with her plan to doom the girl. Not the kindest thing to do, but it could not be helped, could it, once a powerful goddess decided to ruin your life? It wasn't Psyche's fault, of course; she hadn't done anything, except get caught in a web of divine conflicts, or perhaps, shine too hard. Such a shame that this should be a crime. Eros felt for her but brushed the thought away. At times, her duties were messy. She got her hands dirty. It couldn't be helped. She tried to avoid it, she tried to be kind, except when trickery rose up in her and she saw red and let power fly from her bow, tipped with heat and the promise of chaos. Her gold-tipped arrows could defy the very Fates, they could save lives or destroy them, be gifts or tools or weapons, but she told herself that in this case (unlike other cases, unlike the case of Daphne, which still stung the edges of her mind), her conscience would be clean. She was a messenger, nothing more. It would not be her own hand that caused destruction, but the hand of Aphrodite as it steered her daughter's arrows. Let it be done. Let the aim be sharp and swift, a purpose finished by the time the sun sank behind the hills, and then she could rest easy in her mother's favor and forget the whole affair.

But then she landed, and saw the girl.

Sitting in that fetid sheep enclosure, thronged by men.

The girl: Psyche.

Something collapsed inside Eros, the border between her conscious thought and the infinite primordial dark below.

It was clear why the men had gathered—her features were exquisite, that was plain—but this alone would not have brought Eros to her knees. She fought to stay standing, fought back tears. The spark of this girl burned bright and furious. It tore into the core of Eros's being and claimed a place there. The girl's hands were folded in her lap, at times still, at times tapping against each other as if one were delivering a secret message to the other's bones. She kept her face composed, but beneath that calm, dutiful exterior she seethed with rage; how could the men not see it? Why weren't they trembling? How could they look so easily on her when her fury was a lamp to sear the skies? All those men crowded around her, gawking, saw her as a sculpture, as something to be looked at and controlled, they would almost have preferred her to be stone if it weren't for the fact that stone was too cold and hard to fuck, the bastards, the vermin, staring at her without bothering to wonder how the poor girl felt or what she wanted, nor bothering to see what she really was. Wild. Wildness in its purest form. It was utterly clear. In her eyes, in the way she perched on that cursed stool. A presence in her, untamable and vast. And as for Eros, what did she know of fury, of wildness, of power? How had she thought she'd known the world without seeing this girl's soul? She longed to see more, to see everything, longed to get close to the heat of her and hear her every secret. She wanted to give her all the treasures of land and sea just to watch her touch them, one after the other, in curiosity and delight. Treasure had no more important use than to be fondled by this girl's hands. And she felt in that instant that she existed to bring pleasure to this girl, to bask in her, to offer her all the passions, all the world.

In short, she'd fallen for her target.

She could not yoke her to a despicable man.

Gruff laughter rippled around her, the result of some ribald joke among the men. She wanted to cut them down for it, and that urge brought danger into sharp relief. She'd come here with a mission that she now had to betray. She wanted the impossible. She had to think. She had to devise the trick that could make the impossible true.

I could still shoot, she thought, get her to fall for me—but no. She did not want to enchant her way into Psyche's heart. That was too easy, too incomplete. She felt the weight of ages inside her, what she'd lost, what she'd given up. No. No arrows: the girl must come to her in her own way, spurred by her own strange and mortal spirit. Either she'd earn the girl's love honestly, or she wouldn't earn it at all.

Meanwhile, here was the arrow she'd brought for her mission. If she wanted to deceive her mother, she shouldn't bring it home.

She nocked the arrow, raised her bow, drew. Aimed at an arrogant young nobleman and fired. She caught him perfectly, just as he was idly gazing over at a bent old merchant in the crowd. There it went, his face, the nobleman's face, melting into tenderness and hunger. When the merchant caught him looking, he was befuddled at first, then curious. Good. Let those two men tangle their stories and bodies and lives, let them revel or weep, let them soar or let them burn. That was up to them. She turned away, finished with their destinies, mind elsewhere. Up into the air she launched, scheming as she flew home.

She had to love this girl.

She had to save her.

She had to find a way to hide.

It was the only way to defy the gods and carve a space for herself and her beloved from the cold rock of the world.

And so she'd done it.

She'd set it all up and now it was ready.

She was proud of herself, why deny it?

She, Eros, known to be a trickster, had devised the most elaborate trick of her life. Nothing in the past compared to the complexity and ambition of this plan. So many twists and turns, dead ends and portals: the message sent down through the Oracle, transmitted to the father at a slant by a frightened and strategically inebriated priest; the mysterious instructions to leave Psyche at the rock as a lone bride; the transport of wind down into a ravine concealed from the roads and whims of mortal men; the glory of what waited in the ravine, just for them. Brilliant. If she'd been vain, she might have had to boast of her accomplishment, the way Odysseus did after besting the Cyclops, breaking his own anonymity and baring himself to Poseidon's long revenge. A dumb mistake. A mortal man's mistake. She would not make it. She wrapped her plan in utmost silence: nobody would know, least of all her mother, who was usually her closest confidante but in this case would be deadly if she saw.

From a distance, she felt Psyche rise from the rock, borne aloft, held and carried by the wind. Cradled in a nest of air. She longed to approach her, to trace her arc against the sky, but she pulled her sight away. Not yet. For the magic that surrounded Psyche's destination was no ordinary shielding spell, the kind you pulled around your own body to hide from fellow gods; this magic encompassed a whole valley. A dazzling scope. It had required extra powers. Eros had stretched her skills and was proud of what she'd done. She had integrated a layer of dark to keep the magic securely in place, shrouding the palace from divine eyes. Genius, really—but now darkness had to be her mantle. For the spell to work, for her to go unseen, Eros could not visit in the light.

She would wait.

Still, she felt an electricity move through her, a bright vertigo. *It begins.*

PART TWO

Palace

5

I couldn't tell how long we flew, the wind and I. Forever; an instant; it seemed an infinite instant in which there was no time, no earth, only air everywhere, rushing past, waking my skin. I might have dissolved entirely into air, might have believed my body was gone if I hadn't finally felt ground beneath my hands and knees. Soil. Sudden, damp, alive. Eyes closed, I crouched and dug my fingers into earth until the whirling stopped, rose away from me in a curved goodbye. Slowly I stood. Opened my eyes.

I was in an unknown place, a beautiful meadow ringed by trees. Before me stood a house more grand and elegant than anything I'd ever seen. A palace, it seemed. Marble pillars flanked the broad double doors, which were made of a wood so dark it was almost black. The walls sang their iridescence, like the inside of the conch shells I'd seen in the hands of traders from the southern ports. The windows boasted curtains of fine cloth.

I stared at the trees, the palace. Was I supposed to enter? What came next? Was I anywhere near the monster's lair? I could try to run, I thought. But no—it was useless to try to outrun my fate, and also dangerous, especially when there was no place of safe return.

The wind turned, nudging me in the direction of the house. It felt gentle, not at all like a monster or a monster's servant, but even if it was, I had nowhere else to go. I balled my hands into fists, unfurled them. Approached the door and went inside.

Such riches. Beyond my dreaming. A great hall radiating finery and space. Marble columns rose from floor to ceiling; I longed to run my hands over them—to revel in them, to make sure they were real—but I did not dare. The floors preened with delicate mosaics of tile and precious stone, yet felt smooth beneath my sandals. The walls were painted the color of sunlight; the ceilings bore panels of intricately carved citron wood, ivory embedded in the swirling designs: spirals, vines, stars in their constellations. At one end of the hall lay the hearth, with stools and pillows arranged around it, as well as two high-backed chairs as if for royalty, engraved with scenes of wood nymphs dancing among the trees. How was any of it possible? Everything glowed, as if lit from within. Alive with its own being.

At the end of this great room, a doorway. I walked through it into a hall. Down the hall, a dining room, where a long wooden table stood laden with foods fit for a wedding feast. Platters of nuts, plums, berries, cheeses, breads, meats in various sauces so fragrant I felt my stomach lurch with want. But where was the groom? Where was anyone? I did not yet know the rules of this house, and feared to break them.

And then a voice came, so ethereal it seemed to rise from the air itself, as if nothingness could speak. *Welcome; eat.*

I looked around me. There was no one.

This is for you, all for you.

I waited for more, but nothing came. I drew in a breath to speak to the voice, to ask it a question, but my tongue wouldn't move. So I sat down at the table, and feasted. The sauces were still hot and fresh, perfectly spiced. The meat was so tender it melted in my mouth. Crisp endive, sweet cherry, charred lamb. I ate and ate and stared at the food, more than I could ever consume at once, foods I loved, foods I'd never seen before, more than I could taste in one day. Never in my life had I felt so ravenous.

A voice rose up inside me: Psyche, be careful. You don't know this place, nor how it relates to the monster for whom you've been delivered as a cursed and wretched bride. What are you doing, Psyche, have you forgotten how you got here and the dirges sung this morning, have you forgotten what happened to Persephone when she ate pomegranate seeds in the underworld, how it yoked her to the realm?

But so what? spat another part of me. Those dirges mean I'm dead anyway, at least to the villagers who sang them and the family that walked in time to that music to let me go, it's too late for any other fate to save me and I'm hungry. I'm in a strange and shining place, full of urges and about to die, so let me have my feast!

Even so, I did not touch the pomegranates, cut open to display succulent seeds.

When I was finally sated, I stood from the table. No one had come to meet me. Before I left the room, I took a knife from one of the serving dishes, a small one I might hide in the folds of my skirts, under my pillow. Any effort to defend myself would be futile, I knew, but still my hand curled tight around the handle. Even if I died tonight, on my marriage bed, I could at least harm my murderer along the way.

There is a bath for you. That voice again, the instant I crossed the threshold of the dining room. *Fresh water, come.*

Nobody appeared to guide me, so I searched the house until I found the bath, which was not in the kitchen but in a room of its own, standing ready, already filled. It was nothing like the ceramic basin we used at home. At what used to be my home. It was made of gold, and large enough to submerge the whole body at once, with four feet in the shape of lion's paws. I'd heard of such riches in tales of goddesses and queens, but I'd never thought I'd see it with my own eyes. I approached, gingerly, almost afraid, though of what I did not know. White petals floated on the surface; I dipped my fingers in; the waters were crystalline, and hot, as if freshly taken from the fire, even though no hearth was to be found.

I had never in my life bathed twice in a single day, but the heat and fear had coated me in sweat, and the luxury was too much to resist.

I took my clothes off and stepped into the bath.

The animal pleasure was so intense I almost forgot where I was.

I sank into the wet embrace, and the grief-songs, my mother's face, my wailing neighbors, the rock, the chafe of rope and fear all melted from me, dissolved in the heat. Petals on my skin, thighs, fingers. Warmth in my bones. Clear as water, clear as life.

Your marriage begins tonight, said the voice, breaking my trance. *The bedchamber is upstairs. Bring a lamp, but when you enter, blow it out and leave it behind.*

I shivered, for I understood. My husband would arrive and deflower me, make me his wife. I could fight him if I wanted, but even so, he'd do it. Whether a bride struggles or submits, smiles or weeps, the marriage begins. And in the case of my marriage—what would—how would—I saw monsters, slithering or leaping or lumbering toward me. I saw myself torn limb from limb, ripped open in this or that place. Teeth. Claws. Red eyes, though without a lamp I wouldn't see them. Why had I been asked to leave the lamp behind? So I'd be disarmed, more defenseless, bereft of sight? What kind of palace was this? Beautiful. Haunted. Rife with dis-embodied voices and dark corners. Luxuries and secrets. Petals and what else? I cupped my hands for water, rinsed my bare skin, and wondered what scars would mar it in the unlikely event that I survived the night.

I went up the stairs with a lamp from the bathing room, and reached a narrow landing. I paused. There was no hall, only a single door. I raised the lamp to better examine it. Dark wood, solid, perhaps the same material as the front door. As instructed, I blew out the lamp and put it on the floor. There were no torches on the walls, no other sources of light, I could not see as I stepped into the bedroom. The door shut itself behind me as if by a fingering breeze. Darkness. A shroud of it, so plush and absolute it took my breath away. Where were the windows? Where was the moon? It was almost full tonight, but there was no sign of its silvery glow. I tried and failed to stop shaking. Come on, Psyche, collect yourself.

"Hello?" I said into the darkness.

No answer.

I held my breath, listened for the slightest motion; I seemed to be alone, unless a man or monster lurked somewhere in the stillness. I heard nothing, not the slightest rustle, not the slightest breath. I was flooded by fear, I could not see, the dark was everywhere. What next. If I had a few moments to myself before—before what came next, then I should try to get my bearings, feel my way around the walls and learn what I could of the room that held me. I grasped the small knife from the banquet table in one hand as I traced a path along the wall with the other, and the wall, I realized slowly, was curved, there were no corners, it seemed the room was a great circle rather than four straight walls. One long wall with no beginning and no end. Stone, stone, then thick tapestries, hung from ceiling to floor as far as I could tell, for my hand could not reach their upper limits and did not know the ceiling's height, but here they were, the tapestries, vast, thick, dyed with deep colors surely to keep out all the light, a great luxury that whoever created this place could easily afford, or else not easily afford but still insisted on in order to keep the room so dark. Why? Don't think.

More stone; more tapestries. And here, behind the fabric, a depression that suggested a window, ah, yes, there it was, covered by a cloth so thick and long it would take two strong people to move it aside and let in the sun. A window shielded by the heaviest possible cloth. Why—again, no, no thinking, on to the end of the window, wall again, fabric, stone, more and more until I reached the headboard of a bed, curved perfectly to fit the shape of the room, carved in some sumptuous pattern my fingers slid along but could not translate into image. Curiosity stung me; what pictures had been grooved into the wood? Below the headboard, a bed. A proper marriage bed: wide and soft and lush with supple blankets. There was no one in it. I'd been right; there was no one else here. I continued past the bed along the wall and finished my encirclement of the room on reaching the closed door, which I for an instant pictured throwing open and running through, down the hall, out into the surrounding valley and then—what? Then nothing. Then nowhere. There was no clambering back up the wind that had brought me here. I had no choice but to face the night.

Back to the bed. Inside. The blankets enfolded me in welcome. I was wearing a sleeping gown I'd found beside the bathing tub, made of a finer and more delicate cloth than anything I'd ever worn, and the luxury of both gown and bedding disoriented me. Should I be on top of the bedding, rather than under it? Which was safer? Did it matter? What could I really do from this point on to keep myself safe? I tucked the small serving knife under the pillow and closed my eyes, though I knew I wouldn't sleep.

I am dead, I told myself, though I could no longer bring myself to believe it. Up on the rock, lashed by my father's ropes, I had felt the truth of my death, the end of my life in the village as an end of life itself; it had been a feeling strong enough to overcome me, a sense of falling from the raw edge of the world. How could this still be the same day? Did secret powers lurk in the food of this place? Had the waters in the bathtub come from an enchanted spring? Why did I hum with the insistent sensations of existence? How could I feel so vibrant at the door of death? Was life so stubborn, even in a spurned girl? I felt my breath moving in and out of me, a river of air connecting me forever to the world. My heart drummed against the inside of my chest. I was not dead. I was afraid, full of dread, in a state of shock and wonder—but dead, no. Never had I felt more alive.

Time passed, an hour, maybe more, before I heard a shuffling behind the great tapestry that covered the window. I held my breath. The window? What kind of husband does not use the doors in his own house? Especially when this window stood so high above the ground—how— Shut up, Psyche, I told myself, don't be stupid, it's obvious what kind of husband would do that and it's the kind you have, a monstrous one. I fought the urge to reach under the pillow for the knife. Not yet.

Steps, close, closer. I forced myself to breathe again, in ragged gulps.

A voice said, "Psyche."

I gasped audibly—then regretted that the sound had escaped me, that I'd let my shock be heard. A woman's voice. A *woman*. What was she doing here? What was her purpose? Where was the husband?

"Good evening."

Not any woman's voice. It was both deep and melodic, tilting each word toward song. I'd never heard a voice like that before, so sure of itself, so easily fluid. Some part of me wanted to hear it again, longed to sink into its sound, a terrible temptation given the danger I was in. My fingers groped the mattress as if to make sure it was still there.

A woman. What kind of—

—she must be—

—a servant. At this thought, I breathed with more ease. A servant preparing the way for my groom.

But the voice spoke again. "I've waited so long to meet you."

Not a servant. But then what? Why would she be—no.

No.

"Who are you?" I said.

"I am the one who brought you here." She sighed, long and soft in the darkness. "You are surprised?"

"I—"

"Of course you are."

Rustling in the dark; I could almost hear the stranger thinking. I for my part could not think, for my mind was overtaken by a rushing sensation, as if I'd been pulled to the depths of a river, caught among the pebbles.

"Psyche: you are my bride."

"Yours?" Immediately I regretted my tone. This was the owner of the palace, as far as I knew; either she owned it or had full use of it for some reason beyond knowing. A woman with such access was to be feared, for she surely had the favor of the gods. And just because she was female did not mean she would be soft. There were all kinds of females in the world. Stories abounded. Gorgons. Witches. Hags. She did not sound like any of those—or at least, how I imagined they might sound, for I'd never met any such creatures and had only heard their stories told, what did I really know of the world—but until I knew the scope of the danger I was in, I had to be careful.

I felt as well as heard the stranger pace the room. Back and forth. Stirring the air, stirring her mind. I braced myself for shrillness, violence, anything. If I'd angered her, I could be doomed. I sat up against the headboard and slunk one hand under my pillow for the knife, raising the other hand over my chest, instinctively, as if to shield myself from any blows or danger, as if my bare hand could keep me safe as I lay friendless in a dark room in the flimsiest of gowns.

The woman finally stopped pacing, approached the bed, and sat gently at the foot. "No and yes," she said, and only then did I remember that I'd asked a question. "I say no, because you are not mine—you do not belong to anyone but yourself. I did not bring you here to be in chains."

Then why in the name of Zeus did you bring me here? I thought.

"But there is also a yes, because your wedding is to me. This is our marriage bed. I want nothing in the world more than this, Psyche, to be with you."

I felt frozen inside. I'd prepared for so many different possible monsters, but no part of me had prepared for this.

"You do not have to want me back. You do not have to love me—not yet, though I hope one day you will. This palace is yours. The days you spend here are for your pleasure. I will provide for your every need and want. All I ask is that you follow two rules."

The dark, the burgeoning dark, it swirled into my mind. I was a whorl of thoughts and darkness, a person crumbled, come apart. *Do not. Have to. Love. Your pleasure. Provide?* What woman could provide? Queens, perhaps, though only under the blessing and authority of their kings. An unmarried woman could never wield such power, but—and here my mind hurled impossible lassos, snagged, tangled into knots—the woman before me was not an unmarried woman; if her words were to be believed, she was in fact, according to her own declaration, married, newly married—*to me*. My thoughts collapsed and twisted beyond recognition. I might have lost myself in that chaos, but I had to focus, had to pursue the one thing I wanted most: to survive. And for that, you have to know first where you are. "What are the rules?"

"First, you must never see me in the light. We will meet only here, in the darkness. You must never bring any lamps into this room nor let in the moon or sun."

What possible reasons could she have for such a rule? Scars, disfiguration, secrets she was keeping veiled—stop it, Psyche, stop thinking, keep to the thread.

"And second?"

"You must not ask me who I am."

In the quiet that followed, I listened to the syncopated rhythms of our breathing. Strange, how easily we sank into shared silence, as if silence were a friend we had in common. But it could not be. She was a stranger. What did she know about me? My name, that much was certain, she'd spoken it as soon as she arrived. Other things as well, it seemed; perhaps she'd caught wind of rumors about the Oracle, my reputation, forged her own judgments, laughed or scoffed or reveled in my humiliation. People did such things, drew entertainment from the woes of others, as any bard who knew how to earn his bread could tell you. Perhaps the stories had made her curious, those tales about the hordes of men, those horror-days—but if so, why would she forbid light on our meeting? Hadn't that been all the crowds wanted to do, lay eyes on me, eyes and more eyes? It was what made me worth talking about. Worth anything. The looking at me.

Yet here was a person who'd arranged a place for me to live without laying eyes on me at all. Why? Why would a woman bring me here and how would a woman get a place like this and what did she care about some cast-off girl, it made no sense, none of it fit with any possible shapes I could give to reality. To never know who she was. What a rule. How would I ever understand my own circumstances, if I managed to survive this night? It was starting to seem possible to do so. I'd have to find a way to map my surroundings. Her two rules didn't seem impossible to follow; they were not the raw wool from which nightmares were spun. A prick of hope at the thought—but still: it wasn't possible that there were no more confines in this palace. Not for a second could I allow myself to believe such a thing. There were always more than two rules to contend with; life was a long chain of hours spent surviving gauntlets of rules. There had to be more, and I had to understand as much as I could. My stomach was a fist, tight with determination.

"Can I ask you other things?"

"Do you want to?" She sounded almost amused.

"Yes, but I do not wish to—" I broke off, stopped short of saying *offend, insult, accidentally step on unstable ground that might give way beneath my feet.* "Violate the second rule, without meaning to."

"I see."

A whispering of bedclothes. She seemed to be making herself more comfortable, perched on the bed, though she did not come any closer.

"Well then. You may ask, and I will answer if I can, and if otherwise, I will say no. There is no violation, so long as you respect that, and do not ask again."

"All right." I strained to shape a question from the clamor of my thoughts. "Is this your palace?"

She laughed, sharply. "That's your question?"

"The first one." I tensed, the way I always had when my sisters mocked me, and for an instant my caution wavered, and I felt the flare of my own dignity.

"Who else would it belong to?"

For a moment, I feared I'd upset her.

"Other than you?" She laughed again, easier this time.

"There is no . . . king? No nobleman?"

"No. There is no nobleman, nor un-noble-man, nor any man at all. There is only us."

Us. "And . . . we are married?"

"You're a bride, are you not?"

I nodded, then remembered that I couldn't be seen, a thought that raised more questions, about the first rule, the dark, the motive and purpose of banning lamps. But I dared not muddy one question with another.

"Yes."

"You were sent out for your wedding day?"

And also to my symbolic burial, I thought, to a union hailed as tragic, to a union also thought of as my death. "Yes."

"Well then, we are married."

"You will . . . make me . . . your wife?" The words escaped before I could restrain them.

The air between us changed. In those moments of silence, my heart thumped so hard against my ribs that I was sure it must be audible, and I was mortified at the thought.

There was only one way for a girl to be made a wife, and it was an act of which girls were told little, an act we saw the farm animals engage in yet could never fully translate into human form with our conscribed imaginations, an act that stayed shrouded in mystery and silence even as it loomed enormous in the future paths mapped for us in the world, an act that had to do with the parts we were supposed to keep closed and that could only be performed by a man.

"Is that your wish?" Her voice came so deep it sounded like the voice of another person, or another part of her.

I would choose my words carefully. I only knew two rules of this place and had not yet found its unspoken laws, but I would not ignore them, so determined was I to stay alive. It would not be a serving knife that kept me safe, I saw that now; even with so many questions still unanswered, I could tell already that if I survived, it would be by my wits. A hot tide in me, the will to live, sudden, welcome. I kept my voice as steady as I could.

"It is a bride's duty to be made a wife," I said. "It does not matter what I wish."

"It matters here," she said sharply.

We sat together in a long, slow silence. I wondered whether I should fill it but could not fathom what to say.

"Ask me another question."

Again I searched the cacophony of my mind for a thread. A single word arose. "Why?"

"Speak more."

"Why did you choose me?"

Now she did move closer, forward on the bed, and her hand alighted on my hair. It hovered there at first, as if listening for stiffness or a flinch. None came. My body seemed to know this stranger better than the rest of me, though how could that be so? What was this leap inside me, a lift toward her touch, a welcome? It seemed a betrayal, for my body to be so far ahead of my mind, already running toward this woman as if toward

a long-lost friend. You don't know her, I tried to remind myself. And
she doesn't know you. And yet. That hand, on my hair, as if a palm were
capable of listening through touch. When had anyone last reached for
my hair with such tenderness? My mother, perhaps, when I was still too
small to groom myself, four or five, and my sisters were too busy with
some other task; a memory welled forward of my mother pausing, laying
the brush aside and stroking my hair with a gentleness that bordered on
reverence, as if the greatest blessing of her life was this chance to stroke
my hair, and I felt myself transformed by it, made into something precious and radiant and good.

But this was not my mother, and this woman's touch was not the same.
I could not have found words to describe it. Even now, years later, as I seek
a way to tell my story, to give voice to that moment and all that followed,
not knowing whether anyone will be able or willing to hear, I find myself
at a loss for words to even begin to encapsulate what happened in that
first experience of her touch, let alone what would happen in the touch
to come, for language has not yet found the words or shapes to hold such
tellings; yet even so I'll try, for only language takes the truth of who we've
been and what we've lived and clasps it to the great necklace of time,
keeps it from being forever lost. What can I say. That the hand against
my hair was honey on a thirsty tongue. The glint and shudder of fish in
a stream. Silk rippling through sunlight. I was sunlight, in the presence
of her hand. I had not known, before, that this was possible, that a body
could be transmuted into light by another person's touch. I gleamed, I was
lost, I was vast inside. Some part of me must have known even then.

"Psyche," she said. "Psyche."

My name in her mouth, a song.

6

She didn't dare move, not a muscle, not a hint, nothing that could disturb the girl's sleep. How sweetly she'd drifted off to the sound of her own name. Gods could rest if they wanted, but didn't have to, and Eros preferred, now, here, to stay awake. A thrill to be near her. To breathe in air that knew her lungs. It had gone well, had it not? Better than it could have. She'd felt Psyche's curiosity, the beam of her excitement, and even the desire she would not or could not name, though above all what radiated from her was fear. Vast fear. Like that of a cornered animal, desperate to live, scanning for claws. I want you to live, she thought toward her in the dark. I want you to thrive here, to make this your home—but words would not be enough. She'd have to be cautious, gentle, slow. For what she wanted was not just to possess the girl, but to share with her a mutual joy. Could it be done? Did it start this way? With a care for her so deep it hurt. Eros could be maimed by the tenderness, pulled entirely apart.

She took a deep breath, exhaled into the dark, the good dark. By meeting only at night, with no lamps or flames, they kept the shrouding spell intact; her mother would not see. Already, Aphrodite had been calm today, the news of Psyche's miserable fate having spread across the land. She'd watched the sad procession up the mountain with a gloating glee, all the way to the girl's disappearance down the cliff, a swift obliteration. She was either dead or being tortured by some monster, hidden from view. *So who is he?* she'd asked Eros, handing her a cup of nectar. *Did you find him on the farm amid the crowds, or in the dungeons of Tartarus or what?* And Eros had waved her hand and said, *Come now, Mother, you don't really want to know all my secrets.* Her mother had squinted at her for a beat, as if to say, Of course I do, and in that moment Eros did not breathe. But then Aphrodite laughed and raised her glass. *It doesn't matter, she's gone. Toast with me!* Eros had complied, stretching a smile across her face. How had she done it? How had she kept up the lie? A stab of guilt at her betrayal. She'd lied before, of course, plenty of times, but never to her mother. They'd always been united. Them against the rest of the gods. And her mother—well—she did not deserve this. She was no monster, after all. Vain, yes, and easily offended. Temperamental. But she could also be generous, streaming beauty into the world, a radiance that nourished the spirits of gods and men. And from the beginning she'd been fiercely loyal to her daughter, and so she told it: *We arrived together, Eros my light, my joy and spark, it will always be us against the rest of the Olympian world.*

No other gods had been born like Aphrodite. Nor had any others been born like Eros, who ruled over a primordial force that had existed long before she became embodied, had existed when the world began.

So the story went.

In the beginning, Gaia breathed. Breathing, she experienced Eros, the force itself, the deep cosmic pull. This made Gaia long for coupling. Which made the earth goddess reach for Ouranos, the sky. Which brought about a birth, then another, then a thousand more, and so the living world began. It had always amazed Eros that the tale of life's origins had included the force of her, before she herself was born—that the force of her ran deep and primal in a way that stretched far beyond her reach, her time, her knowing. Other deities might have swaggered at such a truth about themselves, seen it as a cause for boasting, but she had always found it humbling, for it yoked her to a vastness she carried within, yet whose depths could never be fully plumbed.

In any case, the story of their birth, Aphrodite's and Eros's tandem birth, held violence in it too.

For the children of Gaia and Ouranos, the Titans, rose up in rebellion against their father. And one of them, the Titan Kronos, slashed off his father's genitals and threw them into the sea. The broken genitals of Great Father Sky roiled in the water. They dissolved. They turned to foam. The foam frothed, swirled, caressed the fish, spat toward the stars. For centuries, through the reign of Kronos and then of Zeus, the foam glittered and churned, pink and vibrant, its own unbridled substance without name. And then, at last, at some moment only the foam itself could understand, it coalesced into a new being. It frothed and leapt and shaped a body out of its own rhythms, a body more beautiful than anything this universe had ever known. The body of Aphrodite. Celestial, complete. Rising from the foam, beauty itself, so alluring the wind immediately caressed her and could not stop. She walked out of the sea, taking her time, already formidable, and already pregnant with her first and most important child. *You, Eros,* she'd purr in the early days, *you were in me then just as you're ever beside me now. I have never been without you.* That was how Aphrodite told it, relishing the tale of how Eros had arrived, already in her mother, born without a father. *As it should be, daughter, for you embody a force that was here long before Zeus or Kronos or any of the other fathers came to be. My birth contained your birth inside it. We will always work as one.*

And so it had been. They were ever enmeshed, their spheres of power so intimate as to sometimes overlap like ripples in a lake: Aphrodite reigned over love and beauty, while she, Eros, reigned over love and desire. Most of the time, they worked in tandem with no conflict, loyal to each other in the face of other gods. They took good care of each other. Aphrodite defended her daughter among the most powerful of gods, and Eros had needed the defending, as from the beginning she'd leaned toward the wild. Some of that was natural enough. Desire itself belonged to realms of wildness; it could be deep as mountains or quick as river currents, could flicker and change like the turning of the weather; it had the power to warm a house or burn it down. Eros would never have the steadiness of Hera, goddess of marriage, with her carefully tended hearth and skilled amelioration of Zeus's tantrums, of course she wouldn't, and Aphrodite was glad, for she could not have abided such tedium in her own child.

But still. That did not mean that one could simply do whatever one chose. For the gods were an intricate nexus of forces, of interchange, of balance and compliance, and you had to know how to caress the threads of power like the strings of a lyre, to make them sing. You could not smash them and keep running—yet Eros wanted to, wanted to hoard her arrows to herself as soon as she'd grown tall enough to shoot them, wanting to aim however she saw fit, refusing to hunt down nymphs for Zeus when he felt like fucking in the grass. *But Mother,* Eros would say, *why should I? I don't want to, and that poor nymph-girl doesn't want me to either.* And so they'd fight. How they fought, in that time when Eros was just rising into her strength. *Child,* her mother would say, *you have to understand, you're part of an intricate webbing of power*—but Eros would interrupt, would say, *What if I don't want to be part of it?*

"You are, child."

"Why should I submit to the squabbles of the gods? Why can't each of us reign over our own existence and be free?"

"That would be Chaos."

"So?"

"Chaos did not serve this world. Not the way the Olympians do now."

"How are you so sure? Maybe Chaos was better than this."

"Eros! Lower your voice."

Young Eros swept a shield around them so no god could overhear. Some words could be seen as treason. "Sorry, Mother. But truly, how do we know the time of Chaos, or of Gaia, or of Kronos, wasn't better? You weren't there."

"Neither were you."

"You've said I was."

"Not in your incarnate form. I was there too, as foam, roaming loose, but I don't remember that, just as you don't recall a thing about existing as a primordial force."

"I wish I did." She wondered whether it were really true that she recalled nothing. Under the surface of her thoughts, a deep darkness moved and breathed, endless, inscrutable. Was that memory? A knowing? Or did all beings possess such rich black infinities inside?

"It doesn't matter," her mother went on. "We are here now in Olympian times, and we must work within the web of Olympian power."

"But why?" Thoughts swirled in Eros, deep below the surface, nebulous and dim. About working with a web, or pushing against it, stretching what existed or shrinking to fit. It was more than she could synthesize, yet also more than she could easily cast aside.

"Because you endanger us both with your recklessness. You think you can ignore the other gods and let your arrows fly as you please. Trust me on this, Eros: the last thing you want is to fall from Zeus's favor."

"I don't care about that."

"Well, I do."

"So this is to protect yourself—that's all that matters to you?"

And before Aphrodite could reply, her rebellious daughter spread her wings and flew off to shoot arrows into mortals until her blood cooled.

Her mother's rage must have been vast that night; looking back now, from the dark round room where she lay beside her hopefully-bride, Eros could imagine it. She'd been so young then, expansive, ready to flout limits. But her mother had been right. There was no such thing as independent power, not for her, not for her mother, and not even for Zeus—though that last one would take far longer to understand.

She'd capitulated, eventually, after a long standoff. Eros learned to train her arrows on behalf of others, not always, but sometimes, when called to and offered the proper favors, and over time she came to enjoy the benefits of such a system, the racking up of debts. It was almost too easy to keep the gods pleased. She relished her particular sphere. The sphere of lust. The spiky shifts of it, the surprises. The joy and turbulence. The way it could bring beggars and kings, gods and lions to their knees. She'd pierced hundreds of generations with her arrows—both the gold ones and the lead ones, the sweet and bitter pricks—and laughed as her targets went mad with passion or jealousy or heat, as they destroyed or renewed or built or exploded their own drab lives. She toyed with some, uplifted others, settled scores for fellow gods if they insisted and knew how to repay a favor. Her shots were clear-eyed and true. It wasn't the worst work, as divine assignments go, and in fact she knew that on Olympus, envy sometimes barbed the words of the gods, *lucky Eros, the bitch, look what she gets to do*, but the truth of her work was more complicated, for sometimes it was dull to watch mortals fall into the same traps and patterns over and over, which was how she'd become a trickster, known for shooting arrows into people's destinies just to watch tangles ensue. To liven up the scene. Heat up the story. She'd done it to gods too, made her power known. Made wild things happen. Such episodes caused their scandals in the halls of Olympus, then subsided. Her tricks were frowned upon but not deemed a crime.

Her crimes lay elsewhere.

In the dark, Psyche stirred, and Eros held her breath, but the girl was only settling deeper into slumber.

A lump in her throat, lying in the dark beside the mortal girl, whose hand had landed closer to her now, close enough that Eros could reach out and touch it, though she would not. She held still, alive to the rhythm of her maybe-bride's breathing, the soft pulse of her sleep. Psyche's fear was gone for the moment, dissolved in the river of dreams. What was she dreaming? It wouldn't be hard to read—but no. Don't enter her mind. Give her space. Feel her presence in the lush dark and let her be. Bask in her until the night calls you out into the black sky, before dawn's rosy fingers paint the world.

7

I don't know how much time passed before I fell asleep. I must have drifted off during the long crooning of my name, as I have no memory of the voice falling to silence. The day had been long and the terror of impending death had worn me to the marrow, for that is how terror works, it takes every ounce of our energies and leaves exhaustion in its wake. Still, I slept fitfully. Once, I stirred in the night from a feverish dream—winged snakes descending on my village, bridal jewelry dangling from their bloody teeth—and felt with my hand that the woman lay on the bed, also asleep, or so it seemed, though we had not been touching. I felt more than heard her breathing in the dark, the quiet glow of her. Woman. Stranger. A form blurred into the night. Naked. Was she naked? It seemed so but I wasn't sure. I wanted to reach out, why I could not say—curiosity, perhaps, or to learn what I could for my own protection, it was that, yes, surely, but even in my half sleep, my curiosity was drowned by caution. What if she woke? What then? I held back, did not move, and soon I drifted back into slumber.

When I woke again the room was still dark, shuttered against the morning sun. I was alone.

I spent the next day wandering through the house, coming to know it or at least attempting to, as the more I explored, the less I knew. Mysteries at every turn. Two more rooms with bedding in them, as if ready for guests or progeny. Rooms shouting with treasure: lyres, flutes, goblets, jewelry, statues carved from stone, spears and arrows and bows for hunting, incense and driving whips, tapestries folded at the ready, pots full of paint, and—my breath stopped when I found it—a single chair placed in front of the most beautiful loom I'd ever seen. It stood tall and solid, gleaming in the light through the window. I stroked it and my fingers reveled at the smoothness of the wood, surely sanded by the finest craftsman or the patient hands of time. Beside it lay piles of ready thread, dyed in rich colors, greens and reds and even purples of various shades. Colors I'd never felt move beneath my hands before, never woven with; how would they feel, where would their winding dances take me? I fingered them and imagined what I might create. One day. Perhaps. Not yet. For even weaving, my great happiness in my old life, had come with a sense of duty, with being told to sit and recall the cloaks or robes that needed making, and it thrilled me to think that here, in this place, I had hours of freedom, with no one to control the way I used my hands or mind or time.

When hunger came, I went to the dining room and found the table ready, laden with delicacies. I ate with abandon. Bread, cheese, figs, grapes, fresh goat's milk, salted fish. The pomegranate sat in the same place as the day before, and I touched it, cradled it in my palm, admiring the beautiful fruit, a rare delicacy in my valley, but still I avoided its seeds. There was even roasted meat on the table. Perhaps I'd eat some later in the day. Meat every day if I wanted it! Like royalty! I licked milk from my fingers. It still seemed a dream, this new place, this new life, as otherworldly as the visions that had come to me in sleep. And yet I was not asleep. In the past, whenever I'd been dreaming and realized that was the case, I'd immediately been able to wake myself or change the story, to suddenly appear in a new place or move backward through time. Would that I'd had that ability the night before, to banish those bride-eating creatures that had stormed my village. Well. Sitting at this table, I tried to wake myself, tried to appear outside, summon my mother to walk into the room: nothing. This was real. I was awake. I'd fallen into a secret ravine of reality, and here I was. I wiped my mouth with a cloth from the table, satisfied by my morning feast. What a place. Every day a feast. And every day completely alone, a solitude I relished: after the hordes of suitors, it was a heady gift to have the whole house, to shout myself into so much space. Whichever way I turned, I found more room to breathe. I could be loud if I wanted, sing if I wanted, whirl my limbs through the air if I pleased. I stood from the banquet table and spun my arms through the air, made sounds like a goose, like a dove, like some fantastic bird I'd never seen before, squawk! squawk!—flying about the room and down the hall, majestic and impossible, all claws and brilliant feathers and keen-eyed hunt and nobody came to stop me. I laughed, delirious, drunk with the freedom of it; never in my life had I felt so free.

But I was not free.

I paused in my game, dropped my arms to my sides. What was I doing, playing like a child, when I was still in a foreign place I was only just beginning to understand? Stop being silly, Psyche. I had to stay alert, had to keep learning the rules of this new terrain and what my life could be.

I spent that afternoon pacing the house and the groves around it— there were orchards, clearings, a sinuous stream—thinking, feeling the dizziness of new luxury subside and give way to thoughts of the coming night, of what would come next, of what I knew so far about this place and still needed to know. It was more than I could fathom. The house, but also the woman and above all the things she'd said. Two women. In a marriage—it was preposterous. A horror. Not to be accepted. Outside the bounds of the possible—further beyond the possible than anything else in this house, the disembodied voice, the miraculous food, meat every day, and the smoothest loom. Even outside of marriage, two women could not be together, it was unheard of.

Or almost so: there had been a milkmaid once who'd been caught with the weaver's daughter, out in the forest, for which they'd both been punished with public whippings and then quickly sold to the first traveling merchant to arrive in town, a sour-faced man. The village had shunned the girls on their last day despite their weeping. I'd thought that after they left, their transgressions would feed the local gossip for a season or more, growing larger and more prurient in the telling, as gossip often did, but to my surprise nobody spoke of them, not the servants, no one. It was as if the girls had never existed, as if they'd been erased from the world. This was the only instance I knew of where two women had joined—had tried to join—in the way that men did with women, and in this instance there had only been stolen moments in the forest, nothing like a marriage, not even close. For men, it was different. I'd heard whispers of it, men who consorted with each other or with boys, as their wives stayed mute and pretended not to see. The weaver himself, who'd banished his daughter, was said to have favored the boys who joined him as apprentices. But that weaver had a wife. Any men who sought such pleasures that I'd ever heard of still had wives. That was marriage: a man taking a woman for a wife, never a man taking a man, much less a woman taking a woman or taking anyone for that matter, for a woman never did the taking—such things couldn't be called marriage, or called anything at all.

So what was this?

Something monstrous, as the Oracle had said?

Perhaps.

Must be.

But this palace.

That room.

That hand in my hair.

They did not feel monstrous.

What, then, was this palace? If not monstrous, then something else that vaulted far beyond words? This palace blasted all the words apart. I had to find another way to understand. And questions filled me, starting with the question of that first rule, the rule of dark: What did it mean? What did my—husband—it did not seem the right word, but no other word could be—have to hide?

That night, she arrived earlier, almost as soon as I'd settled into bed. Again I heard her alight across the room, before the tapestry that covered the window, and then approach, so gracefully she almost seemed to glide.

"Good evening."

My body warmed at the sound of that voice, and I realized that I'd missed it, had been waiting for it eagerly. This made me nervous. I still didn't know this person, my benefactor, didn't trust her; so why this animal response, this urge to reach out my arms? Was it because for the first time in my life I'd spent a day without seeing another human soul? Solitude had been delicious, but also disorienting, new. Perhaps it had left me off-balance, and that was why the woman's arrival had this effect on me. It must be that.

"Good evening," I replied.

"How was your day?"

I smiled, despite myself, even though my face could not be seen. "Lovely."

"What did you do?"

"I ate, dreamed, explored the house."

"Does it please you?"

"Very much. Especially the loom."

"Ah. I am glad." A smile seemed to permeate her voice.

I wanted to ask about her day—how had she spent it? I couldn't begin to imagine—but before I got the chance, she spoke again. "What is your pleasure?"

The darkness seemed to split open around us.

"I do not understand."

"What do you crave?"

"Crave?"

"From me. Or from this night."

"I—" I said, then stopped. My mind as dark as the room. I craved nothing from this woman, but I could not say that, for I was her bride; but also I could not say that because it was untrue, or rather, it was not the whole of the truth, it was a surface truth that barely covered the pulsing naked truth below. I was full of craving. I didn't know what I craved. I craved nothing and everything, I carried a tangle of longings inside that never saw the light for they were not to be looked at, I didn't want to look at them or at her question, had been bred all my life to erase my wants, to crush them to nothing, to exist for the craving of others. Of men. Of men deemed worthy of it by other men. Strangers, fathers, eyes and eyes and eyes. I was a thing, I was supposed to be a thing, I saw it clearly for the first time and it gutted me. I could have wept a river into being, but I shoved that impulse down for there was no time, I had been asked a question by a person who was right in front of me, invisible, waiting. "I do not know."

"I see."

"Are you . . . going to make me your wife?"

I heard her rustle closer. Now she spoke slowly and in the gentlest possible tone. "Is that your pleasure?"

I could not say no for it would not be true—how could it not be true, what was this thought growling inside me, who was I becoming—and also because *No* was a pebble caught in the throat, far from the tongue. But what would happen if I said yes? That single word, *Yes*. My body felt blinding, like a stream catching raw sunlight in a glade. "You truly wish to know."

"I do."

Moments passed in which the world seemed to empty of light, over and over, becoming the black sphere of this room, a black that could absorb the sun and moon and stars, a black into which I breathed, for I was alive, wasn't I, enfolded in black, enfolded in the moment as the past and future vanished in the distance. She waited for my next words in perfect stillness. I felt, in the calm of her presence, that she would honor anything I said and accept it without ire or blame. How could it be? When was the last time anyone had asked me about my wanting and listened for an answer? *Pleasure. Your pleasure.* I searched my mind, all the unsayable thoughts, for one I could name. One that would respond to her question and test it at the same time.

"Sing to me," I said.

Silence rose between us for a beat, two, and I held my breath, readied myself for a reprimand, *that's not right* or *why did you say* or even Iantha's *stop it, Psyche.*

But then she sang.

She began with my name, crooning it again, *Psyche, Psyche,* until it shifted into a wordless melody that moved around and through me, merging with the dark. The music of her voice, a revelation. In the village, she would have become famed for such a voice, begged for renderings at every wedding and funeral. Crowds would have gathered in wonder and hung on every lithe or sumptuous note. But there was no crowd. We were alone, and all this music was for me.

She was closer now, her breath on my cheek, the heat of song on my skin. I felt keenly aware of that heat, its sound, from deep inside the singer's body, and stop thinking about that, don't imagine it, why can't I rid it from my mind? Her body. Unknown curves, slants, secret places, through which this voice moved toward me, into me, as if song were its own form of touch. A song that sprang from my name. As if I myself were music. Or as if music could bring me newly into being, unerased from the book of time.

That was how it went for the rest of that night, and the next one, and the next.

Each time, she arrived in the dark room through the hidden window and said, *What is your pleasure?*, and each time I asked her to sing.

I thrilled to her voice, at the thought that it came for me and no one else. I wrapped myself in a sound that draped its beauty around me and also slid right into me, for sound enters through the ear and seeps directly into the mind, the bones. With sound she entered me and reached my core. There she hummed, vibrated. There she coaxed sleeping beasts to wake. I had not imagined before that sound could wash the soul the way water washes a body, but that was how it felt those early nights: that this mysterious woman's music cleansed away the layers left by sadder days, washed the stains of old invasions, eased sorrows I didn't know I had. I became lighter in the presence of her song. I came to crave it in the course of the day, waiting impatiently for night to fall so she could return and open the world to me, or more accurately, open me gently to the world.

But for all the joy I took in her song, there were other reasons I asked for it too.

I kept these reasons hidden, even from myself.

It took me five nights to finally see what I aimed to do. I understood it as I strolled through the groves outside the palace, breeze on my skin, a storm in my mind. Birds laughed, high above the valley. Tree-tops brushed lazily against the sky. I was trying to push her. To test her patience. To force her to—what? To shed her pretense of wanting only whatever her bride did, and to reveal what she really meant to do, for surely she had plans, wants of her own, aims regarding her bride; for all her insistence on doing no more than my bidding, there had to be more to it, and wouldn't it be better for those wants to be made known? Wouldn't I have more sway in this new, uncharted life if I could see the owner of this palace's intentions more clearly? It was still a riddle, after all, what I'd been brought here for, beyond that strange question *What is your pleasure?* No. That could not be the whole truth. That could never be all that was required of a bride, because what were brides for? To serve, to be enjoyed, to bear children, though that was impossible with a husband like her, this I did know, and if that third purpose of brides could not apply, I thought, striding toward the stream, it must make the first two all the more important. That was what I meant to do. Try her patience. Be coy. For it could be that way with men, or so I'd heard: tempt them, with a word, a glance, a sway, a veil, and they'd turn rapacious and lay all their hunger bare.

And then they would—do something.

What they wanted.

And you could finally know what it was.

But my husband was not a man. So would it work? I had no idea. I was lost in an unknown landscape, wandering without path or guide.

In the nights that followed, I kept at it, denying her anything but the singing, even as her question *What is your pleasure?* landed in me with increasing heat, as if it could catch flame. I would not let it. More nights passed. My plan seemed to be failing, for she showed no sign of impatience, not the slightest ebb in her warmth toward me. Night after night, she met my request and sang to me with the same willingness and artfulness as ever, wrapping me in music, filling me with her voice.

Ten nights passed. Eleven. I grew restless. I still loved her song but something else rose up in me, an undercurrent of frustration, like the hum of a bee trapped in a house. She sang and did not touch me. Not even the hand on my hair of the first night, fingers tracing grooves in the strands. She did nothing I had not asked for. I ached. I fumed. The hum swelled in me. At night, by her side, my body shouted for her, desperate to press close to her, a sensation that dizzied me, for I'd never experienced it before. My own body, a stranger to me, a greedy wailing stranger. What was this? What was I? During the day, I paced the groves, splashed my legs in the stream, skin bright with something I could not name. I yearned for sun, wind, touch, monstrousness. I yearned to feel alive—I felt alive, hounded by my own aliveness. I cupped stream-water toward me with both hands, drenched myself, thought of her and could not breathe. What's happening to me? I thought. And what's possible between me and this woman? Was she fine with continuing this way, with endless nights of singing and nothing more, had she not wanted a real bride after all? Had I been a fool to imagine she wanted something else? Or had I been a deviant? Wild Psyche! Rotten Psyche! You invented a monstrosity all on your own.

Over meals, on walks, as I sat at the loom weaving a tapestry out of finer thread than I'd ever used before—a simple design, two alternating colors, for fear of what would happen if I let my imagination merge with the motion of the threads, given the tumult inside my mind—I saw visions of what else I might ask for, what else might be *your pleasure*, things I should not think of and should not want, even now as a bride could not allow myself to want: her hand in my hair as it had been the first night, her body near mine, her body on mine, her hands on me, her hands moving along me, would they be hard or supple, fast or slow or—her mouth on my neck—then what? I fractured, felt some part of me buckle and sweetly come apart. I had to leap up from the loom and pace to stay inside my skin. I was not entirely inside my skin. I ached at the edge of *then what?* I could not disentangle the threads of my curiosity and desire. They twined into a rope so fierce it took my breath away. I was taut with it.

On walks, the sun seemed to pierce right through my skin, reaching the core of me.

At the loom, the tangle of my mind spilled out into the weave, creating chaos. Loops and spikes of wool appeared beneath my hands. For this I scolded myself, undoing the gnarls and knots with trembling fingers. Careful, Psyche, you might be wrong about all of this, it could be that you've completely misunderstood. She might just be a rich woman driven mad by loneliness, who in that madness devised a plan to ease the solitude, a bride in a room with no light. It made no sense, but nothing about this palace made sense, not without stretching my understanding of reality into new shapes. I was stretching into new shapes. I'd become large inside, hungry, unrecognizable to myself.

On the thirteenth night, I finally broke our nightly ritual.

We began as usual. But after a few moments of her singing, I said, "That's enough."

"It is not your pleasure?"

"Not now."

"Then?"

Then. A single word and yet to me it thundered. I'd spent that afternoon prowling the halls of the house, wondering, thinking. What did I crave from her? With her? I did not fully know, but I knew some things. I knew that when she was close, I came alive. That in the morning, her absence hollowed me. I knew that the longing for her hands on me had become intense, a thirst that swallowed me whole and filled my days. I could not deny it anymore, the crushing need for her hands on me. None of this fit in the realm of the real according to the world I'd known before this palace, but that didn't matter. I was no longer of that world, and what my body knew eclipsed all the things I'd been taught, obliterated it all, shouted for space. I wanted to press against her more than I'd ever wanted anything.

Still I could not speak. How to shape words around the unspoken. How to make any sound. Unthinkable to give voice to anything so dangerous. Unthinkable to stay silent and risk losing this chance. This chance. At what? My mouth opened in the dark, sound caught in my throat. Darkness in my throat. A chance at everything, I thought, to hear only what's inside me shouting true, I want to let the rest of the world's noise dissolve, even if only for one night, I don't know what I am or who I am but tonight, right now, I know what I want, and so what if the laws of gods and men would slay me for it, who cares, they already tried to slay me and here I am. "I want you to show me."

She went completely still. She seemed to be listening, as if waiting for further explanation, as if the obvious question hung already in the air: *Show you what?*

But I could not speak it.

She could not make me speak it.

If she tried to make me, the gate would close.

But she did not. Instead a hand arrived on my cheek, with the delicacy of a bird's wing. Hovered there. My breath caught in my throat. I arched toward her palm and that, my body's language, was enough response to the question the hand was asking, for it could work that way, I realized, a body had the power to ask, answer, speak. She fell upon me. Kissing my face, neck, chest. Her body on mine, naked, her hands on me. Seeking. Finding. Stroking gently and not gently at all. What startled me most was not her ferocity, but my own thirst for it, the way the ache in me intensified, expanded, as if in recognition. I felt alive, like a plant suddenly doused in light. I burned for her in the places where she touched me, burned to know what she'd do next. She did not bother fumbling with the laces of my sleeping gown; instead, she ripped it open with her teeth. Her strength astonished me, I had not imagined it. All the way down to the skirts she tore, and I felt the cool, dark air on my bare skin. I clamped my legs shut, as if the posture could rescue some shred of modesty, as if that were something that I wanted—it was not, but the gesture was instinctive, trained into my body all my life, *protect this*, even though I longed for her to touch me there. She made no move to part my legs; she hovered for a moment in which I pined to see the expression on her face, to read her features even though I'd never seen them, what would her face say now? I'd thought her forcefulness would extend to this moment, to my legs, to prying, but instead the rhythm shifted and she hovered over me, all the fire of the world reduced to her hand on my thigh. The air between us thick and vital, our breath a ragged music. I wanted her to rip me open as she'd ripped the gown. I shocked myself with such a wanting, but I knew it all the same. How could the urge to be ripped keen with so much life? Was this death or the longing for it? It felt nothing like death or what I had always imagined death to be, the approach, the river-crossing, this had to be a different river, an entirely different force, I did not know its name. She descended to my feet, kissed them, traced her gentle tongue along my ankles, toes, calves, leaving wetness in its wake. Every part her tongue touched was more alive for it. To be damp with her was to know life, to gleam. Her mouth traveled slowly up my closed thighs, and when she reached the thicket at the meeting of my legs she buried her face there and inhaled as if breathing in the salt air of the sea, a sensation of which I'd only heard tell by servants who'd heard the traveling merchants speak of it: the briny air, rich with underwater life, fresh and vibrant, you can't imagine, so it had been said but this, this was something else, I kept my legs shut and thought, no, it can't be, it's too shocking, her nose in those curled hairs I can't bear it, too much, not enough. In all the whispers of what men did to brides, I'd never heard the slightest hint of such a thing. I felt the world shake, stretch open. What kind of world was this, where such a thing could be? Her face had risen now, was near my own, our mouths met long and slow. I felt the pull of another woman's want, her mouth, slaking itself. Slaking me too, though I felt I'd never be done. A thirst in me so vast it had no end. Sky-thirst. It shocked me, the clarity of my own wanting, its brightness on my tongue and on another woman's tongue, after all these nights of patient singing, now the swift burst of a dam. Her mouth, her mouth. Her hands in my hair, at my breast, waist, hip. When she pulled back to move elsewhere, I reached up and grasped her face, violently, and pressed her lips back to my own. She let out a surprised laugh, spilled it into my mouth, and that was the moment I became her wife: when I gripped her face and crushed it to my own; when I drank her laugh; when our mutual want shone as clear as a flame.

We kissed on, for an eternity. I could have kissed her forever. We moved against each other, my husband's breasts against mine, a thrill and revelation, so this was her, this naked body all curves and muscularity and I wanted to know all of it, feel all of it, the lean and the sumptuous, the firm and the soft. *What is a body?* I thought. *What is a life?* I was life, pure life. My legs melted open of their own accord, for I was fiercely awake now and a new thought had risen to the surface: I had nothing to lose. I'd faced death to reach this night, I'd faced horrors to reach this night, I'd lost everything to arrive here. I would not surrender any part of it; I would taste it all. I wanted more of my lover, this woman, this husband, wanted her everywhere, wanted in my hunger to consume the world. My husband between my legs. My husband's hand. Moving. On me. In me. In me. Soft at first, then sweetly brutal; we rocked against and with each other, found a rhythm, or one of us found it and the other became it. Dissolved. Heat rose in me and I broke open, I was breaking and breaking like the sea against rocks, and what to call it, this good-sweet, this explosive force, this shower of splintered light. On and on it poured before it finally came to rest. Sound returned; when had it gone? My breathing and hers. She fell against me, slick with sweat. Her weight pinned me back into my body, pulled shards of light back into woman-form. I felt the urge to weep, but instead I licked my lover's shoulder for the salt. She moaned; I bit her; we laughed, both surprised at the sharp teeth of the bride.

The laughs subsided into other sounds as, slowly, we began again.

We chased the dawn, that night. She made me new, there in the absolute dark. She rode and rode me. And did not disappear until I'd finally fallen into dreams.

8

She left through the covered window just as the sky's edge grew pale, hinting at morning. *Alive.* Every part of her alive as she soared from the valley, her bride's sweat on her tongue. Limbs amazed. Every part of her amazed. Psyche had welcomed her, the welcome had been true. And it had been—

She rose from the valley, left it behind.

Aloft in the cool air.

Sublime, it had been sublime.

She flew until gold and orange ribboned the horizon.

Where to go? She wanted to shout, to celebrate, to stay in the euphoria for as long as she could. Wanted to boom about it to the heavens, *My bride!* But she could not. She had to keep it hidden, keep it silent. And if she went home, would her mother read the thrill on her, the lingering glow of sex? And then what would she say? No, not home. Too dangerous. Better to land elsewhere. She had no urgent duties calling her yet; she could go where she liked. She flew without thinking. She flew in a daze of joy.

Only when Mount Olympus loomed before her, high and shining, did she understand whom she sought. Not Zeus, or Athena, or Apollo, or any of the others—she avoided their halls altogether and landed right at the door to the basement, the lip of the forge.

Down the winding spiral stairs, down, down. The fires of the smithy hotter on her skin with each step. She heard the clank of his great hammer before she saw him. Turned the last corner and there he was. Hephaestus. Already at work, clanging at what seemed to be an exquisite, enormous shield.

"Good morning."

Hephaestus kept his eyes on his artistry. "Eros! Welcome, daughter."

She was not born from him, of course. He'd married Aphrodite after Eros was born, at Zeus's command. The king of gods had intended the match to contain the power of this new goddess risen from the waves. In the end, Aphrodite spent little time at Hephaestus's side, accepting his hand-forged gifts as her due while bedding any god she wished. Her dalliances were widely known. Yet Hephaestus, god of fire and metalwork, remained a gentle presence in the life of Eros, treating her as his own child.

"To what do I owe this visit? What do you want?"

He had always been blunt, direct. Not conniving like so many other gods. "Nothing. Just to watch you work."

Now Hephaestus glanced up. Face streaked with sweat and char. "Hmm."

He seemed to wait for more, but Eros said nothing. The fire crackled. He searched her eyes—they had always had this, the ability to understand each other without speaking, perhaps because they shared a core connectedness to passion, he for his work, she for desire itself—and then he grunted and returned his attention to the forge.

She settled into a chair in the corner and watched. The chair was forged by him. As were all the thrones of Olympus; those gods possessed immeasurable powers, but without Hephaestus, they had no fancy place to sit. Some spurned him, her somewhat-father, because he was lame in one leg and had once been exiled from Olympus for defending his mother, Hera, when Zeus had tried to rape her—you don't get between Zeus and his intended rapes, everybody knew that, Eros herself had felt the sting of such punishments—but no. She wouldn't think of that, not on this day. Stay with the reason she'd come to this place, which was what?

The forge. The incandescent power of the forge.

Hephaestus's thick, rugged body, crouched in concentration, hammering beauty into being.

She could never get enough of the sight. Hot metal as it yielded and curved, the swing and aim of his great tool, a god's virility making something new. Male strength, used to create rather than destroy. *What am I?* Clang, sang the hammer. Clang. *What can I be?*

Oh my husband, Psyche had cried in the night, in the throes of ecstasy. The words had sent shivers down Eros's spine. Shivers again as she recalled it now, her body still humming with last night's sensual delights.

The heat of the forge filled her lungs.

Fire licked the air.

Husband, she thought. Turning the word, attempting to taste it with her mind. *Husband.*

9

Morning. I lay awake for a long time, eyes closed, clinging to the hem of sleep. The night returned to me in a hot rush. I ran a hand along my body, felt it new. This body, which was not what I'd imagined it to be. Hand. Skin. My drumming heart, stubborn, alive. When I opened my eyes, there was no light, though surely dawn had come by now. I felt renewed. I rose slowly, still clinging to the languor of my marriage bed, driven only by an urge to see the sun.

That day, all day, she seared my mind. I ate at the table and I felt her inside me and rocked my hips against the chair, remembering being filled, hungry for it. I walked beside the stream and knew her hands again, roving my body, lighting it up. I stopped many times to lean against a tree and catch my breath, overcome with need for those hands. I tried to work on a tapestry and the strands in my fingers called back her hair, her skin, her firm limbs, so that everything felt impossibly sensuous and I found myself stroking the wooden loom instead of weaving. I was restless. Lit up. I gave up on the tapestry and sank into a bath. In the clean hot water I imagined her again. Gliding up behind me, my husband, my woman-husband, leaning close, her breath at my neck, hands plumbing down to find me. I longed to be found. But there was light in this room, it was still day, she would not come. I'd have to wait. The bathwater cradled me in a warm embrace. I could lie in it as long as I liked; I could lie there for hours with no one to berate my laziness or call me to chores or duties. Wet, naked joy. I could rest here. Even think. Let the mind roam. It roamed to the night before, to what she'd done, what the two of us had done together. Unscripted. Untethered. Unimaginable yet somehow true. Her breath in my ear. The press of her. Mouth. Scent. Hands on me—I succumbed to my own touch. I slid against myself beneath the water as if my hand were hers, though it was not, it did not know what hers knew; how could a near stranger know my body so much better than I did myself? Could I learn to know it too? I'd never touched myself like this before. This body. My body. An unmapped place. What is a person, what is a woman, what is this curve, this one, this. I slid and pressed and let my hand swim as it would. Ravager, ravaged. I made the sensation rise, rise, break. I lay back, breathing hard, water-warm, knees loose and open, leaning against the tub walls. Drunken knees. Hands hovering under-water like slippery creatures of the deep. My own hands had done it; pride swelled in me.

But as I returned to myself, to the room, a sweep of fear. Exploring had its dangers. Endless stories warned against it. Don't enter labyrinths unless you're ready to face the Minotaur, the monster in the maze. I heard my father's voice, repeating the prophecy, *Her marriage will be monstrous.* What happened last night had not felt monstrous at all—it had felt natural, ripe with strength—but it might be seen so by others, temple priests, the gods, my village, my father—

I took that last thought between my teeth and cracked it in two.

My head sank deeper into the water. My hair swirled like that of sirens, wild and lethal to mortal men.

My father was not here, and he had cursed me. Had lashed me to the rock and left me to what he thought would be a violent death. Why should I bend to his disapproval? He no longer ruled me. A thrilling notion. A married woman need not answer to her father, for she belongs to her husband—though here again my thoughts began to fray. Was she a husband? And even if she was, I did not know her yet and could not yet measure all it would mean to belong to her, if such a belonging was to be. I had so very many questions, about where I was, who she was, how food could regenerate itself, what would happen to me if she didn't return. There was so much I did not know. Despite everything that had happened last night, all she'd shown me and given me and revealed, I could not even call her by name.

That night, when she returned, I thought I heard the beating of wings beyond the tapestry in the moments before she appeared in the room. Wings. I pictured how she might have arrived here, riding what kind of beast: a great eagle, or a Pegasus, resplendent in the light of the moon. How can that be? I thought, and then, just as quickly, How can any of this be?

"How are you tonight, beloved?"

Not *wife*. Not *Psyche*. Simply *beloved*. I cradled that word in the palm of my mind. "I've thought of you all day."

"Ah yes?" A smile in her voice. She was on the bed now, close, though not yet touching. "Good thoughts, I hope?"

All the plans I'd had to talk to her, to ask questions, to find out more of who she was, were drowned by the great force of my want. My body blazed already. I reached out to her. "Come here."

She did not tear the cloth from me this time. She rocked against me as my body shouted for her, refusing to unclothe me. *Shh, shhh,* she said instead, her thigh between her wife's legs, a rock to crash against, and I crashed and crashed against it until I broke. I clung to her, recovered my breath.

"You're eager, aren't you," she whispered in my ear.

"And yet you deny me."

"Deny? Did you not just take what you wanted?"

"I—"

Her laugh hot on my skin.

"I want more."

"Ah."

Her tongue on an earlobe. Teeth. I gasped at the strength of her bite.

"I have so much more for you."

"Really? Like what?"

Daring spiked in me. I reached out, but she caught my wrists and pinned them down. I writhed against the restraint, want flaring open in me so fiercely I thought I might burst out of my skin.

"Poor Psyche. So hungry."

Her mouth on my neck, shoulder, biting wet. On my nipple through the flimsy nightgown. She suckled there, still holding me down at the wrists, locked to my breast no matter how I thrashed and bucked. The joy was sharp, I could not bear it. I thought I might crest again, but before I reached that place she released my breast and kept moving down, biting at my belly through the thin gown—next time, I thought, I'll come to bed naked—and then her hands moved to lift my skirts and she was kissing thighs, trailing her tongue toward my sex. Reaching it. Her mouth. Another thing—like two women together, like a husband with breasts, like a wife who answered to no man—that I had not known was possible. Something in me cringed against it: What was it? Shame. How would I smell, what would she do when she caught my scent, surely she'd recoil in disgust? How could she want to—but then I could not think because her mouth overtook me. Hands roved my hips, waist, thighs, what is this, she's everywhere, at the core of me, is that my core, what does that mean, what can you call this place, this thing she's doing to me with her mouth, a long kiss? A speaking? A kind of devouring dance? A mouth is a soft wet thing, is it not, how can it be so muscular, so absolute? Shame slipped away, sank into a hot blind sea.

I shattered into pleasure. She did not release me. Instead, she held me in her mouth until the shaking stopped, then began again.

She stayed and stayed there. Forever. For a great roaring sea of forever, wave after wave.

Afterward, I tried to talk but could make sense of nothing.

"Shhh," she crooned, and held me gently for a long time until I pulled her onto me and then she was not gentle anymore. I did not want her to stay gentle, craved her force, conveyed this with the press of my hips. She gave my body all it asked for and more. We grew sweaty and slick as fish. Creatures of another world. We slid against each other, glided and crashed, then collapsed after what must have been hours into a thick, damp sleep.

When I woke in the early morning hours, she was gone.

I had so many questions still. The next night, I was determined to ask them, at least to start, so when she arrived and reached for me, I kissed her back but then managed to push her away.

"What is it?"

"You haven't told me your name."

A shuffle in the dark. "Do you need a name for me?"

"We are married, are we not?" Even now, a knife of danger, saying these words to a woman.

"What do you think?" Her words hot against my skin.

I wanted to succumb, to fall toward her: Where would she be taking me tonight? What would she awaken, what would she reveal? But I had promised myself in the bath that I would try to find out more, for it was still my mission to stay alive as long as possible. So Psyche, I told myself as I soaked in the hot water, you'll have to tamp it down tonight, keep your urges in check, just long enough to get some questions answered. "Well, that raises another question. What is marriage?"

She bit my shoulder. "You tell me."

"Is it not the sharing of a life?"

She tensed; I could swear I felt her tense; but perhaps I'd imagined it, for in an instant it was gone.

"It is, my love."

"So how can I share my life with someone whose name I do not know?"

Silence. A hand stroked my naked thigh, for I'd made good on my decision to leave the nightgown behind, and my legs were right there for the stroking, now they began to part, without my meaning them to, without my mind deciding, greedy legs, greedy Psyche. What had happened to all my pure maiden keep-your-legs-shut training? How could it melt so fast? Had it been so flimsy after all, or the body's urges that strong? I wanted to succumb to that touch and what it promised. Stop. Hold back. Focus or you'll never learn the things you need to know. I held still, waited.

Finally, she sighed, as if realizing the conversation could not easily be put on hold by other things. "You ask what marriage is. But let me ask you this: What is a name?"

"A way to know a person."

"Don't you know me?"

"Do I?"

"Why would you doubt it?"

"I've never seen you."

"What does it mean to see?"

"Well—"

"Can it only be done with eyes?"

My mind reeled back to the sheep enclosure, men who stared without seeing me at all. "Sometimes eyes fail at it."

"Yes," she said, with a tenderness that made me wonder how much she knew about my past. "So is the opposite true also? If eyes can fail to see, can seeing be done without them?"

"Yes."

"Ah." Her hand had been resting on my thigh. She moved it now, soft, pensive strokes. "And what does it mean to know someone?"

I moaned at her touch. I couldn't help it. I rocked against her, but my mind carried her question like a leaf along a stream. I thought of Iantha and Coronis, with whom I'd shared long days of childhood and whose faces conveyed worlds to me; reading their faces had been as natural as reading the wind; and yet, for all of that, we'd kept so many thoughts hidden from each other, especially toward the end. They hadn't risen to mind in days. I realized with a flush of shame that I hadn't wondered about their well-being, how their new homes were treating them, the curve and taste of their new lives. How were they faring? And how could I have forgotten them so easily? I thought of my mother, unfathomable, yet also as familiar as breath. I knew and did not know her all at once.

"I don't know. I'm not sure how possible it is to know another person. But I want it to be possible."

"This is what I love about you, Psyche—"

"Only this?"

"No! Much more."

She pulled me close and kissed me. I welded myself to her and returned the kiss. My hand thrilled along her arm, its firm muscles and smooth skin. Every time I touched her was a revelation. Without the ability to see her through my eyes, my hands took up the role of learning her, of experiencing her physical self. I touched her gingerly, but with eagerness. I felt the sharp, elegant line of her cheekbone under my fingertips, wondered how the color of her eyes gleamed in the light. Every part of her amazed me, for she was exquisite, but also because it was still new to me, this touching of a naked woman, and every time I braced for a thunderous reproach that never came.

She pulled back, breathing hard. Ran tender fingers along my face. "What I mean to say, Psyche, is that I love the way you seek what does not yet seem possible. Knowing someone, for example. If it could be possible, what would it mean?"

"To become open to each other."

"Haven't we done that?"

"Yes," I said, and meant it, though I also thought but did not say, *I have opened to you at least, but perhaps the reverse is not as true.* But no; how could I express that? What *did* I mean by it? My mind spun. Stop. Focus, Psyche. There are things you do understand. Hold on to your knowing. Namely this: She knows your name, and you do not know hers. She knows where you were all day and you don't know the same for her. She came here on some winged creature through the night sky, she is a woman free to roam the sky, a woman with a palace, a woman whose days are hidden from you, a woman who can do outrageous things to another woman's body, a woman whose power is mountainous, whose strength is vast, whose charm is boundless, you'd never imagined such a woman could be, yet here she is, and far be it from you to anger her when she's already given you so much, how could you ask for more, when she has chosen you for this adventure for some inscrutable reason you'll never understand, just as it's impossible to understand how this adventure can exist or what the scope of it will be, but there it is, the need to clasp it close and not let go because you want this life she's offered you, want it with every fiber of your being, yet also want to hold on to your own knowing, however tiny it may be compared to hers. "In some ways. We've started to."

"You're not pleased."

Genuine hurt in her voice. I flinched in surprise.

"No. I am. Truly."

"It's not enough? The palace?"

"Of course it is."

"Or our nights?"

"Oh no, oh no, the nights are enough. They're—" I cut off my own words.

"They're . . . what?"

"I don't have words for it."

She was silent.

"I don't have words for any of this. On my wedding day, I thought I was going to die—"

"Die?"

"Yes."

"Why?"

"Because I was marrying a monster. Or so the Oracle had told us."

I paused, waited for her to laugh at my outsized fears or quip that she was not a monster, what a silly thing to say, but she stayed quiet until she finally said, "I am sorry."

"It's not your fault."

She was silent again.

"But I didn't die," I said softly, hoping to draw her back to me. "I'm here, in a place beyond dreaming."

She took my hand in the dark. "I want you to be happy, Psyche. I want nothing more."

"I am happy." I stroked her fingers, felt them curl in response. They were long and delicate, though also forceful when they wanted to be. I had more to say. It reached beyond the sayable, but it was better to speak. I closed my eyes, took a breath. Moved her hand to my waist, where it stirred want in me, greedy body, how could it ever have enough of her? She seemed to sense it, for her fingers grew firm as a promise, then soft again. "Not happy, or not only that. It is something far beyond happy. What happens when I'm with you is more living than I thought could ever be mine." I traced my fingers along her shoulders, felt her shudder, though whether from my touch or my words, I did not know. "It's as if the whole world becomes this room or this room becomes the world."

"Mmm. Really."

"Yes."

"Good."

Her hand on my belly now, moving ever so lightly, hunger in its wake.

What was she afraid of? Perhaps it was safer not to know. "I'm not asking about your name out of unhappiness." Concentrate, Psyche. Hold the thread of your thoughts, don't fall, not yet. "It's just the opposite. I want to know you in all the ways I can, as deeply as I know anything. To hold your name inside me like a jewel. To keep you with me through your name. To speak it, roll it on my tongue when you are gone."

She made a sound of surprise, or what seemed like surprise, a sharp intake followed by a sigh. She lowered her head to my breast and came to rest there, not in the way she had before, thick with desire, but in a softer way, almost childlike, a young bird seeking the comfort of a nest. I had not expected this; it was a side of her I hadn't yet seen. This formidable woman, full of strength and power. Vulnerable. Could it be? I felt a rush of tenderness. My arms rose to cradle her head. She stiffened, then relaxed against me.

"You dissolve me, Psyche. You cannot imagine how."

Her words left me mute. The dark rose around us, petals of a great black flower. I stroked her loose curls. Learned them. Silken, coiled vitality, I could spend a lifetime sifting through the strands and it would not be enough, I could lose my fingers there forever. Was that what she meant by *dissolve*? A loss of self? A rearrangement? I still longed to know her name, but I longed for other things too. I longed for so much that

I almost longed for everything, which is a feeling so vast it curves in on itself, toward the start of the circle, where everything becomes nothing and the longing for everything blurs into longing for nothing, a subsuming in the longing itself, pure, raw, swallowing you whole.

So what if she's a woman? I thought the next day, strolling through the groves around the palace.

So what if I still don't know her name?

So what if this marriage has no clear shape respected by the men who run the world, so what if it takes place only under cover of dark?

Do I need a name, respect, a shape to things that could be recognized by fathers and villagers and priests, when instead I can have this?

All around me, trees reached their green arms toward the sky. A small animal shivered the grass and fled unseen. The stream sang of its perpetual journey over stones. The edge of the valley seemed distant, the enclosing cliffs an afterthought, like guards keeping watch so far from you that you forget they're there.

For now at least, I'd been given the chance to live. And to be a wife, of some kind. To have a home, food to eat, nights of utter joy.

It was so much more than what I'd resigned myself to just weeks before. Why ask for what couldn't be given?

A wife's duty is to fulfill her husband's wishes, whatever they be.

What were my husband's wishes?

To stay in the dark, that much was clear.

To not be known by name.

A reasonable sacrifice, I thought, when I had been given so much.

But my husband had other wishes too, unnamed. She was hungry. For what? For the astounding things we did together, and what else?

You dissolve me. Her words in my bones and in the murmur of the wind.

She had everything: riches, power, knowledge, freedom. Skills in the arts of love. Surely she'd had previous experiences, had brought many other women to the edge of mercy, it had to be so. How else could she be so sure with her hands, her teeth, her tongue, her rhythms, her everything, what women, where, who had they been, had she married them too, was she married to them even now, and how could I, an ignorant country girl, ever measure up to all these other women? Jealousy bright inside me as a flame.

I paused by the stream, where a fig tree basked in the afternoon sun. I reached out to caress one of its leaves.

There may have been other women, there may even have been other wives in this palace or in other palaces in other valleys, but right now this woman spent her nights—all her nights—with her one bride.

She had everything. She could have anything. And yet, I thought, she wants me.

Me.

And look what she gives me in the night.

How could I ever ask for more? Had any woman ever received more?

The fig tree leaves preened in the sun, a deep green, I had not stopped touching them. Broad leaves, smooth, the nubs of small, hard fruit scattered among them in a promise of ripeness to come. I felt sensual. Everything made me feel sensual now, and she had been teaching me to let my want be known, to reveal it to myself without balking. To swim in it. Could I do that also here, in the full light of day? I tore a piece of leaf and ate it, and it was good, bitter, not enough to satisfy. I wanted to be satisfied. It felt good to want, in a clean way that was new to me, unadulterated by rules or shame. Want climbed inside me, green and riotous, reaching for sun and shadow. I was a mystery to myself. And surrounded by mystery also. This tree. I touched its bark, wanted to be closer. I sat on the ground and wrapped my arms around the trunk, legs too, sex pressed up close and moving the way I'd moved against my husband's thigh, and there was no one to stop me, no one to scold me, no one to bear witness but the birds.

That night, as we lay together, catching our breath, sweat cooling on our skin, I said, "It doesn't have to be your real name."

"No?"

"No. Perhaps it's better this way. I'll have a name for you that's all my own."

"I like that."

I could hear the smile in her voice. She was still stroking me, and we both knew we were not done, I had crested only six times, while she—had she reached it? What shape did her own satisfaction take? She seemed to lose herself in my ecstasy, join me in it, growled and moaned and shook against me. She seemed satisfied, but I wasn't sure. I would have liked to ask but had no idea how. I still hadn't touched her in the way I'd been touched. I hadn't even thought of doing so until now, a realization that filled me with amorphous shame. Did she want me to do those things to her, too? Did I want to do them? Curiosity flared in me, followed by fear—how would I know where to begin, what if I failed and she laughed me out of bed into the cold dangers of the world, what awaited if I failed, perhaps I was failing already as this strange woman's wife. Unless this woman wanted to be always the husband. Unless some things were for husbands, some for wives, even in a situation like this one. How would I know? I knew so little of the world, and of bodies, my own body included, and about situations like this I knew even less, a thought that made me feel small, lost in the great sweep of my own life.

For now, there was another matter in the air.

"So what would you like to call me?"

I'd considered this, in the forest, lying sex-drunk under the fig tree that I'd taken as a lover, staring at the sky, thinking of my husband, thinking of us. "Pteron."

"Pteron." Slowly, as if tasting it. *Pteron. Wing.* "Am I your Pteron?"

"Are you not?"

"If you say it, it is so. Psyche, everything I am is yours."

Nights of wonder. Nights of bliss. Nights of blind exploration. I came to know her body, her rhythm, the shape of her wanting and my own.

Her hands on me. They pierced me. Roamed me. Or simply touched me in one place and held still. Waist. Hip. Thigh. The small of my back. Hand holding still as pleasure poured through it, filled me, tore me beautifully apart.

Hands like beings of their own. Birds, flown right from heaven, full of sky and thunder, alighting on me. Nesting on my body. Burrowing for food.

Hands like light, gilding me. Soaking me. Turning me translucent in the dark.

Hands with their own language, their own speaking. Communicating directly to my body with no need of words. A language so ancient and primal it transcended human tongues, the known ones, the lost ones, all of them.

*   *   *

And yet she kept inviting me to words.

"What do you desire?" Her voice through the dark.

"I can't always say it, Pteron."

"Why not?"

"I was never supposed to speak like this. The words I have can't contain . . . this, what we are, what we do."

"Then make new words."

"What!"

"You're afraid, but you don't have to be. Words belong to you, and you can do with them whatever you wish."

"What if I don't want to use them?"

"Words are power. When you speak what you know, or what you want or what you are, you give it power, more existence, more shape inside the texture of the world."

"The world has a texture?"

"Doesn't it? To you?"

"I'd never thought about it that way. But I'm still not sure I want to put words around the—all the things we do."

"Why? Are you ashamed?"

"Of course not!"

"Then?"

"Then—I don't know." I reached for her hip, stroked it. Her smoothness a joy to my palm. She rocked toward me in response, I filled with heat. It always thrilled me, the way we could exchange not only sensual delights, but also words and ideas, all at once, as if we were conversing with both mind and flesh. "Do I seem ashamed?"

"No."

"I just think there's power in silence too. Just like there's power in the dark."

"I see," she said.

"Do you?"

"Mortal girls aren't raised to wield power at all, are they? Of any kind."

My thoughts snagged for a moment on the word *mortal*: Why the emphasis? But my own questions had a stronger pull.

"Are words power?" I said. "Or do they express what's already power-ful?"

"Both."

"I feel like anything I could say about what we do—what we are—would diminish it."

"Nothing can diminish what we do."

"Nothing?"

"Nothing," she murmured, sounding sure.

"All the noblemen of this land would disagree."

Pteron laughed, and I marveled at her bravado. How had she learned to so easily scoff at powerful men?

"But it's true," I said. "To them what we—do, are—is the worst thing. Two women together. Even two men together is more possible. Not for a marriage but—for—bed."

Even now a word like *sex* wouldn't leave my lips; this very skirting of the word might prove her point. I braced for teasing, for a declaration of triumph as my sisters might have done, *you see, it's as I said!*, but none came. It wasn't Pteron's way, to mock me. It was one of the strangest things about her and among the hardest to get used to: she treated me not like a silly child, but as if I were a great philosopher, white-bearded, surrounded by disciples, worthy of the gravest attention. Only not white-bearded at all. Neither old nor male. A young woman, naked in her bed, desired and desiring, yet still philosophically profound. In what kind of world could such a thing be true? In this one. Only this one. The world of this round black room.

"It's true," she said. "Two women is less seen. And I know why."

"Oh? Tell me."

"It's because women are not supposed to want."

I reached for her and stroked her back, which was smooth and muscular, her shoulder blades long and pronounced and sensitive, so intensely sensitive that if I caressed them too much now we'd lose the thread of talk to the tangle of something else. And why not. Let us lose it, I thought. Let us be lost. "And yet," I said, "we do."

Pteron inhaled sharply in that way that signaled we were almost there, in the calm before the torrent, the beautiful torrent—and that I'd managed to unlatch something inside her, buried deep beyond sight. "Yes. We do."

The days grew languorous, rich with memories of the night before that I could roll under my tongue in all my hours. Long days. Evenings sultry with heat. I soaked in the bath, strolled the groves, foraged for berries and mushrooms, lay in the grass and learned the song of birds. Who are you? I asked my own reflection in the stream. Psyche, what have you become? I didn't know. I laughed at the wildness of my own questions, the even wilder answers that flocked to mind. I was nothing, anything, colors in the water that the lightest leaf could rupture into brilliant shards the stream carried away.

My mouth on her. Between her legs. The first time, I'm afraid; of what? Of failing. Of not knowing what to do. I'm tentative and she's patient, lying back, thighs spread wide for me, at rest. Those muscular thighs. I trace them with my tongue on my way in. Explore. Go on. She moves sinuously, makes a sound. She tastes like the river on a hot day, like berries drenched in sun. And the shape of her. Every fold and crease a revelation. I become my mouth, I long to take her in, farther and farther. She moves and I move with her. I cup her thighs, her behind, the great bowl of her from which I drink and drink. My tongue becomes a living thing, a being all its own, pulsing, ravenous. I paint her with my tongue. All the possible colors spring from its tip. My tongue creates. Gives birth to worlds.

Her explosion in my mouth remakes the universe.

She tries to talk, stroking my hair, unable. I rest my head against her thigh.

"That can't have been your first time," she finally breathes.

"Of course it was."

"Tell the truth. Who taught you?"

"You did."

"There is no one like you, Psyche," she says as she pulls me up for a long kiss.

Later that night, when we finally drift to sleep, I dream that I am doing it again, my mouth on her, fused to her body as it writhes in joy— in the village square, on my childhood bed, on the dining table of my childhood home, floating in the sky among stars.

"I want you to show me everything," I murmured into the dark.

"Everything?"

"Yes. Everything about you." *And everything about myself,* I thought but did not say, for it made no sense; how could she show me that? Myself? Yet it was exactly what she'd been doing.

"You're delicious."

"Don't change the subject."

"I mean it."

"I know how you are."

In response, she stroked my body, long, deep movements along my thighs and waist and breasts that always sent me to distraction.

But I would not be distracted tonight. "Tell me a secret about your-self, one you're afraid to share."

I thought she'd laugh and dive right into the game—for she was bold, my husband, afraid of nothing—but she was silent for a long time. Her caresses slowed, grew lighter.

"Pteron?"

"Yes."

"What are you thinking about?"

"A secret."

"Tell me."

"I can't."

"Of course you can."

"I don't think so, Psyche."

I was struck by two things at once: she'd put up a wall between us, and also, she'd admitted to the secret's existence. Some part of her resisted telling me, but another part of her longed to tell. Instinct rose in me; I followed it. "What if you try? There's nothing I can't hear from you. I'm not afraid."

"Is that really true?"

I wasn't sure whether it was true. Perhaps I had no fear, or perhaps I had plenty of it but my curiosity was stronger, able to wrestle fear to the ground. "Of course it's true."

Silence stretched into the darkness. Her hands lingered on my hips. I waited.

"I'm not a normal woman."

What could she mean? Could it be true? Not a woman . . . Could it mean—my husband, a goddess? It would explain a great deal, the palace, the comment about *mortal girls*, the irresistible charm that radiated even through the dark. But if she was a goddess, then—

"I mean to say, I am a woman."

I inhaled slowly. Not a goddess, then. How quickly my mind slipped away from that thought, chiding itself as it went, *Who do you think you are?*

"I am a woman and also, at the same time, I am more."

My thoughts spun with such intensity that I clung to the bedding beneath me as if to brace for a fall. What's more than a woman? A man; so it was always said; men were better, stronger, superior, so at least went the accepted logic of the world. But even men, with all their power, could not be *more* than a woman, and also *be* one. "I do not understand," I said. "But I want to."

Pteron kissed me, long and slow, and at first I wondered whether this was her response, an explanation offered in the rhythm of her tongue. It would be enough. I wouldn't press further. I'd become used to this from her, the sudden drawing of a veil, you can't know that or that, no more questions, back to the beauty of the Now. But then she said, "Are you sure?"

"Yes, of course." And I meant it. With every fiber of myself I wanted to understand.

She guided my hand to her sex. I moved there, intrigued, delighted, for it was a thrilling place for my hand to be, and it seemed that perhaps this was what Pteron meant, that she was more than a woman because normal women did not do such things, did not ask directly for other women to touch them, an idea I could swim with, could swim through, though it also implied that I too was not just a woman but also more than one, a thought I'd have to ponder later as I wove or walked or— Pteron took my wrist gently, stilled it.

I would have asked why, I opened my mouth to form the question, but then I stopped. Held my breath. What was this? In my hand? Change. Metamorphosis, swift and smooth. The nub of her grew large and long, into a shaft, still warm, still firm, alive against my palm.

"What—"

"It's what you think it is."

But I had no thoughts. I was all thought. My mind became translucent and filled with the dark, as if I suddenly had no skin, no borders, no defenses at all, and I could only feel the rush of it, succumb to a great black swirl of night.

"Like a man's?"

"Like a man's."

I drew my hand away, instinctively. Brought it slowly back.

"Are you afraid?"

"No," I said, though I wasn't sure. Inside me, an inscrutable darkness, *something monstrous*.

"I can ungrow it—"

"No. Don't. Unless you want to."

"I want—" She broke off, and I felt her hold her breath, release it. "I want to know what you're thinking."

Where to begin. This palace, this dark round chamber, had dismantled all I knew of the world or thought I'd known. Wonder. Curiosity. Exhilaration. A slash of fear. "Does it hurt, to do that—to change?"

"No." She laughed. "Not at all."

"But how is it possible?"

"Psyche. Beloved. Who defines the possible?"

"The gods," I said before I knew my own mind, before I could reflect on whether it was true.

"Ah, so—the gods." She sounded amused, though there was a hoarseness to her I hadn't heard before; my hand was still wrapped lightly around her phallus; was that pleasure? "Let's say for just a moment that this is true." She paused, sighed, for I'd let my fingers move lightly against her.

"Shall I stop?"

"No, please—don't."

I couldn't resist teasing. "Are you sure?"

"I beg you."

"Then you'd better keep talking." A thrill moved through me at this reversal of our usual roles, the power of my hand.

"All right."

She paused as if to steady her voice and thoughts. Inhaled.

"Let's say the gods . . . define what's possible. Well, rumor has it, does it not . . . that they can metamorphose? Zeus into a swan. Nymphs into trees."

"Yes."

"Well . . ."

I stopped my hand. "I said keep talking."

"I can't, Psyche."

Rare words from her.

I thrilled at them.

I pulled my hand away.

Pteron moaned. "I see. So. Hmm—take Zeus."

My hand curled back around her phallus.

"The feathers, the beak, the lengthening neck. Isn't that all a more drastic change than this?"

"I suppose."

"Then why shouldn't this exist?"

Her logic only raised more questions, but I could not tame the chaos of my thoughts. I wanted to rove over Pteron, discover her body anew. Who cared about the why and what and is it possibles, when there was this, the simple *Here it is, what next?* What next? *Everything next,* I thought. The crush of Pteron's breasts against my own, her rich, deep woman-voice, I wanted everything, all of her, every bit of Pteron that she'd give, look what she brought me tonight, more surprises, secrets older than the earth itself or something brightly new, what to call it, what can it mean, who knows, who cares, Pteron, I'd go anywhere with you, I'd follow you right into the underworld if that was where you were going. It touched me too, the sudden shyness in Pteron, who was usually the incarnation of daring, the one who taught me how to unlatch, the one who boldly forged the way to ecstasy along a thousand paths, now revealing this new dimension of herself, as if she'd feared that I would spurn her, that her bride might shrink away in disgust, as if there were a vulnerable spot inside her that she now was making known and that evoked in me a fierce love along with a wave of relief that I was not the only one to bare those soft parts like a snail venturing out of its shell, easily crushed yet craving the sun. Pteron was waiting, holding back her desire, I could tell from the tension in her hips as she kept them absolutely still. And yes, we could keep talking, as always there were droves of things I longed to say to her and hear her say, questions roared through me, but so did lust, and why not dive toward it, for this was our palace after all, a house where wonders already formed the center of our lives. What was one more? Everything we did and everything we were already defied laws both human and divine. I drew her in for a kiss. Our mouths met deep and slow. I wrapped my legs around her, used them to pull her hips toward mine.

"You don't have to," she whispered into my ear, breath ragged.

"I know."

We moved against each other and soon she was inside me, as she had been before with her hands and tongue and it was her, still her, ever my Pteron in her many-shaped hungers, my same lover continuing the same music we'd been making all this time, and I could welcome her with all my being, could wrap my thighs around her and pull her in deep, as together we rode and rode the mare of our delight.

We crested brutally, at the same time, as we had done before, for she reached her own crest inside her lover or against her with hand or thigh. She'd told me many times that her pleasure lived in giving. Now I finally understood. It was this, it was absolutely this, the same clasping, the same bellow and near-weep, the bite of my shoulder that would leave marks for me to bask in the next day, I reveled in the thought of those marks tomorrow even as I pressed close, closer, I could never press in close enough, wanted the merge to last a lifetime. Though it would not. It always ebbed. So instead—I thought as I dug nails into her back—this is what we do. We seek it over and over, tangling our bodies into shapes of our invention. How many forms can we make together, are they infinite, are we infinite, I wondered as she collapsed against me, teeth still buried in my flesh.

We lay together in a sumptuous silence for a long time.

"So," she finally said. "You're not . . . disgusted?"

"Ha!"

"What?"

"Did I seem disgusted?"

She laughed tentatively. "Not exactly."

"How could I ever be disgusted by you?"

She was quiet.

"Pteron?"

"You constantly amaze me."

I smiled, remembered I couldn't be seen, made a sound of delight.

"You are like no other woman, Psyche."

"I assume you've known a lot of other women." I marveled at my own boldness at bringing up her life outside this room.

"Not . . . not like this."

I relished the thought. Me. Giving her something no one else had. "What's different?"

"Your . . . embrace of me. It's more than I'd imagined. It's—" She fell silent for a time; I held my breath. "It's everything. You are everything."

"Pteron. Sweet Pteron."

"Sweet?"

"Sweetbitter. All the tastes."

"That's better." She hummed a sound of approval. "I thought perhaps you might not take kindly to such parts—that it wouldn't be to your liking."

"And what about your liking?"

"You are my queen. Your joy is my joy."

I laughed, loose-limbed, still drunk on her. "Liar."

"How dare you!"

But she was laughing too. Our laughs twined together in the sweat-thick air.

"I do want to know your liking, Pteron. You can't hoard it away from me forever."

"You don't believe me, Psyche, but it's true. Your joy is my world. My ecstasy."

"I don't know what to say to that."

"Whatever you want to say."

"Well, there is this: if I'm to tell you the truth, I used to fear it. The wedding night, a man's thing, the first time."

"Because of what the Oracle said?"

I lay back into my pillow, reached out for her. She still had her phallus, now a soft, curled snail without a shell, damp and satisfied. More shape-shifting, I thought. This softening its own enchantment. I felt it twitch and swell a little beneath my hand. "Before all that, too."

"Because you hadn't seen one?"

"I had. On goats, and sheep, and dogs. But there were stories in our village of wedding nights that could turn violent for a girl."

"I see." Her fingers at my waist, in my hair, and it was a game, I thought, to test how long she could keep her voice steady while I held her this way. "You're right about those dangers, believe me. But they're not caused by a man's phallus. The mind is where violence begins."

I made a sound of doubt, but I was listening.

"Consider a different body part: hands. Men have killed with their hands but also built with them, loved with them. You don't fear all hands, do you?"

"I think I see what you mean. But"—I tried to pull together my thoughts—"it still doesn't make sense."

"What doesn't?"

"What you said about Zeus. When he became a swan, as legend has it, he was still male. That was the whole point, after all—he did it to ravish Leda."

"Ha! And he thinks he has to be male to do that."

"Pteron!"

"What?"

I thought of what might happen if the gods could hear us, the scoffing in her voice. In my village, no one would have dared to mock Zeus. "You're right—you don't have to be male to ravage someone, well I know it now, my love. But what I'm saying is, when he changes into a swan, eagle, serpent, any animal form, that part of him as far as we know has stayed the same."

"Perhaps he gives it plumage."

"Poor Leda!"

She laughed, and I joined her. Psyche, I thought, look what you've become, daring to laugh at Zeus himself, the god who rules the gods. I was amazed by my brazenness, enthralled by it, scared of where it might lead.

"Yes," Pteron said. "Poor Leda. But that's a different matter. It's not that Zeus *cannot* change that part of himself, but that he *does not*."

"Does that really make a difference?"

"Of course it does! Do you know what it means?"

"What?"

"That it's Zeus who suffers from a lack of imagination."

"What a thing to say!"

"Shall we imagine it? Zeus devising a female sex on his swan-body to pleasure a woman?"

"Is there no limit to what you'll imagine?"

She leaned in close. "None."

"Don't you ever fear punishment?"

I felt her body tense, though she kept her voice light. "For what?"

"For crossing a border that even Zeus has not crossed."

"And which is that? The border of male and female?"

I strained to think through words I'd never pulled together before. "Yes."

"It's not such a deep border, after all." She traced delectable lines along my skin, as if she could not resist me, though later I would wonder whether the roving of her hands was also meant to distract from the edges of our exchange. "Or perhaps the border is a mountain range, the kind people declare impossible to cross, but whose ravines are full of green and secret life."

I thought of the mountains that lined our valley. "Perhaps it is."

"You don't like my example."

"No, I love it. It's just that I mean something else."

"Then say it."

"It's not that this change, this crossing, is harder to realize, but that it might be . . . a deeper crime. Not to me. Never to me. I'm just afraid for you."

"Me? *You* are afraid for *me*?"

I nodded, unseen. "I couldn't bear for anything to happen to you."

Pteron made a sound that could have been tender or something else, rooted in some hidden place inside her. "Why not?"

"Now you're just teasing."

"Perhaps." She was still stroking me, speaking gently to my skin. "But a deeper crime against whom?"

"All of them. Men. Gods. Who could ever accept such a thing?"

"Can you?"

"Yes."

"Are you sure?"

Her voice came delicate now, cautious, the closest I'd ever heard to childlike; I wondered what she'd been like as a child, what kind of girlhood possibly led to an existence like this one, like hers. I couldn't fathom it.

"I think it's"—I searched for the words—"beautiful." I paused; there was more than that, a great deal more, but to wrap words around what she was, what she'd shown and was still showing me, of herself, of the world, seemed a Herculean task, a conversation that could take lifetimes. "But I meant people beyond this palace, who would not wish us well." I feared that if I said more, I'd start to paint the terror into being. The whole world, it seemed, both man and god, would be against the metamorphosis Pteron had shown me. After what I'd seen of my suitors, I could no longer believe in the hearts of strangers, would never trust them again.

"Psyche." She leaned in close so I caught the warm scent of her breath. "Don't worry about that. About any of them."

"How can I not?" I wanted more than anything to be persuaded, to believe her brash vision of the world.

"They're not here in this palace—none of them. And that is precisely why we have it. I built this palace for our freedom. I built this palace for you."

"In the mountains of the borderlands?"

She replied with the sheer force of her kiss.

10

She had not prepared for this. Could never have been prepared. All day she soared from place to place, fulfilling her duties, shooting arrows to shape the energetic balance of the world—a woodcutter and a widow, a princess and a thief, a traveling bard and his own wife who'd been waiting for him to come home—a normal day's work. Nothing grand, nothing taxing. Meanwhile, inside her, a thousand thoughts vied for space.

Borderlands. The mountains of the borderlands. How had Psyche known to say such a thing? Did she know, could she imagine, what it rattled inside Eros? How the very landscape of reality was expanded by her words? How could such a night have been predicted? Even in her wildest hopes for this unsanctioned marriage, this marriage beyond the bounds of law, she hadn't imagined she could be so thoroughly transformed. So thoroughly seen. Seen! In the dark? In a marriage forged entirely in the dark? If anything, she'd thought perhaps some distances could never be crossed, that they'd have to adapt to some limits in their knowing of each other, so she'd gone into that round black room knowing that without her arrows she was just as vulnerable to rejection as any mortal might be (though of course she knew her powers; her voice; her presence; what her hands could do, what happened through her hands; the way a woman or nymph could be pulled into her orbit; the sensuous arts she'd perfected over centuries). Her highest hope was that they'd connect in some authentic way. Any authentic way at all. But this Psyche was taking it further. She invited Eros into deeper and deeper spaces, a flight akin to falling. Never had Eros thought she'd feel so out of control, so drunk, euphoric and torn open. Never had she thought she'd reveal her full self, reveal the secret she kept hidden even from the gods—especially from the gods. Dangerous to do so even under cover of night, even in the strongest shielding spell.

But she'd done it now. Revealed it. Her secret, and her crime.

Long ago, when she was young, it was a natural part of her, welcome and full of ease.

How free she'd been, before the trouble began. Her body fluid, perfect, itself entire. How true she'd been and how alive.

But then the trouble found her.

It began when, one afternoon, centuries ago, she idled by the river with a wood nymph. Her name was Rhanis. Eros should have known better: Zeus had had his eye on this same nymph, and he'd told Eros to prick her with an arrow on his behalf, but Eros hadn't done it, for Rhanis had eyes like liquid joy and Eros had seen too many nymphs go dead-eyed after Zeus was done with them, arrows or no. By that time, Eros had had passion at her beck and call for centuries. She'd lain with thousands of nymphs and mortal women and even a smattering of mortal men, drawing in her wings to take human form or swooping down on them in dreams. She'd satisfied her curiosity about all the permutations of desire, the hungers of this orifice or that one, the various shapes and avenues of sex—there were so many pathways—for sex was a city with infinite gates surrounding it like the facets of a jewel, hello, welcome traveler, there's plenty for you to find in our town, you can enter here or here or here.

She knew what her arrows could do. But now, she also wanted to experience desire without her arrows, to approach someone in a way that was unenchanted, pure. Someone like Rhanis. Defiance, to lie with her now, in the sun-drenched grass, catching their breath after running along the bank, hand in hand. Defiance to let her hands roam the nymph's body, leaving streaks of ecstasy wherever they went, for that was the nature of her hands, Eros's hands, energy flowed through them when she intended it, and that energy could melt a lover into utmost bliss. *How do you do that?* Rhanis breathed as she rode the waves, as she climaxed many times. *How do you do it?* And then, after a long while, *What else have you got?* The nymph grew bold, her hands roved, *Ah, the famous Eros,* she said, *let's see what you've got between your legs, is it made of gold?*—laughing—and as she rubbed, boom, there it was, before Eros's mind could catch up with her body, a phallus growing in that sweet palm.

It had happened before, often, all her life. As a child, she'd thought it a normal gift, possessed by every god. Even now that she knew better, it seemed ridiculous that it should matter much, when divine life teemed with metamorphoses, why such a fuss about this one? The molding of the vitality between her legs into different shapes? Where was the harm? Hidden from the gaze of Zeus, there was none. *What's this?* Rhanis said, delighted. *What's this?* And before Eros could delve into the cosmic layers of that question, the girl found her way to her own answers, for this particular wood nymph was not prone to philosophizing, not with carnal matters at hand; she had her own way of seeking knowledge and she sought it with abandon that afternoon. In the throes of that happiness, Eros forgot to cast a veil over their tryst, to shield it from divine eyes. Zeus saw almost immediately, for his attention had not wavered from Rhanis, and he'd been looking for the right moment to chase her. Before the wind could carry the news up to Olympus, he'd already opened his seeing and watched them for hours, stirring his cauldron of rage.

The next day, Zeus summoned Eros and Aphrodite. Thunder rang at the center of their minds: *Appear before me.*

"Child," Aphrodite muttered as they soared up the steep face of Olympus, "what did you do now?"

They stood before him in the great shining hall. The throne room of Olympus, which always filled Eros with awe and nausea. Vaulting gold ceilings. Marble pillars, impossibly tall. A colonnade on either side that let out to the whirling sky. And at the center, gleaming stairs to the platform that held the thrones, the long row of them, with Zeus's seat at the center, the largest by far, blistering with lightning bolts and intricate mosaics of gems. Hephaestus's handiwork, of course. There he sat, Zeus, glowering, his bad mood rippling across the hall. Hera was beside him, in her smaller throne. Hera, with her quiet glow and hair in glistening braids.

Of all the gods and goddesses, none formed a greater mystery to Eros than Hera, for they oversaw such different realms. Vied over them. Though Hera never vied directly, at least not in Eros's presence. She could lash out when she wanted, as brutally as any god, Ares included, but unlike that god of war she had no need for other gods to see; in fact, perhaps thrived in the unseeing, fighting her battles in underground ways not visible until it was too late. Blood spilled. Cage closed. Some battles were waged with so much secrecy they might not even be called battles at all, but something else, tending her sacred hearth, perhaps. Protecting the hearth. Protecting the bonds of marriage in the face of their defilement. Hera was fearsome. She'd punished her husband's lovers with all the savagery of Ares, even—and this was the part Eros could not forgive, for it clawed at her mind like a trapped ghost—even when they'd tried to resist Zeus's advances. Hera had tortured the girl

Callisto, who'd wanted nothing more than to stay free of men and roam the forest with Artemis and her fellow virgin huntresses, who loved the hunt and the wild and female friendships; Callisto had fought Zeus's embraces as hard as she could yet still bore the blame for carrying his child and was doomed as a result. Poor Io, the river's daughter, had also run and run from Zeus, for she did not want him, and on seeing his firm member and outstretched arms she was not excited but afraid. For days she ran. Her terror built and did not soften when he seized and took her. But even so, Hera understood that punishing her husband directly did not serve her own interests. When you are married to the king of the gods, and you want to keep your queenly power, the most convenient path is to prop up your king, even when he crosses you, even when he hurts others, and this was the path Hera chose (except for once, when she plotted to overthrow Zeus, a story blurred by rumor and conjecture and retold only in the hush of secret voices). Because of this, because it suited her, Hera gave Io all the rage and all the blame. Poor Io, imprisoned in a cow's body, guarded by a monster with a hundred eyes. How she'd suffered. How droves of girls and nymphs and women had suffered under Hera's hands. There was no mercy from Hera when she felt under threat. Her revenge was swift, sharp. And she had little affection for Aphrodite and Eros, for she saw their realms as sources of the problem. Desire. Unruly love. Disregard for marriage. The gold-tipped arrows that could tempt husbands and wives alike to shun their vows in the arms of a lover. For Eros, this was her work, her realm, and her delight; for Aphrodite it was the inevitable outcome of her power; for Hera it was enemy territory. This made every visit to the throne room tense. Including now. The air crackled, grew taut. Before anyone spoke, the battle lines were drawn. Hera smiled peacefully, yet Eros could feel her gathering energies like a storm.

"Great Father," Aphrodite said, and knelt.

"Why can't you control your daughter?" Zeus shouted, and Eros felt him glaring down at them though she didn't dare raise her head. "She's using more than she was granted. It's an aberration. She has no right to claim the territory of both goddess and god."

You're just jealous I pleasured her better than you could. She bit her tongue to keep from blurting out her thoughts.

"She was born female; to defy that is a crime."

"Great Zeus—"

"I'll strip her of her powers for this!"

Eros scanned the other thrones on the platform, wondering why they were empty. Where were the other gods and goddesses? Perhaps they'd had business to attend to; perhaps Zeus had made them clear the hall to conceal this challenge to his power. Would it be better or worse, if they were here? She didn't know. Her mind had snagged on one phrase, so that the rest of his threats and criticisms landed as if at a distance. *Using more.* More what? Power? Space? Divine force? What was the element she was using, was it a *more* to shift the way she did? If she had no right to claim it, why did she have it, how had it been made to exist? If no god had granted what she was *using*, then where did it come from? Did it really need granting, or did it simply spring into being within her, a natural existence that some powers, his powers, sought to thresh or cage or kill? Could it be—could it even be—that this natural force rose up not only in her, but in others as well? Goddesses, women, girls? That she wasn't the only expansive one?

She might have tried to shape these thoughts into words, but it was her mother who spoke first. Her mother, who knew her better than anyone else, and who for all their quarrels had stood beside her as she grew and revealed herself, who understood that her daughter would shrivel if forced to keep inside a single realm, even the realm of the feminine, a realm of great magnificence, as Aphrodite well knew, for she ruled it herself. She had a daughter for whom the feminine was not her only home. *I have known this,* she'd croon later, when they were finally alone, *since you were small, that you are female but also—you; understand?* And when Eros said, *No, I don't understand, tell me what you mean,* her mother would go silent for a few beats before finally saying, *Free.*

"Good Father," Aphrodite said. "I beg your mercy."

She pleaded the case from every angle. It was good, she said, to respect nature, even in its oddness, such as misshapen fruit that yielded perfectly fine juice. It was good to have leniency. A sense of humor. Some things were silly, after all; even the ridiculous deserves its worldly place. As she spoke, the throne room warmed, filling with the rich honey of her voice, and Eros felt Zeus's rage not exactly dissipate but soften its edges, grow malleable, while Hera's silent storm grew more intense.

"Consider," Aphrodite added, "the benefit to immortals: the better Eros knows the male realm, the better she can serve the desires of male gods."

"Hmm!" said Zeus, stroking his beard in a manner that struck Eros as lascivious, though she immediately buried the thought. "Go on."

Beside him, Hera seemed to tremble almost imperceptibly, though her face remained composed. It was a risk, for Aphrodite to mention such advantages so bluntly in Hera's presence. She was, after all, offering the very thing Hera sought to prevent. It would not do to incur a goddess's wrath while trying to escape that of a god. Eros watched the sunlight catch on Hera's black braids, and thought of darkness, the shroud it could provide. She had spent her early years in darkness, Hera. She'd been born to the great Titan goddess Rhea, only for her father Kronos, the Titan god, to consume her. He devoured all his children to prevent a prophecy—that one of them would overtake his power—from coming true. Only Zeus had escaped, when Rhea, too heartbroken to face the loss of another child, had hidden him in a Cretan cave and given her husband a swaddled stone to eat instead. By the time Zeus grew into immortal manhood and returned to free his brothers and sisters from their father's belly, Hera too had reached her prime. All those years, growing up in the dark. All those years in the abyss inside Kronos, wished dead, clinging to life. What had that done to her? Now Kronos and the Titans were long defeated, and she reigned. Or sat beside Zeus as he reigned. Sat beside him and seethed, deep below the surface, in a dark as whole and bottomless as the one where she'd been raised.

In that moment, watching Hera, Eros felt a new idea stir deep inside her. Darkness as protection. Darkness as a refuge for what burns to be free.

Meanwhile, Aphrodite was not fazed. If she sensed Hera's displeasure, it only encouraged her, a sign that her argument would hold water where it counted.

"Great Zeus," she continued, "you could let my daughter's nature keep on, in your infinite mercy, and in return she will serve you, serve all of us, all the better with arrows as steady as hawks."

Zeus settled his gaze on Eros, who kept her eyes lowered to the gem-encrusted floor and forced herself to let him study her. To be looked upon by Zeus was no small thing. It was an experience to be borne. Mortals never came out of the experience unchanged, and even immortals could be shaped by the intensity of his looking, blessed or warped or tumbled. She inhaled. She held her breath. She drew her senses inward but resisted throwing up a shield, for Zeus would sense it and would surely not grow more generous as a result. Better to appear open, small, unthreatening. Defang your thoughts. Shrink into yourself. Pretend to be flimsy, susceptible to the winds. Time stopped, under Zeus's gaze; time swooped, collapsed, broke open. There was no time and everything was time; there was no you, only a subsuming. He wanted to reduce her. She would not let him. She would fake a smallness she did not feel.

"You're lucky, goddess," he finally said. "I am in a generous mood. I'll give this child of yours the freedom you request."

"Great Father," Aphrodite began, still on her knees, "you're too—"

But Zeus was not finished. "On two conditions."

Aphrodite's flinch was so subtle nobody but Eros could have sensed it. "Of course, Great Father."

"First: when she becomes a man, she must be fully male. None of this in-between, blended nonsense. One thing or the other. The full disguise or none at all."

Eros looked away, at the sky beyond the colonnade, streaked with a single white cloud. No birds in sight, for this was too high for their flight to reach. She railed inside at the word *disguise*, at the stifling rule, but she felt her mother send a flare of warning as clear as if she'd spoken: *don't protest.*

"Second: when she takes females as a man, I get to watch."

Eros's skin crawled. "No," she said, "absolutely not."

"Daughter." Aphrodite's voice rippled with warning.

"I am being lenient with you," Zeus said.

"We understand that." Aphrodite rose, took a step forward. "We'll agree to it."

Eros opened her mouth to contradict her but stopped at her mother's stern look. She closed her mouth. She understood. She was no longer young but she was still her mother's charge; this negotiation was out of her hands, the tides of power rippled far beyond her reach.

Aphrodite turned back to Zeus. "But only the first three times."

Zeus grunted. He turned to Hera. "How did Aphrodite get so spoiled?"

Hera, drawn into the conversation for the first time, regarded him for a long moment, as if relishing the hall's attention on her, as if to say, *Finally, here it is, my due.* But it could not last, as she well knew. She seemed to weigh a range of possible answers for their consequences; should she be direct, lash out at Aphrodite, who might one day be needed for a favor? Or use this moment to get revenge or strengthen alliances, and if so on whom, with whom? She smiled. "Husband, are you truly asking *me*?"

Zeus laughed.

Aphrodite's spine remained erect, palms open at her sides, turned toward the throne as if to catch its radiance. Eros stared at the backs of her mother's exquisite hands. All of this, she thought, every bit of what my mother is doing, is for my sake. The goddess of love, and look how much love she gives me.

Zeus returned his gaze to Aphrodite. "If only you weren't so beautiful. It's really a problem at times like these."

Beside him Hera went brittle again, her moment already gone.

"Thirty times," Zeus said.

"Nine," Aphrodite said.

"Nine," grumbled Zeus.

And so the agreement was made.

Eros flew from Olympus with that number spearing her chest, all pain and horror. Nine. No. Impossible. Nine.

Back at their own palace, she erupted at her mother. "How could you? I don't want to do it! I won't!"

"Daughter, calm down. Look at all I've done for you. Can't you see that I have saved you?"

"I can't go through with it, Mother. Not nine times, not even one."

"It'll be over before you know it, and then you'll be free. Is this not what you wanted?"

It was not what she had wanted. *Then you'll be free.* Those words opened a terrible longing within her. To have what Zeus had forbidden forever. To be whole, to express herself as she saw fit when she saw fit and allow her body its own song, not only for sex, but at other times too, without having to warp herself into a fully male shape or stay in the mold of female, for though she relished each of those forms, neither was the whole of her; she was both of these, she spanned the realms, she held it all. Between female and male, within them and beyond them, lay more than had been given name and more than Zeus himself wanted to see manifest in the world. Play and joy and searching. Ease and art and fluid truth. Body as lake. Body as sky. Body as wind and flow. The unscripted dance of what Eros knew could also be.

How she dreaded the Nine.

How she longed to be dance.

How she wondered what it would take to be free.

11

I spent my time as I pleased. A liquor to get drunk on. I could lie on the floor or on the ground as long as I liked, wrap my legs around the fig tree as often as I liked, and I did like to do so often, it turned out, for the heat of my nights spilled over into mornings, and sometimes I could not wait. The day without Pteron was too long, my body made demands and I fulfilled them, outside, with the fig tree, my daytime lover, secret friend. Sun stabbed through the green mesh of her leaves. I savored her. I savored myself. Most of the time I even forgot to be ashamed. I felt bright inside, as if the sun itself had stolen its way into my body and declared it home.

I reached for other things too, as I moved through the palace and lust rose inside me. Objects I clasped between my legs and rubbed against to blunt the need. A clay jug. An apple I later ate, streaked with my own juices. A ball of wool. The pestle from the mortar in the banquet room, which slid into me with ease, and the mortar too, its lip a welcome rough edge.

These moments sated me but not for long.

To truly manage my lust during the day, I needed something larger, deeper, a channel for my energies.

I found it in the act of creation.

It happened instinctively: more and more, I found myself turning to the loom. My feet carried me there some days before my mind knew where I was going. I'd be thinking of something else and suddenly there I was, sinking onto the stool, hands already starting to weave. My body craved the slow flight of threads, their loop and sway, my hands the wind that made them dance. On some days, I felt so peeled open by the intensity of my nights, so raw and bared to the world, that it felt as though my very soul entered those threads and soared through them, moved through color after color. So much color in this palace, no dyes spared. The colors saturated me; lacerated me. As if my skin were dissolved by what we did in the night and there were no more barriers between my pure sensation and the colors of the world. The world spilled in, I could not filter it. A single red or royal purple could whip my soul awake. I wanted to be whipped awake even though sometimes the intensity made me weep—and even this was a great luxury, to make whatever sound my body wanted, to sob, wail, whisper, or croon in response to color. I did not have to stay composed for the sake of others. Or to seem sane. What did it mean, anyway, to be sane? To shut up and be small? I didn't want it and I didn't have to do it. I made noise when I wished and spent hours, too, in absorbed silence, weaving. I grew instinctive in my use of color, texture, shape. Unlike before, I had no need to make garments for myself or for a household, for all of that was taken care of, which gave me the delirious freedom to make whatever I wished. The riches of it, the riches of a queen, the loom of a queen.

I dared myself to behave like a queen.

Every day I thought it, sometimes even said it aloud: *Psyche, what would you do right now if you were royalty?* And then I did that.

I wove my visions. I wove the wild.

If I didn't like the way a tapestry came out, I undid it and began again. There was no urgency, no demand from anywhere but my own inner impulse. I could take ten years on a single piece if I liked—though instead, gradually, tapestries began to pile in the corner, my own visions made palpable, made real beyond the secret chambers of my mind. Colors dipped and churned beneath my hands; shapes sprang into being: flowers, lions, women, winged creatures, rivers, trees, goblets, stars, gates, boats, knives, more women, naked women, dancing women, women with arrows, women with knives, cliffs, rocks, ships, slashing rays of sun. It thrilled me to watch their birth on the loom. I thought of Arachne, a woman who—like me— had been said to anger a goddess, in her case by boasting that her weavings outshone the work of Athena herself. I steered clear of such claims, even in my own mind, for I had no need of any more divine enemies, let alone of being made a spider. Yet when I looked at my handiwork, I felt proud. I wasn't used to the feeling. Ever, of anything. The feeling swelled in me, made my body alive. I was constantly hungry for creation. Even as I wove, I began to dream of new pursuits. New adventures. New channels for the visions that sparked behind my eyelids, seeking home. And yet it was weeks before I finally connected this to the pots of paint stacked along one side of the room that perhaps were not simply left over from the building of this palace, as I'd initially thought. That perhaps could be for me.

"Can I use them?" I asked Pteron, in the night.

"Of course."

"To paint?"

"Yes."

"To paint on what?"

"On whatever you wish."

"Even the walls?" I said, laughing and defiant.

"Why not?"

"You cannot be serious."

"You're not serious?"

"I—" My voice broke off. "I don't know. Today I was staring at the eastern wall of the main hall and saw griffins soaring, women riding on their backs—"

"Sounds lovely."

"—and then they became huntresses, running through a forest under the moon."

"And you want to paint that."

"Yes."

"Then do it."

"Surely not on the wall? I'm just learning and have no one to apprentice to. I could start by painting pots."

"You could."

"I'm terrified of painting on the walls of this palace."

"Why?"

I searched for words. "Because I could mar them. Because I don't know how. I could ruin a beautiful thing."

"Or you could make it still more beautiful."

"I doubt that."

"Psyche," she whispered into my hair, "this palace is yours. Do with it as you will and be free."

I carried those words with me into and through my days.

Free, I thought as I opened the paint pots and peered inside. *Free,* as I stirred and dipped, as I brushed at bowls and jugs, making shapes, practicing. *Free* as women's forms emerged from my brush, one after another, stroke by stroke. Men painted, women did not. There had been one servant at my father's house who'd learned the craft, and I'd occasionally watched him with his brush, the way he touched it to a surface with such lightness it might seem nothing would come of it, no picture would emerge, the surface would remain the same as it had always been, but no: the contact was enough to make a line, a dot, another line, a curve that birthed an arm or an eye or a bird. Just-right pressure. Like this? Like this. No, not like that—a smudge on the pot. It was ruined. I'd ruined it, I couldn't be trusted with a brush! I stalked out of the room, marched outside, circled the orchard. The chant filled my mind again: *As you will, be free.* I had never been so free. I'd never dreamed such freedom could exist, not anywhere on this earth. I didn't know how to inhabit it. But what if such a thing were possible to learn? What would it look like? So what if a free woman ruins pots or bowls or jugs? So what if some of her markings come out ugly or wrong? She can still use the dishware as it is, marred with lines that tell the story of her efforts, of her study, of the shapes she was aiming to create. Because she is free, there is no one to tell her the pot or bowl or jug is wrong. Or that she is wrong.

Except her own self.

I strode back inside. Brush. Pot. Close your eyes, imagine. Light touch, just enough, where is that right pressure? What do you see behind closed lids? Open your eyes, begin again.

I painted and painted and painted.

Over the days, the ceramics gathered, one after another, bearing my paint, bearing my visions translated into the physical realm. Slowly, very slowly, I improved. I waited impatiently for the paint to dry so I could run my hand along it, marvel, thrill at having changed a thing according to my own desire. A few times I could not wait and I smeared the paint, ruined the work. No matter, I told myself. There are many pots. Is that not what a queen would say? I rose in the morning eager to paint, often spending hours in my creation room—as I'd come to call it in my mind— before breaking my fast. Sex at night, painting and weaving by day, from one fulfillment to the other. I rode those rhythms for a long time until finally, one day, I gathered my daring and, brush in hand, turned toward the wall and saw exactly what I wanted to create there, ready to begin.

Nights full of sweet, untampered joys. We played like cubs discovering the world; we twined like ancient currents of the sea. We took delight, drank from each other, grew thirsty again. We laughed, we wept, we bit each other's shoulders and thighs, we slept in the caverns of our loving. Each night I feared she would not come, that she'd tire of me or that the Fates would cut this life too beautiful to be permitted to exist, and each night she kept her promise and returned.

On some nights, we were gentle with each other, moving with a river's sweetness.

On other nights I'd bite and claw at her, draw blood that I felt as wetness in the dark and found in dried remains under my fingernails the next day. I was monstrous with her, unleashed.

She let me tear at her flesh. Took me spread wide beneath her. Took me on all fours like a dog or goat. Took me pinned facedown beneath her, roughly, with the command *don't move* because she knew how forcefully it would make me crest. She turned me on my side, held me by the hips, let me mount her like a steed. With her hands, mouth, phallus, with the rhythm of her wanting, with her body pressed against mine, she satisfied my thirst and woke it terribly, so that the more she gave me, the thirstier I became.

Everything she did, I welcomed. I needed her brutality as well as her tenderness and everything in between. She knew how to push me to the edge of madness and hold me there, quivering, about to fall, falling, always landing in some place that made me want to feel that push again. She knew when I needed softness and when hard teeth might shock me into joy. She knew my hungers before they rose in me. How she could know so much, I couldn't imagine. Sometimes, before we started, she'd run her fingers lightly across my naked skin as if listening to it, seeking signals the way a bear might listen to a river for the shudder of fish. Paw in the water. What's this, what's here. From there she might explode in any direction: I might find myself rocked sweetly or spread wide or on my hands and knees beneath her storm.

She gave me more when I demanded it. She met my violence and did not flag. She was limber, tireless, and astonishingly strong, lean muscularity with a woman's curves. My fingers memorized the shape of her, traced her greedily, imagined what it would be like to lay eyes on her. I crushed her to me, swallowed her with my hungry thighs. Rode her face and gripped her curls like reins. Traced her shoulder blades until she bucked and writhed and gave me what I wanted, which was her bliss and mine, in every form, without end.

There was so much about Pteron that was not possible and yet was true. She did not submit to the accepted logic of the world.

The logic of the world was a metal she melted in the forge of her loving.

Entire armories could be vanquished by her laugh alone.

I learned her body. In all its shapes. I learned the contours of her wanting. The most responsive part of her body was not between her legs but on her back. Her shoulder blades: anytime I touched them, she shivered and made the most beautiful sounds I'd ever heard. Back then, I didn't know why they held such potency, what secrets they kept; I only knew that they entranced me. I stroked them. Licked the length of them. I turned her facedown and climbed onto her back to give myself to those protruding bones, hard beneath taut skin.

I held her arms down and she made a sound of surprise, stiffened, then relented. I laughed. I felt whole and strong, pressed against the naked length of her, her hips beneath mine. I stroked her calves with the soles of my feet. Here was a strength I'd never dreamed was in me. I claimed her shoulder blades with my mouth, my fingers. She moaned and I felt a rush of happiness. Tongue. The shape of those long bones beneath my tongue. She writhed beneath me, tried to talk but there were only incoherent sounds. I'll stay here a long time, I thought, the way she does when she puts her mouth on me; I'll linger here until the waves break and then I'll linger more, until the hours melt into forever, until she's sated, until night swallows the world.

Sometimes, in the mornings, I searched my skin in the gold-framed mirror for bite marks and bruises. I savored the sight of them. She was here, and here, she did that and that and that. I mourned them as they faded. I took to goading her, in the night, to bite me harder, suck or press or slap more brutally, wanting to feel more of her and also to enjoy the medallions of our love during the day, mementos of our time together, a memento of her, painted on my flesh. Through her markings she was with me. Where her teeth had been I wanted more. Where her hands had been I wanted more. I took delight in the bruising, but it did not seem like violence, for I had in it no wish to destroy myself or anyone or anything—except perhaps the cage that I'd been raised to call my place, a woman's place, a cage that had no room in it for all this savage joy and that I often pictured decimated by the force of our loving, reduced to dust on which I danced and danced and danced.

"How did you know," I asked one night, "that I would want you?"

She was quiet for some time. "You do want me, do you not?"

"How can you ask?"

"To hear you speak it."

"I want you more than I can say."

"Mmmm." She caressed me. "You could try. To say, to tell me."

I sank into the richness of her touch. Resisted the river of it, the underwater pull. "But you're not answering my question."

Pteron laughed. "You are too smart for me, my love."

She always toyed this way when I probed into her life before she brought me to live here, or her life in the daytime when she was away. She'd tempt me in ways that subsumed the thread of my thoughts, distracted me from it. Sometimes it worked, but even when it did, I noticed. More and more, I noticed, and some deep, hidden part of me roiled in response, turbulent, unsettled. "You're still not answering."

"All right." She sighed, and I thought I heard a smile in her voice; deprived of sight, I'd come to hear the slightest shifts in tone. "It's because I saw you."

I waited for more, but Pteron only traced curves along my skin. Vibrant curves, glittering, as if her fingers contained stars. "You saw me?"

"Yes."

"Before I came here?"

"Yes."

"How?"

"My love, I think you already know."

"You were there?"

"I was there."

"The sheep enclosure?"

"Yes."

"Disguised?"

"Of course."

"As a man." I didn't phrase it as a question, for it was the only way she could have come. "How many times?"

"Once. Only once."

I imagined her amid the swarm. What day had it been? I wished I could return to the past to scan for traces of her. If I'd known, on that day, that Pteron was among the men, would their gazes have felt less brutal? Or would knowing have tainted her somehow instead, made Pteron part of the ugliness of that crowd? Had my own eyes ever landed on my future beloved's face, even for an instant—this face I'd never seen in the light? If so, I'd never know it, as I had no way to recognize her features.

My fingers knew them but my eyes did not. Even if my gaze had rested on her, I'd have had no way to know. It stabbed me to think she'd been part of those hurtful crowds in any way, though of course her gaze would not have been like the men's, right? She was not them, was she? And at the same time, I was knifed by another thought, that I'd had and lost the chance to lay eyes on a face I longed to see more than anything else in the world, for it was true: I hadn't realized it until this moment, but I now knew without a doubt that there was nothing I longed to see more. Not Olympus. Not my mother. Not the mythical sea. "And what? When you saw me, did you say to yourself, 'Ah, there's a girl who'd really like to wed another girl, I can see it in her eyes'"—my voice shook—"or did you just think I was pretty?"

"It was so much more than that. It was all there in you, radiant. The flame of you. A wild and perfect flame. That's what I saw."

I couldn't speak. Flame? I thought. What flame?

"You don't believe me?"

"Why should I?"

"Why shouldn't you?"

"I don't think any of those men saw that in me, or if they did, they didn't like it." I thought of what my family had always said, how they'd called me a too-wild girl and tried to tame it out of me, how my sisters had thrown up their hands and called me difficult. Whatever this flame was, it was not supposed to be there.

"The fools. The better for me."

"They're all like that. Men. They look at a girl and see only a thing designed to please them. Any wildness, any flame—it all stands in the way of what they want a girl to be."

"And yet the wildness is what you actually are," Pteron said.

I caught my breath; I'd thought such things, but never said them aloud, never even trawled them from the deeper regions of my mind.

Together we listened to the breathing of the dark.

"I didn't know it was possible to be so alive," I finally said. "So hungry and full. Awake to all the incredible ways you make me feel."

"It's not me that makes you that way, you know. It's you. Part of you."

"How can that be?"

"It's natural. The most natural force in the world."

"Well, if it's part of me, I never knew it was there before."

"I understand. You weren't told. Where you grew up, girls are told not to listen to their bodies in that way, not to think."

I laughed. "Was it any different where *you* grew up?"

She laughed too, though it came slightly forced. "I . . . didn't say that."

"It's a transgression, then, to hear your own body. Or to think."

"Yes."

"Men want us not to think. But why? Because we're empty and stupid, that's what they tell us—but what if that's not the truth at all? What if—what if—oh, I don't know what I'm saying."

"You do know," she said with infinite gentleness. She stroked my face. "Whenever you say that, the next thing out of your mouth is pure wisdom."

"Shut up."

"It's true. I'm in awe of you, Psyche."

I leaned into her cupped palm. Felt the comfort of it. After all this time it still amazed me to be taken seriously, to be heard.

"Keep talking. You have all the time in the world."

I gathered my thoughts into new, untested shapes. "What if it's the opposite? Something more combustible? What if men designed the world this way, not because they think we're nothing, but because they sense great power in us and want to press it down or chain it up?"

"What kind of power?"

"This thing you called—what did you call it? A force. A natural force."

"Ah, that." Her hands on me. Long strokes, along the whole of me. I sighed, transported. "Such power," she said, one hand between my legs. I spread open, as wide as I could. Wider.

"Enter me, please."

She hovered at the opening, pressing, teasing, denying me even as I thrust against her hand.

"Pteron, I beg you."

"Mmmm," she said. Matching the thrusts of my hips with her own movements. Lingering, lingering, until finally she pushed into me, and the force of it was so intense the waves broke over me at once and took my breath away, I was not breathing, I was breath, reduced to it, distilled to rushing air. She gave and gave to me as I spiked and finally ebbed and then she gave me more until the waves rose again, whispering into my ear, "Such—power."

Summer flared. Ripened. The sun grew strong across the valley; I dipped my feet in the cool stream.

My hungers had no script, no language.

I wanted—what?

Everything. All of it. To ravage the sky itself.

To buck against the blue, to surge with it.

To claim the greenery with the hunger of my thighs.

To live vitality in its purest, brightest form.

My tapestries grew ever more ambitious. I spent hours at the loom, and even more hours with a paintbrush in my hand, creating frescoes on the walls of our palace that brimmed with images of things I'd seen and wanted to see, pictures both fabled and real, fanciful or perhaps prophetic, evoking what was past and what might still come into being. I painted entire landscapes and then covered them with my brush and began again with another layer, shaping images anew until they sang, until the wall or jug or cup felt right, for I had an abundance of both paint and time.

Or so it seemed. Was this how it felt to be immortal? Alive inside with endless time? I'd found a well of vitality inside myself and drew from it, not because I wasn't afraid, but because the upwelling drowned out the fear. My vitality belonged to me. Every bit of myself belonged to me. Since birth I'd been taught such a thing would never be possible, I would always belong first to a father, then a husband; there would always be a man to steer my days.

But here I was, belonging to myself.

And to her.

To Pteron, who demanded I stay free.

And I felt free, in the palace. There were rules, but that seemed a worthy price to pay. I could circumscribe my life here on this patch of land. Why not?

What did it matter, to have a small outer scope to my life, when its inner scope was vast?

How deliriously happy is it possible to be? I asked myself, in the long stretching days, the liquid nights. Can this last? Is it possible? No, don't think of that, stay in the moment, in the glowing heartbeat of the Now.

I would never need anything else, or so it seemed. In those days, the future seemed far away, irrelevant to our dreaming.

The world seemed ours.

Not the whole world, but the one we'd created here in this palace, the one defined by its walls.

It was enough.

In that time, it still seemed enough.

12

"Eros, my child," Aphrodite said, plucking a pear from its branch. "You seem changed."

"Do I?" They were strolling in the orchard, the Graces just behind them: Aglaea, Thalia, and Euphrosyne, her mother's three loyal attendants, luminous as always, gathering fruit into baskets as sun gilded their skin.

"Oh yes. You're love-drunk."

Eros kept quiet, eyes on the pear tree as if scanning for the best piece of fruit, not daring to meet her mother's eyes. She couldn't deny it. She was spinning, giddy, blinded by her own happiness.

"Who is she? Some nymph? Wood or water? Come now, tell me."

She felt the pull of her mother, the pull to speak. They had always been in tune with each other's journey through this world, utterly entwined, as if the Fates had spun them a single glistening thread. Once, they'd fled Olympus together, when the great storm-monster Typhoeus attacked the palace of the gods. Everyone else scattered alone in those winds, but Aphrodite and Eros clasped hands and careened through the air side by side. They landed in a river, where they turned themselves into fish, linked by the harmony of their dance, tail to head, head to tail. They glimmered through the river until they found two other fish, who led them down the currents to a pool of calmer waters that the violence of Typhoeus could not reach. How they swam, circling, circling, cradling each other in a current of their own making as torrents tore across the land above. How they learned immediately to speak with scale and fin and sense each other's every tremor, decoding every flick and ripple of the water that joined them. When peace finally returned to the land, the two fish who'd guided them became a constellation in the sky, a testament not only to their noble act, but also to the bond between two goddesses. A fluid bond, eternal, as ancient and unbreakable as water. She recalled it now and longed for that shared depth, that liquid radiance between them, but the longing collided with terror of what would happen if her secrets were known. "It could be one of each, Mother."

Aphrodite laughed. "Or ten of each. Certainly. But this is different, child, there is one in particular."

"How do you know?"

"From the light in your eyes."

Eros plucked a pear. Studied it keenly before taking a slow bite.

"It's been a long while, hasn't it?" Aphrodite said softly.

Eros shrugged. It had indeed been a while, one hundred years. She let her mother's compassion fill her, though she stung with guilt.

"Well, I'm happy for you." Aphrodite threw her half-eaten pear, watched it curve through the air and land in the grass. "But do be careful. You know how slippery these nymphs can be."

13

Distant cries, low as whispers, woven into the song of birds. *Psyche!*

I lay by the stream, gazing at clouds. At first I thought the voices might belong to spirits, carried on the wind. But then I heard it again. *Psyche—oh, sister!* Interspersed with caws and the churring of the stream.

I sat up, tense, my hearing pricked to listen.

Torn from us, to such a gruesome death.

Iantha. Coronis. Breath caught in my lungs. How could it be? I burrowed my fingers into the cool soil and tried to think. If their voices could carry down into this valley, they must not be in their homes. They must be at the rock where I'd been tied up on my wedding day; they must have gone there to mourn me. Why? Because it was the place from which I'd been taken and therefore the closest thing in their eyes to my grave? Dutiful sisters, mourning the dead girl. Were they doing it for show? Or did they actually care? Was their grief for me real? Their faces rose behind my closed eyelids, twisted in sorrow. They weren't there the day I was taken to the rock, already in their new homes, with their husbands. What they felt at the news, I did not know. Perhaps mourning had crept up on them, like afternoon shadows you barely notice until the sun tips and they quickly consume the ground.

The day at the rock rushed back to me, sent a surge of horror up my spine. The people's burial songs in my ears. Their thick heat as they stood around me, silent and approving as my father tied me down. Pain. Terror. And something new: What was it? It roared and burned. Fury. It leapt in me, a flame. None of them had tried to protect me, not one. The rules of society had seen fit to stamp me out—to end the drought, to obey the Oracle, to appease the laws of god and man—so stamp me out they would. It was the world I'd been born into, and the people of my village hadn't made the rules, but none of that quelled my anger, for I saw new things inside me now, a worth in my body, my life, the soul inside me, and the more I mattered, the worse their crimes.

Psyche, oh Psyche. Our dear sister, gone. Their voices adrift on the wind.

What had they heard, my sisters, about that day? Did they wish they'd been there to say goodbye? Did they secretly relish any part of the story? I hoped not. Perhaps they'd been overcome by sadness. If they could see me now, what would they say?

This last question stayed with me, clung to the edges of my consciousness, as their voices ebbed and faded and finally fell silent. I stayed on the grass for a long time. The light had grown heavy with gold, shattering on the surface of the stream. The figs on my lover-tree were almost ripe, still hard but swollen with anticipation, for summer was almost done. Soon the wind would turn biting crisp, if this valley's seasons were anything like where I grew up, though of this I could not be sure. It was the same sun and the same green grass, yet everything was different here. I could not know how the autumn and winter would envelop this place, what they would do to the sky, to the wind, to my body. There was so much I did not know. I felt hollowed by all the unknowing.

I went inside, took a bath soft with petals, had my evening meal. As I ate, my sisters' voices threaded through the back of my mind. Against my will I saw myself in a reunion with them. Our embrace. Our clasped hands. The sight of them at this very table, faces amazed at the splendor, the delicacies and wine. How they'd stare when they first entered the palace. How they'd look at me. What it would be like to speak with them, to answer their questions and assure them that I was not dead, to talk of childhood memories and reconjure them with our words. The force of my own longing for this surprised me. The past was gone, but those who lived it with us hold it in remembrance, can offer it back up, a mirror for past selves. Did they have that with each other, and did I dare dream of having it too? If they could visit—

I sipped my wine, swirled it against the roof of my mouth. What would it mean, if they could visit? Perhaps their grief for me was real, perhaps it was not. But my mother was surely grieving me, and every-thing in her was real. If my sisters came, they could take news back to my mother, assure her that I was all right.

My mother.

I stared into my wineglass as if for prophecies.

She was the only one who'd tried to fight the Oracle's pronounce-ments, who saw me as worth saving. She'd shielded me as much as she could. The thought of her grief was almost unbearable, for it was base-less. There was no need for her to mourn. I hadn't been torn apart by a monster, or tortured by a beast. That she would suffer so deeply because of a lie—or a distorted story, though who could tell when one ended and the other began—seemed the worst kind of injury. It hurt me to imagine her, alone with my father in a house now surely awash with bitterness. If I could send word to her, let her know I was well, I could bring her peace and ease her pain.

But if I told you it was only a daughter's love that spurred me on, or the urge to reminisce with my sisters, I'd be lying. And you need to hear everything that happened to me, all my choices and what came next. I will tell you, for I believe, or at least hope, that you are listening. It was not loneliness, despite what would later be claimed; before I heard my sisters' voices, I did not pine for them; my loom and the glades and the forest were good company for my days, along with moments from my nights with Pteron that I curled against the tongue of my mind. My days were full and beautiful, and if there were sometimes twinges of a wish for company, I shook them off easily enough.

No, loneliness was not what spurred me. It was pride. A thirst for dignity. All the shame I'd brought my family, all the doom for which I was supposedly destined, and look what I had. Look what I'd become. If they could see the riches of this palace—all the tapestries and paintings born from my very own hands—they'd glimpse my triumph and I'd see my own flourishing reflected in their eyes. Perhaps then I'd finally get the respect I deserved. Though I would not have dared admit it to myself, it mattered to me fiercely, even with all I'd experienced and discovered, to watch my sisters' faces when they saw the palace and me inside it, aglow.

It still shames me now, that this paltry thing—the approval of my sisters—could contribute to my risking everything, make me forget, even, the scope of the risk. I had grown strong during my months in the palace. I'd come to think that I was free. And yet, even when we change, even when we find power inside us and lift it to the light, we still carry in us the wounded animal of our memory, the bruises and scars, the spurning. We want to be un-spurned. We want the ones who held mirrors for us, whether in solace or in mockery, to see us again with fresh, admiring eyes, as if this seeing could affirm us, mend the shattered parts, and make us whole. Those of us who've been broken have more shards inside us than we know—and who among us has not been broken, as women in this world?

*   *   *

Pteron drew away from me the moment I spoke it. "No."

"Just for a day." I'd never heard myself use this tone with Pteron; but on the other hand, I'd also never been met with such resistance. She granted all my wishes, even the unspoken ones, even the ones I myself did not yet know I had, like the loom and paint that graced the rooms at the end of the hall. That I should ask for something she did not want to give was new terrain for us.

"It's not safe."

"Of course it'll be safe. Why wouldn't it be?"

"Isn't this all enough for you?"

I felt a sting of guilt for seeming ungrateful for all I'd been given. Only later would I realize that her question was anything but an answer. "Pteron, it is far more than enough," I said, though even as I spoke it something tugged at the hem of my mind: *And if it's not? Can I crave more? To see faces, to roam?* I pushed the thoughts away. "It's more than I ever dreamed."

"But?"

"I want to see my sisters."

"I thought you didn't trust your sisters. That they'd spurned you."

"They have. But they also cared for me. Brushed my hair into braids and whispered away my childhood nightmares. Perhaps we can overcome the ugliness now that we are all married."

"Or they might bring bitterness your way—especially when they see everything you have—"

"So what if they do?"

"Bitterness is a poison."

"You think they'll poison me against you?"

"Isn't it possible?"

"No."

"How do you know that?"

"Because what we have, Pteron, can't be poisoned. Not by anyone." I reached out and stroked her, moved by her vulnerability. "There's also my mother. It hurts me not to be able to send her word."

Pteron shuffled in the dark. She was quiet so long I feared I'd angered her. "Tell me about her."

I did so. I told of my mother's dark beauty, said to be like mine; the tenderness she held for me; the story she'd told me of how I'd been born, fast and eager, and how she'd sung me old songs to keep me connected or yoked to the earth because I seemed too keen to fly. "I'm not surprised to hear that about you," Pteron said, and I smiled into the dark and kept on talking. As I spoke, I saw my mother sewing by my side while I wove, coming to release me from the locked room with a fresh gown in hand, weaving by my side in a rich silence, weeping on my wedding day as though she were burying her daughter alive. I told it all, and Pteron listened.

"She suffered at the Oracle's news, and so did you."

"Of course we did. There was no way to know I would not be torn apart and killed. It is what we all thought."

"I am sorry for that."

I reached for her, caressed her chest. "You've said this before. I don't understand. Why should you be sorry for something over which you had no control?"

She was quiet for a long while. "Because I love you."

I let the words sink into me like fresh milk.

"It sounds like you have a beautiful mother."

"I do." I knew nothing about her own mother, the home where she'd been raised, the people she came from. "Is she very different from yours?"

"We're not talking about my mother," Pteron said, in a voice so low it was almost a hiss.

I stiffened with surprise. "Sorry. We don't have to talk about your mother." Something flickered through me, a brush of unease. She wanted me to see our bond as boundless, our refuge in this room as unfettered.

In sex we became a merged, infinite thing. She didn't want me to feel confined; this I did believe. Yet even now, with all we'd shared and done together, I knew far less of my beloved's life beyond this palace than she knew of mine. Usually, it didn't matter. Perhaps it didn't matter now. Or perhaps it did. In some subterranean part of me, my will grew taut.

"Psyche, I understand that you want to show your mother, as you say, that you are well. And I'd want that for you. But this palace isn't here for that purpose."

"What purpose?"

"Receiving guests."

I thought of the empty chambers, their bedding untouched. "But there is room for them."

"It's not for them."

"It's all for me?"

"Yes."

"So, then—what you're saying is, this is my home?"

"Of course it's your home."

"And what I want matters? You don't own me?"

"You already know—"

"You said it before. But what about now?"

"How can you say such a thing?"

"Why won't you answer?"

Pteron went silent.

As the silence gaped on, I fought the urge to fill it with words of fury or peacemaking—if I opened my mouth, which would come out? I didn't know. The world slipped, felt foreign, this blackened room a haunted space, unknowable. Where was I? Was this chamber to shape the rest of my life? Suddenly I felt the constraint of it, its smallness in comparison to the world.

And yet this chamber also blessed us, protected us from a world that would have us not exist. It was a haven. It was my heart.

The silence stretched on so long I thought she might have fallen asleep, though she was sitting up and I hadn't felt her move. The more time passed, the less I knew what to say to bridge the gulf between us.

"We'll talk more tomorrow," she finally said, in a voice more weary than cold, and I heard her turn and settle into sleep.

We'd never fought like this before, had never gone to sleep in anything less than harmony. It hadn't occurred to me that such a thing would be possible between us, though now I plainly saw the absurd naïveté of such a thought. Gingerly I felt for her body; she'd turned her back to me in sleep, though whether she in fact slept or not was impossible to tell. I lay awake in the dark behind her for a long time. I wanted to stroke her shoulder blades where they protruded, as if with memory of primordial flight. But I didn't dare. I don't remember falling asleep that night, though I must have, for I dreamed feverish dreams before my eyes opened to the still-dark morning.

I spent the next day possessed by fear. A cold rush of dread washed through me. What if she threw me out for having asked too much? What else did I have but this? Where would I go? What would I do? The thought of losing her tore my mind to shreds. I'd be losing everything: my joy, my heart's desire, but also, the only scrap of the world I could call home. My village had become hostile to me; no other village would receive a lone young woman without destroying her. I pictured myself leaving and wandering unknown roads, a beggar, unprotected, ripe to be taken by force. Raped. Forced into servitude. I thought of the servant girls on our farm, how they'd kept their eyes down, cowered, even taken horrors as Melia had done. I didn't know where Melia was born or how she came to join our farm, but I did know that often servants had nowhere else to go. Melia. How was she now? What would she say if she saw my life, the radiant palace, what I was now at risk of losing?

I couldn't lose it.

It would be unbearable to lose it.

I should acquiesce to Pteron, accept her rules, keep my sisters at bay.

Yet that seemed difficult. Even as a voice inside me shouted to be careful, to protect what I had and sit down and obey, another part of me insisted on my right to speak my desire. A terrible thing. The doors she'd unlocked inside me had let out forces that now wanted room. Desire leads to more desire. Existing leads to the will to exist. Boldness in the dark leads to boldness by day. After all those nights, I could not shrink myself, nor did I want to. Our argument had made me want my sisters' visit even more, as an enactment of my own freedom, my right to define my life in this home that supposedly belonged, not only to her, but also to me. *I don't own you,* Pteron had insisted and insisted. If this was true, shouldn't I be able to make choices in this life we shared?

I wrestled with myself all day, so that nightfall found me exhausted, worn down by inner battles, yet determined, armed with reasoning and pleas and patient arguments with which I hoped to persuade her.

But it was all unnecessary. As soon as the tapestry rustled and she stepped into the room, before she even reached the bed, she spoke. "It will be as you say, my love."

I felt a mix of triumph and relief, flecked with confusion at the speed of her change. "Really?"

"Yes."

"How?"

"The next time they go to the rock, the wind will carry them down, as it did you."

I longed to ask how she could know this, whether she made it happen, what spirits she called or how she spoke to the wind, commanded it, or was commanded by it. What secret language did she speak with the great wild? How had she learned it, what was the scope of her power? To glimpse the workings of this place was to touch the edge of mysteries. Better not to broach any of that, especially not now, in this moment of fragile victory. My sisters. I would see them anew. "Are you sure?"

"How can I ever deny you, Psyche?"

There was amusement in her voice, and love, but also, beneath the surface, a streak of resignation, as if she saw further than I did, into my motives, into the shape of the visit and what it would cost.

For the next three days, I stalked the front door, eagerly awaiting the moment when my sisters descended in the wind's invisible arms. On the fourth day, I heard their approach before I saw it—two long moans of surprise and fear and thrill, overlapping like ripples in a pond—and I raced to the palace door. What a sight: my sisters, eyes clenched closed, fingers splayed, suspended against the clouds, their robes in whorls as the wind brought them gradually toward the ground. They looked like fish suspended in water for the first time, flapping their limbs in amazement. I began to laugh, then stifled it. They grew closer. Iantha seemed to lean into the supple air with a startled enjoyment, but Coronis was stiff as if bracing against the fall. Only once they'd landed and felt grass beneath their knees and hands did they open their eyes.

They took in the glade, hungrily, and it wasn't until they saw me that the shock set in. They seemed not to know me at first: a strange young woman in fine robes, gazing at them as a glorious palace loomed behind her. I watched recognition dawn in their eyes—and was that envy? Admiration? Disbelief?

They were still down on all fours. I smiled and opened my arms.

"Sisters. Welcome to my home."

They rose. Dusted dirt off their robes. Stared at me. Both of them gaping, frozen in shock.

Finally Iantha said, "Is it you, Psyche?"

"It is."

"You're alive."

She hadn't asked a question; I didn't answer.

"This—is your home?" Iantha continued.

"Yes."

"But—" Coronis said, then went quiet.

Iantha broke into a sob of relief. She stepped toward me. "We've been so worried about you, dear sister."

My heart quickened as we fell into each other's arms.

"I can't believe it," she said.

Coronis approached too and embraced me. "What happened?" she murmured into my hair. "How did you live?"

All my plans for what I'd say, how I'd tell my story, melted in the face of this, my sisters' arms around me, two women who smelled like home. I pulled back to see their faces, make sure they were real. To look into a human face. How I'd missed it. Guilt slashed me at the thought, for it seemed a betrayal of what I had with Pteron, the bond where we did almost everything but that. We'd been innocent together, my sisters and I. Unable to see the future that awaited us, the forces that would twist us into shapes expected of women whether we wanted them to or not. We'd been so much to each other, for each other, and also in spite of each other. I wanted to pull them to me and run from them at the same time.

"Come inside," I said, "and we can talk."

They followed me and gaped at the glowing walls and ceiling, the gilding, the delicate inlay, the soaring marble pillars. Coronis gasped, mouth open, while Iantha took in everything with ravenous eyes. It was all as majestic as the first day I'd entered, only now I'd hung tapestries of my own creation along the walls. I watched my sisters keenly, full of an artisan's pride. I tried to decipher their expressions. I searched for admiration or approval, envy or awe. Though I didn't want to admit I craved these things from my sisters, crave them I did. I stood still. Waited for them to turn their attention to me.

Instead, Iantha smiled tightly, eyes on a place just behind my shoulder.

I felt an ache in my chest. They seemed to hover, waiting for my cue. I was their hostess, after all.

"Let us feast," I said, "to celebrate our reunion."

I led them into the dining room. At the sight of the table, richly laden with meats and fruit and bread, their eyes grew wide, and satisfaction rushed through me.

"You had all this prepared for us?" Coronis said.

"Of course." I didn't mention that the feast was no more luxurious than what appeared on the table every day. It wouldn't do to appear boastful.

"How did you know we were coming?" said Iantha. "Did you know what the wind would do?"

I faltered at the directness of her questions. She sensed my hesitation, as a crow senses the scurry of an insect. "Have a seat." I tried to keep my voice even. "Enjoy the meal."

While they ate—Coronis greedily, reaching for one delicacy after another with an enthusiasm that suggested this banquet differed greatly from the tables in her husband's home; Iantha carefully, but no less keen—I had the chance to study them more closely. They had changed. Marriage had changed them. Iantha was as intelligent as ever, but she was not the loquacious girl she'd been before; she sat erect as a soldier who'd been on guard duty too long. There was something sour about her now, as if the trace amounts of sweetness she'd possessed had been leached from her by life. Coronis, too, seemed closed in a new way, though what lay beneath the veil she'd drawn around her, I could not say. I'd spent the hours before their arrival thinking about how my marriage had changed me, but the truth was that all of us had entered marriages, each of which was a closed sphere, shrouded from public view, intricate in ways no one on the outside could see.

"Where are the servants?" asked Iantha.

I hesitated.

"Surely you have them." Coronis gestured around the room as if to say, *Given all this finery you've got.*

"I—yes. They are away right now."

"As is your husband?" said Coronis.

I nodded. "We have the place to ourselves."

Iantha bit into a piece of roasted goat leg and studied me as she chewed. "This husband; tell us about him."

"What does he look like?" said Coronis.

"He's handsome." This first lie was an easy one.

"Oh?"

"Is he young?"

"Young enough." I'd planned and practiced my story about this phantom husband, and yet now, I found myself fighting down panic, throat stiff. What if they caught me in a tangle of untruth? What then? My marriage did not seem precarious, but Pteron's worry, her resistance to this visit, made me feel it had to go smoothly—all suspicions avoided—to protect what we had. I could not fail. "Young enough to be strong."

"What does he look like?"

"He's of medium height, with solid features, and curls," I said, remembering my fingers through Pteron's hair.

"What color is his hair?"

"Dark."

"Black?"

"Yes."

"And he's rich, it seems," said Coronis, failing to keep envy from her voice.

"Yes."

"A king?" Iantha asked, scanning the room as if it served as evidence.

"Yes." I was relieved to hear the certainty in my voice. As a kindness, I added, "Like your husband, Coronis."

Coronis's smile was tight, almost a sneer. "Not really."

"Now, sister—"

"Don't chide me, Iantha. Surely we can finally speak honestly of our husbands. We're far enough away from them, wherever we are, whatever this place is."

Iantha pressed her lips together in disapproval but said nothing.

I waited for Coronis to go on.

She looked at each of us in turn, then at the tabletop, as if searching its smooth wood for something she'd lost.

"It's not that my husband isn't rich—though there is nothing like *this* luxury in our home. But he isn't young and handsome along with the riches. Those were the terms of the deal. Wealth first, and status. Fine. That's what Father wanted and that's what he got. But *he's* not the one living with an old man whose feet are crusty and festering with sores that stink when I wash them—"

"Coronis!" Iantha placed her palm firmly on the table. "Enough."

Coronis seemed about to go on, then leaned back in a sulk.

Silence fell between us.

"I'm sorry," I said.

"Are you, though?" Coronis picked up the bread on her plate and started shredding it into small pieces. "You can't tell me that you'd rather switch places."

I couldn't. I kept my mouth shut.

"And you're the one with the prophecy about a monster!" Coronis's eyes glazed with tears. She looked as if she'd tasted venom. "That's what makes no sense. What happened?"

Panic stabbed me. Had I made a mistake? Why had I fought so hard for this with the person I loved most to bring them here? The space between us tore open, into a chasm through which my village roared back to life, a swirling wheel of pain, a rock, a dirge, a crowd mourning the bride, a father walking away as if he'd just shed a deadweight, the home I'd never see again, the dining table, the halls, the loom, the sheep and their enclosure when it held them, when it held me, the pain of too many eyes, the meadow, the path to the river, the dirty linens rubbed against rock, waves of laughter from girls who would never be small again.

I felt cold, but I kept my voice even. "Do you wish I were with a monster?"

"Of course she doesn't." Iantha glared hard at Coronis.

"Of course I don't." Coronis shoved a piece of broken bread into her mouth.

"Psyche," Iantha said, "we're your sisters. We're very glad to see you safe and sound, the wife of a rich and handsome man."

I nodded.

"What a relief, that the Oracle . . ."

". . . was wrong?" Coronis said, to finish her sister's sentence.

We didn't dare look at each other, for Oracles were never wrong, and to suggest as much was to tempt disaster from the gods.

". . . that the Oracle had spoken in riddles more mysterious than we knew," Iantha ventured.

I smiled gratefully, thinking, Yes, maybe that's what it was, a mystery hidden in layers of meaning that mortal minds strained to unravel, the temple priest's mind, my father's mind, all the villagers' collective and individual minds. That explained the incongruity and shocking turn of events, did it not? But if so, what were the layers beneath the layers? The mystery was what? The monstrousness not yet properly decoded was where? My head hurt from the attempt to decipher these meanings.

Iantha's voice broke into my thoughts. "When can we meet this husband?"

Something in her tone sent a shiver up my spine. I met her eyes, but they revealed nothing. "He won't be back until tomorrow."

"Oh?"

"Yes."

"Alas, we cannot stay the night."

"How unfortunate," I said, secretly relieved.

"Where did he go?" Iantha's face grew focused, as if searching avidly for a crack in a wall she aimed to break.

I squirmed inside, for the truth was that I had no idea where Pteron went during the day, where she was this instant, how she filled her time. Not that a wife had to know such things of her husband, or that I could have shared the truth with my sisters if I'd known it. "To take care of business dealings."

"So he's not a king?"

"He is! Of course he is."

"But if he were a king," Iantha said slowly, "wouldn't his business dealings come to him?"

It was a crude trap, really. Kings can go wherever they please and have plenty of business reasons to travel from their homes. But I knew little of such things at the time, and, more important, I was poorly prepared. My silence was too long and they both knew it. Coronis sat taller, perked up by the tension, while Iantha kept her eagle gaze on me.

"His dealings take many forms." I hoped I sounded confident.

"Mmmm," said Iantha. "I am sure they do." She looked around the room, more slowly this time. I braced myself for more pointed husband-questions, or perhaps a return to questions from before—whether I'd known about the wind, how I'd survived—but her eyes fell on a fresco on the far wall. "What an interesting painting."

I could not help but beam. "I did it."

"You?" Iantha stared at it more openly. "You painted this?"

I nodded proudly.

Coronis stared at the painting also, and as the silence wore on, I realized they were not impressed by my artistry, as I'd wanted them to be—for as my brush grew more sophisticated, I'd experimented with animals and human forms, far outstripping any painting I'd ever seen and rivaling, I thought, I hoped, frescoes on the walls of kings—but rather, troubled by the picture itself. As if it might be laced with subtle poison. I looked at it again, tried to see it through their eyes. Two women under fig trees. Naked. Their nipples tight clusters of dots, their black hair cascading in coils. They were not looking at each other as they both faced the same direction, though the woman on the left might have her gaze fixed on the other woman's hair, for I'd intended it so, intended a mystery as to whether the woman on the left was staring at another woman or directly at the rising sun.

"Well, sister," Iantha said slowly. "What does your husband think of your . . . pursuit?"

"He doesn't mind."

"Was it . . . his idea?"

I sensed the edge of peril. She was too sharp-minded, that Iantha. "Why does that matter?"

"Because why else would he let you paint?" Coronis broke in. "On the walls of his own house!"

"I suppose your husband doesn't." I tried to sound neutral, no hint of gloating or triumph.

Coronis scoffed. "No. Obviously not. He'd have me flogged for touching a brush."

"Coronis!" Iantha said.

"What? It's true. He loves his house too much for that. And anyway, fresco painting is the work of men, especially when—" She gestured at the wall.

"When what?" I challenged, though we all heard the rest of the sentence, *when painting naked women*. What I'd done here in the dining hall was unseemly for a wife on three counts: because we were not supposed to paint, because we were supposed to cede decisions to our husbands, and perhaps most importantly because we absolutely should not portray naked women, much less two of them, standing in a grove in arm's reach of each other for reasons undiscerned. I'd been gone from civilization for too long and lost track of its rules. I'd gone feral; I'd forgotten, or rather, I no longer cared how the world might perceive what I did or said or painted, for in this palace I believed myself fit for anything I wished, and I was too caught up in my accomplishments with these complex designs to fret over whether they were presentable to other human beings. Anyway, my paintings were good. I had practiced in the long course of my days, and had grown in form and style. I could make a wall beautiful, make a picture spring to life, despite the fact that I was not a man; any king would be glad to have such quality of work on his walls, and we all knew it. Yet even so, the work was wrong. I had transgressed.

Iantha studied me as if I were an unsteady loom she meant to either fix or topple. "Well! It's very nice, sister."

The victory felt sour on my tongue.

"Tell me," she said in a newly genial voice, "does your husband like your paintings?"

Pteron. I longed for her to see my work, longed for her to enjoy it with me, to dream into it together. But of course she'd never laid eyes on it, as far as I knew, and if she had, it was in some secret moment—by the light of a lamp, in the depths of night, when she crept away from our bed? Before the winged creature arrived to carry her into the sky? Was it possible that she'd prowled the halls, then, and seen my paintings, keeping those excursions hidden from me? So much was hidden; there was so much I did not know. I felt flattened by the weight of secrets. Why could we not love each other by light of day and in sight of the world? I'd thought seeing my sisters might alleviate the crushing weight of shrouding one's true life, but instead, in their presence I felt it all the more.

Iantha had been watching me.

She seemed to glow with vindication.

I straightened my spine and smiled, battle-ready. "Oh yes, he loves them. He's proud."

"Proud," Iantha repeated, as if examining the word for shadows.

Coronis looked sullen, but as the pause wore on, she tuned in to Iantha, as if trying to read her mind.

"Why not?" I said, feeling that I had misstepped somehow.

Iantha smiled at me, a smile so false it made me nervous.

"Your husbands afford you freedoms too, do they not?" I said. "You visit each other, after all. And you've left home to be able to come here."

"This is true," said Iantha. "We have nothing to complain about."

Coronis's face tensed. She clearly understood those words as directed toward her, and, I thought, she was right: our elder sister meant to scold her. There was pain on Coronis's face, which she tried and failed to hide. I watched her war with herself, war with Iantha in her mind, as she sat and said nothing, and suddenly I saw the truth as plainly as if she'd painted it across her face: her marriage was a nightmare. Her days were full of suffering. And, marriage being what it is, women's lives being what they were, there was no door to the cage, no way out, no relief but death. A tide of sorrow rose in me. "You can complain if you wish. In this house, you're free to do so."

I'd meant this as a comfort, the only one I could think to extend. But Coronis glared at me, and the raw pain on her face was replaced by something harder, a wall of defense. I was stung, though I tried not to show it. I'd wanted to offer kindness, yet somehow, perhaps because of how our marriages differed, the way my joy contrasted with her pain, she seemed to take my words as a humiliation.

"Free," Coronis spat, and made a gesture as if throwing a dirty rag aside.

We were quiet, the three of us. I picked up a platter of dates and extended it to each of them in turn. They both took dates, though Coronis placed hers on the rim of her plate, untouched.

"Well," I finally said, "won't you tell me about your new lives? What are your homes like? How do you spend your days?"

Iantha spoke first, describing the many rooms in her house, which stood among rocky crags overlooking the sea; the beautiful colonnade where her husband liked to stroll and think, and where she joined him when he wished it and she had the time, though she almost never had the time (and whether or not he wished it seemed below mention); the cadres of servants whose everyday tumult and quarrels often kept her occupied for hours; her four stepchildren, three of whom were children still and looked to her with a mix of distrust and yearning for maternal care, and one of whom, the elder son, was married and whose young wife battled with Iantha for territory on an almost daily basis, as if she thought her youth gave her some sort of claim to power, a ridiculous notion since Iantha was only one year older than the girl, and, more important, it was Iantha who was married to the man of that house and who therefore reigned in the female realm, and if this girl thought she could maneuver her way past that fact, she had an ugly realization coming. The best part, she said—and here her voice went soft—was that sometimes, when the house finally went quiet in the night with everyone asleep, and if her husband was not snoring, she could hear, from her bed, the sound of the sea: waves at the shore, moving, moving, one after the other, a sound she'd never known as a child and that at first had haunted her with its strangeness but now gave her such a comfort that she sometimes strained to stay awake through her exhaustion, just to linger in its song.

"Does it sound like water falling from a jug?" I said. "Or like our river?"

Iantha shook her head. "It's nothing like that; it's beyond explaining. It's something you can't imagine until you hear it for yourself."

It stabbed me, the desire to know what she knew. It was the first time in the visit that I'd felt jealous of one of my sisters, a strange feeling, given that I didn't want any part of their lives; it was clear now that it was I who had the most enviable life and it seemed that they both knew it, but the yearning I felt now—this yearning to hear the sea—gave me a taste of how they might be feeling as they looked upon my life, a taste strong enough to haunt me.

Iantha was still smiling her veiled smile, now edged with triumph.

She'd wanted me to feel that way. She'd seen the envy on my face and knew that for the moment, she'd won.

"And you, Coronis? Tell me of your new life."

Coronis shrugged. "Not much to tell."

"Oh, go on," said Iantha.

Coronis reached for a fig and turned it in her hand as if searching for doors or gems or worms. "It's a large house. He's a terrible man. Don't look at me like that, Iantha, it's true and well you know it. He's petulant and demanding and he lies whenever he thinks it'll get him what he wants. I see through it, though, and that's my shield, that I learned early on not to believe what he says. The servants hate him and he doesn't seem to know it, which makes him a fool. The worst part is pretending I admire him, pretending I just love to obey his every word, because anything less and—" She stopped. "Well. Anyway. He's not like your husband, Psyche, let's just put it like that."

"I'm sorry," I said, and truly meant it.

Silence bloomed over the table. Coronis put the fig down on her plate but did not let it go. I waited for her to say more, but she did not.

"And our mother?" I finally asked.

"She is well," said Iantha. "Given the circumstances."

"Which circumstances?"

"She's been ill ever since your wedding."

"Oh." I felt gutted by the news, though not surprised.

"On some days, she does not rise," Coronis said. "The servants bring her food and she leaves it untouched. She's grown too thin. When we visit, we sit with her and cajole her to eat, which sometimes works and sometimes does not."

It cut me to think of my mother this way, drowning in a sorrow I had caused.

"When she hears that you're well, perhaps the cloud will lift," said Iantha.

Hope billowed in me. "You'll tell her, won't you?"

"Certainly." Iantha leaned in close to me. "But sister, won't you go to her, and visit? You could tell her yourself. It would do her good to see you with her own eyes."

Coronis glanced at her with a bitterness I could not help but see. It was easy to decode her meaning. Here they were, the two faithful sisters who'd visited their mother, and yet their devotion was not enough on its own; it was the younger sister, the difficult sister, the supposedly-cursed-yet-suddenly-not-cursed sister who would do their mother good with her mere presence.

They were both looking at me now. I felt my throat go dry. I had not spoken to Pteron of traveling away from the palace. It hadn't seemed part of the parameters of this marriage in which, she always said, I was meant to be free. Free within these walls? What would my sisters say to that? But that was the wrong thought, for surely there was far more than that about this marriage they weren't poised to understand. If I could show them the whole story, they would see a new meaning of free, would they not? If they could see it fully. If a full seeing were possible.

"Perhaps one day." I smiled as sincerely as I could.

We talked on as the light grew heavy and golden all around us.

Finally, Iantha rose from the table. "We should go before it gets dark. We still have the walk back."

I felt glad to be reaching the end. I picked up Iantha's cup from which she'd been drinking wine, and held it out to her. "Here, take this with you, as a parting gift. You too, Coronis, take yours."

A shadow passed across Iantha's face. "You're sure?"

"Why not?"

She looked at the cup with furrowed brow, while on Coronis's face eagerness seemed to war with jealousy, and only then did I understand that the gift, a solid gold cup, seemed lavish, even boastful, implying as it did that my house had plenty more such treasures for the taking. I felt myself blush. I'd meant to be generous, not boastful—or had I? I thought of snatching them back, but that of course would only make things worse. It was too late to take it back. It was too late to take anything back, to undo any of what each of our lives had become. For an instant my chest hurt for the girls we'd once been, vibrant and unwed, linked to each other by our daily lives, our futures nebulous on the horizon. I took hold of the third cup, the one I'd drunk from, and gave it to Coronis. "Here. For our mother."

Coronis took the cup gingerly, as if it were a wild animal that might bite her and give her a disease. A bitter taste flooded my mouth; I didn't know what I wanted more from my sisters, for them to enfold me in their arms, or praise me, or disappear.

"We'll want to return," said Iantha, as she took hold of her cup and rose to her feet.

"Of course." I strained to sound as certain as I could.

I walked with them to the front door, and out to the grove where they'd landed.

"Do we just stand here?" Iantha said. "And wait?"

They both turned to look at me. Panic tore through me, for I didn't know what to do next; I'd never exited this valley and didn't know how it could be done. But Pteron had told me they could visit and leave the same day, the way they came. Surely she knew something of the ways of this valley and could be trusted. I trusted her with my life. She was my life. I kissed my sisters one last time. "Yes, stand here and wait. The wind will come."

"Don't forget us, Psyche," Coronis whispered into my ear, in a raw tone tinged with despair.

"How could I?" I smiled at her as I pulled away. I stepped back, toward the house, and felt the wind rise up around us as if welling from the ground. It caught their skirts, whirled their hair, but did not lift them.

"Close your eyes," I said.

Sure enough, no sooner had they done so than the wind bore them into the air.

What a sight: my two sisters caught in the arms of the wind, rising toward the sky, skirts forming beautiful shapes against their bodies as they fluttered. My sisters, afloat, as if they could belong to air. Rising and becoming small, then smaller, then disappearing behind a high crag like featherless birds.

I stared for a long time at that crag. At the sky behind it, empty and blue.

They were gone, and I had done it.

I felt relief, and a hollowness for which I had no name.

"So?" Pteron asked, when she arrived that night. "How did it go with—"

I interrupted her question with a hard kiss on her mouth. Dealing with my sisters had made me miss her terribly, and I hungered for her with an insistence that surprised us both. She moved against me, moved in me. I spread my thighs wide, dug my nails into her back like claws.

"Dissolve me," I said.

"What do y—"

"Just do it." I clung to her and she did as I asked. Even when I drew blood she did not stop. In moments like these it seemed that Pteron gave me everything, all the warmth and succor I could ever need, the whole of life in one dark room: How could I ever ask for more?

Afterward, she collapsed on me and we caught our breath. "So, it was all right?"

"Yes, that was—"

"With your sisters?"

"Oh." I laughed. "I'd forgotten about my sisters. You do that to me."

"Mmmm," she said, a hand idling through my hair.

"It was—good." I searched for words. "Strange. It made me miss you."

"Oh? How can that be?"

"Their lives are very different from mine. They're not faring well in their marriages, or at least, my younger sister isn't. She has a terrible life."

"I'm sorry."

I nuzzled into her in the dark. "It hurt to see it." This was true. But it was not the whole of the truth.

"And?"

"And . . . it made me see how fortunate I am."

"We both are."

"Yes. I suppose. I hope you feel that way."

"You know the answer to that, Psyche."

There was more I wanted to say; it throbbed in my throat, but I could not form another sound. "Don't leave me, Pteron."

"Never."

"No matter what?"

"You know the answer."

It seemed to me that I didn't know the answer, but her hand had traveled from my hair down to my shoulders, breasts, waist, and I wanted to float back out onto the river of pleasure, I wanted an end to thought; I stopped thinking; I pressed into her hands; it was only later, much later, when we were finally finished, that I wondered at the edge of sleep how she'd known without my telling her that my sisters had visited that day.

14

Centuries ago, when Zeus laid down his decree about the Nine, it took Eros three human generations to begin. She could not bear the thought and held it off, thinking Zeus might pressure her, rallying herself to resist his needling. But in the end, he did not prod about it when they saw each other at the banquets of Olympus, perhaps because their negotiation mattered little in the scale of his concerns, or perhaps, she thought and hoped, because he'd forgotten (he had not).

Nine times. Full male form. And Zeus would watch.

When she finally did it—for much as she loathed the thought, the longer she waited, the longer the demand hung over her—it was worse than she'd feared. She went to the nymphs. Made herself a strong and lean young man, waited in a grove beside a stream. A cluster of river nymphs rose from the water, swirling into flesh form, damp and sparkling. They all eyed the beautiful stranger. The boldest among them approached almost immediately, claiming her terrain. She clasped Eros's hand and said nothing, letting fingers speak. She smiled, glanced back at her fellow nymphs as if to dismiss them; grudgingly they swam away and left the two to their delights. Eros had had a name prepared but the nymph did not ask it, nor did she offer her own.

No words.

Sun and skin and dappled shade.

As they tangled limbs, Eros fought the urge to pull a shield around them so Zeus could not see, to shut him out, but she had to obey or she'd be forever trapped in his demands. His gaze was on them. *Finally, took you long enough,* his laughter prickled the back of her neck, he kept talking, and his bawdy words landed in rhythm with her thrusts, as if her thrusts belonged to him, had been delivered for him, were thanks to him and paled in comparison to his own. Mockery in his voice, and triumph, and arousal. The only mercy was that Eros alone could hear him while the nymph stayed lost in her own joy. At least she could be spared. At least she did not know they were being watched; that the Great Father was turning them into a show for his own purposes; that in a place beyond this riverbank, they existed to be consumed. Horror grew slowly inside Eros, and she sped up to make it all end sooner. The nymph seemed pleased enough, but not entirely transported, eyes still gleaming with hope for more, but Eros felt a sickness in the pit of her stomach and could not go on. *You're beautiful,* she murmured to the nymph before she kissed her forehead and flew away. In flight she softened her chest back into breasts, curved her hips, and dutifully shifted her phallus to the condensed nub of its female form. Zeus's voice still in her ears, against her will, why wouldn't he leave her? *Eros, you fool, that's all you've got? You grow an oar and don't even learn to row?* Thunder echoed across the valley, his rolling laughter, the weather pattern of her humiliation.

For the next time, she sought out a mortal. She appeared at the edge of a forest, near a small house, where a widow harvested apples in the orchard. She lived in that house with her daughter and grandchildren, who were down at the river washing linens. The men had long since gone to battle and died. Eros chose her partly because she'd read the dreams inside the woman's heart and knew a tryst would bring her happiness, and also because she knew it would confound Zeus, sabotage his expectations. This latter reason stabbed her mind with guilt as she lay on a rock, naked, waiting for the widow to approach. It wasn't right, she knew, to use mortals as weapons to spite your fellow gods. Others did it all the time, but she liked to think of herself as better than that. Perhaps she wasn't. Perhaps she was just as prone to pettiness as the Great Father, as Hera, as Apollo and Athena and Ares and the rest of them. She tried to tell herself her main mission was to give this old woman a gift to savor in her twilight years, a memory like a fruit pit that could be sucked for juice.

Young man, the old woman said, close to him now, *are you lost? Hurt?* Kindness in her voice. *I don't know,* said Eros, *perhaps I'm dreaming. Tell me, beautiful lady, are we in a dream?* The woman snorted and said, *Beautiful what? Ha. We must be.* And then she watched the phallus on the young man before her swell and harden, larger than any she'd seen. *Dear gods,* she said. *Where are your clothes? I have none,* said Eros. *Who are you?* the woman said. *I have no name, either,* Eros said, *I am simply here. For you.* The woman's eyes grew wide. She laughed. She slapped her own face to see if she would wake. *I am dreaming,* she said, bewildered, in a daze. *If that is so,* Eros said, reaching out to caress the woman's face, *I beg you not to wake.* They said no more. Their bodies twined and found a dark rhythm, like the pulse of water deep below the earth. In the woman's hips, death and youth, the future and the past, grief and vibrant love blended and simmered and brewed. *What is this?* Zeus's voice, at Eros's neck, prickling. *After all that waiting, this is what you're going to give me? So this is how you like them, Eros, you dog, you horse? Let's see, child. Let's see.* He did not relent, as Eros had hoped. He did not withdraw his attention. The rite between Eros and the widow would have been beautiful, even transcendent, were it not for Zeus's mocking voice at the nape of her, laughing at the paltry entertainment. Eros burned. Even as the widow bucked and crooned and drenched her lover's muscular chest with tears, inside Eros felt her own pleasure singe with shame.

Years passed, human generations passed, before she could bring herself to do it again. The next tryst loomed, impossible. But she had to. She'd be trapped as long as the rest of the Nine loomed ahead. So she readied herself, gathered her strength, and in the meantime the Greeks set sail to Troy, dreaming of war—an act that would be pinned on Aphrodite, for offering a Trojan prince the love of a married woman. As if the Greeks had not harbored dreams of pillage and conquest for years. As if the violation of a marriage bond were a worse offense than the slaughter of thousands. Absurd, for Aphrodite to take the blame for the Trojan War. Eros stood by her mother in those times, and flew beside her too, helping her withstand the fury of deities across the battlefield, though Eros herself took neither side, invested only in the stories of desire. Haunted by the violence she saw. That her shape-shifts should be deemed a crime when these horrors were allowed to stand—how could it be? To the blazes with divine law. She hated it. She chafed.

In a lull in the fighting, she scanned the lands and found a woman burning with a passion severe enough to decimate a warship. Clytemnestra, queen of Mycenae. In her palace, abandoned by the king and his men, she had taken to her chambers in a grief shot through by rage, for her husband had sacrificed their daughter so that good winds would come and sail his ships to war. Agamemnon. He'd killed her beloved girl to serve his greed. Deep in her spirit, Clytemnestra was already brewing her revenge. Eros could see the flame of it from many mountains away. That was it: where she should go. She alighted in the palace of Mycenae, in the servants' quarters, where she disguised herself as a handsome young man. Pure. Wide-eyed. Ready and eager to serve the queen. She brought a tray of freshest fruit to the royal quarters, placed it by the queen's bed, and waited to be dismissed. She was not. Clytemnestra looked at her for a long time before asking, *Where did you come from, young man? I would have remembered a face like that.* Eros shrugged, said only, *Not from far, my queen.* Clytemnestra did not smile, but her eyes shone as she replied. *Not far, you say? Hmm. You're too far now. Come close. Closer. The door is locked? Come here. Such sweet eyes. Look at me, don't be shy, shyness is not what I require. I require many things. You are loyal to your queen, yes? Prove it. Let me see.* She kept talking as she pulled the servant closer, kept talking as her chest began to heave, talked and talked and did not stop as they made ferocious love, as if their loving were a ship she could steer with her words. Her pleasure was volcanic, a bright obliterating force. Eros rode the eruption, and as she did, she saw what this woman had already decided she would do, the murder she fantasized each day, tending it like a climbing vine, and Eros knew it would be so, that the mighty Agamemnon did not stand a chance. He would survive the war and be cut down by his fearsome queen. It was many hours before Clytemnestra finally sent Eros away, saying, *Servant-boy, return tomorrow,* an order to which Eros did not respond, knowing she would not obey. Off she flew from the cliffs of Mycenae, into the star-flecked night. *Well,* Zeus whispered at her neck, *you filthy girl, you're an odd one, that was certainly interesting.* Eros suppressed her bile, suppressed her thoughts so Zeus would not sense them, for she did not want to give him anything more than he'd already taken.

The next ones came soon, in the wake of the Trojan War and the chaos of the Greeks' return home, for it seemed best to get the whole thing done. She rushed through it all, numb inside. Finally, one day, the Nine were complete. Zeus kept his promise and left her alone. She was free to pull a shield of privacy around herself and her lovers, whether in a male or female form, as long as she kept to one or the other and did not mix what was forbidden to be mixed. She should have been glad. She should have been grateful, relieved. But something in her had broken and she saw no possible repair. There were times when she couldn't bear the thought of taking male form with a lover, because she'd been forced to do it, because the act had become tainted by Zeus's gaze and mockery, so that the thought of it now turned the pit of her stomach sour. She couldn't imagine how she'd return to the sweet joy she'd felt with Rhanis, that wood nymph who'd drawn her phallus out all those centuries ago, before Zeus enforced his rules. The innocence of it, the playful abandon. Even sex in female form could be fraught, though she engaged in it often, until finally, one day, she stopped. She, the goddess of desire, made love to no one for one hundred years.

She'd earned her freedom but could not bring herself to use it, despite the fact that now, at last, Zeus no longer seemed perturbed, even joking about her shape-shifting at Olympian feasts with the gregariousness of an indulgent grandfather, as if it amused him, tickled his imagination, and even fed his pride: *That Eros, you know how she is, she wants to seduce women the way I do, and who can blame her? Can I help it if some females dream of being more like me? It's understandable, a longing to be indulged,* he'd say, and look at her with a blend of pity and amusement. The other gods would laugh. Such was the hubris of Zeus, the god among gods: he thought virility could exist only as a tribute to him. As for her lying with females in her female form, it would never measure up to what men could do with women (not in his mind, the mind from which Athena herself had sprung and so nothing to be trifled with, he liked to say, as if her arrival through his forehead were a compliment to his intellect when in fact, though he never told this part, he'd swallowed Athena's mother to imprison her, forcing her to give birth inside him, after which she rebelled and clanged and clanged to forge the raging headache that split him open and set his daughter free). A woman could never satisfy a woman as successfully as a man. The obvious falsehood of this was something no goddess wished to point out to Zeus, not for lack of evidence but simply to avoid his rotten moods. In divine as well as mortal realms, no one wants to deliver bad news to a king. It was easier for all of them to allow the lie to stand, to raise their banquet cups and smile, to pretend that it was true that women who lie with women couldn't really do much with each other, nothing to look at, nothing to worry about, nothing to curtail or police.

Meanwhile, Eros's other shape-shifting—a phallus on her woman's body, natural and true—was still unsanctioned. There was no place for it; it had to be denied, hidden from sight. For this was the transgression that would make Zeus shake the very skies, the one that would break the promise Aphrodite had made on her rebellious daughter's behalf. Why this simple thing, which came so easily to Eros, should be so dangerous, was a mystery she could not solve. Who cared if that particular append-age, the phallus, appeared sometimes on women too? Who cared if the male and female were not always separate, but sometimes melted into each other in fresh and curious ways? Who cared if a female embraced her own body as everything? Or became male, or semi-male, or pure ungendered starlight? Whom did it harm? Zeus, apparently. Or so Zeus seemed to fear.

He could not see that Eros had never under the surface stopped shifting, knew these tides within her as her most authentic self—not their height or their depth, but their very flow. Movement. Her truth was movement, ever-changing, as vibrant and essential as breath. She kept it all hidden, allowed it only when she was strictly alone in the dark with a shielding spell swept hard around her. She shared it with no one, until she built that palace in the valley for a bride she never should have claimed, a bride unsanctioned by the heavens, a bride she'd risked her entire universe to love.

15

Days passed. The warmth of late summer yielded to cool breeze. The autumn sun coaxed orange and yellow from the leaves. My fig tree grew rich with fruit and I ate her sweetness, freshly plucked, between bouts of loving. I licked my fingers, paced the grass. All was well. I had everything. There was no reason for the restlessness that propelled me across the grove and along the stream, on long walks searching for nothing or for something unnamed. I was filling my senses for the frescoes. Every leaf and scent, every shiver of water over pebbles, every bird cry gathered in me to later course down my arm and through my brush. It was a gift. It was enough. I told myself it was more than enough.

I'd been gone so long from village life that it seemed less of a memory than a dream. Had I truly sat before those droves of strangers, eaten by their eyes? It didn't seem real, though my sisters' visit had stirred the feeling in my body again of sitting in that sheep enclosure, the swell of ugly heat. All those grown men watching a girl sit still as if it were some great spectacle, more entertaining than the bards. How ridiculous. What a waste. And look what my life was now, what I'd become! If only more people could see! My sisters had seen. They had admired my life before their feelings splintered into envy, had they not? It shamed me that I kept remembering their faces and searching them for admiration, for a reflection of me as happy and strong. Was it approval I wanted, or only company? When I'd first arrived at the palace, the solitude had been exhilarating, a welcome freedom. But now, after my sisters' visit, I was aware of the emptiness of my days, the urge to fill them, though with what I did not know.

I tried to broach this with Pteron, lightly.

"What?" Hurt beamed through her voice. "You're telling me you're lonely?"

I caressed her shoulder. "My beloved—"

"Psyche, I'm here every night. I've never left you on your own."

But I never see your face, I thought but did not say. *The days are long without you, without a village, a women's room, a kitchen where gossip swirls over the boiling pots.* "I know."

"Am I not enough?"

"You are more than enough, my Pteron. You are everything." And then, as I ran my fingers through her curls, which always gave her joy and solace, I had another thought. "But what if one day, you don't come? What will I do without you?"

"That won't happen."

"You could tire of me one day."

"Ha! Never."

"When I'm old?"

"Oh, I'll relish you then."

"What!" I laughed, unable to hide my delight. "But truly, if you didn't come, where would I go to find you?"

Her voice grew gentle then. "The wind brought you to me, did it not?"

"Yes."

"The wind will connect us always."

The silk of her curls, the stubborn spring of them, how I longed to see their color and the way they caught the light.

"As for your sisters, you want to see them again, don't you?"

I tensed, at war with myself. I wanted not to care about whether my sisters returned. "I wasn't talking about them."

"I know. But seeing them made you lonely."

"I don't know."

She sighed. "They'll be back, just before the moon is full."

I almost asked, *How do you know?* but instead we held each other and let our bodies speak and speak.

As the moon waned, to contain my restlessness, I began a new fresco, my most ambitious project yet. A forest scene, right in the great hall, featuring doves and huntresses, stags and fauns, and, at the center, Daphne as she slowly became a tree. I wanted to capture her midway through her transformation, arms verdant, face contorted in wonder or in pain. For many days, I'd been seeking a way, practicing on pot after pot. It seemed impossible, yet urgent, to do it. To convey how it must have been for her inside. It was a story everyone knew: how she'd run from Apollo as he chased her full of lust, determined to take from her what she did not want to give. Daphne refused to be ravaged, demanded to be free. And so, to escape, the nymph became a laurel tree. In some versions, she chose that fate. In others it was decreed by a god. What was her truth? I longed to know. I listened for her. She hounded the edges of my mind.

I thought Pteron would be excited to hear of my painting. She had always met descriptions of my creations with unbridled support. But when I told her, she tightened, ever so slightly, grew tense beneath me—for I'd mounted her, still had her phallus inside me soft and spent—and loosened her hold on my waist.

"Why that story?" she said.

"Why not that story?"

She went silent.

"I just started thinking about her, and then I couldn't stop."

"Even though there are no laurel trees in this valley?"

"None?" I scanned my memory of long walks through the groves, along the stream. It was true. They grew all over the land where I was raised, but I hadn't seen a laurel tree since I'd come here. How had she known that? When had she spent time on this terrain, getting to know its plant life? It crossed my mind to ask her, but instead I said, "How strange."

"I suppose. Every valley is different."

"Yes."

"Yet you thought of that tale." Her hands stroked my hips, leaving trails of fire.

I ran my fingers along her jaw, through her hair, still hungry for her. "Perhaps because she was wronged. She deserved to be free. And maybe, if I paint her, some part of her can find freedom here in this palace."

"Maybe."

"You don't sound convinced."

"You have such faith in the powers of this palace?"

"Of course I do."

In the pause that followed, I leaned down and let my breasts graze hers. She stirred inside me, growing firm again.

"Such faith you have." Warmth back in her voice. Hands on my hips, grasping hard enough to bruise.

"Why not?" I kissed her neck, determined to spark another round.

"Look what it's done for me."

Four days before the fullness of the moon. Three. Two.

I sat before the unfinished fresco, frustrated, stalled.

I'd wanted to finish before my sisters came—at least to fully render Daphne's face—but the creation was taking more and more time. I had to find the exact right balance between woman and tree, limb and branch, breast and bark, leaves and aching face. The more the painting meant to me, the harder it became. But that wasn't the only obstacle. There was a deeper reason I sat here with the brush limp in my hand. I didn't feel well. I had not eaten yet that day because the sight of food on the banquet table had turned my stomach and my blood hadn't come and my nipples hurt and I knew, I'd listened enough in the women's room to know, what this could mean. That I was with child. But how could it be? In a marriage like mine? With a woman?

Not any woman.

Pteron.

Whose body transformed at will, remaking itself, remaking me.

On the wall, Daphne's face shifted, grew. Her eyes closed and opened and fixed on me. She was alive, half tree, mouth opening to speak. I longed to hear what she'd say if she could rise from the wall and move toward me, reach out her branching hand; I'd clasp it and perhaps my fingers would grow leaves and *Daphne,* I'd say, *a child, I am with child!* The future sprawled before me, blurred and gleaming. Birth. Soft limbs. Wails and feeding in the night. A small face to gaze into, hair to brush with the same tenderness with which my mother had brushed mine. How would this palace sound, filled with young laughter? What would Pteron say? Would she feel at all as I did now, this sense of spinning, falling, plunged into a lush, dark sea of future days?

I don't know how long I sat there, brush in hand, watching Daphne in her metamorphosis, not adding a single stroke. The afternoon grew rich with light. Inside, I teemed. Only when human voices wafted in through the window did I wake from my trance.

My sisters.

I heard their voices in the distance. "Psyche, Psyche." Their voyage on the wind.

My heart swelled: perhaps I could tell them. Surely they'd be glad to hear my news.

I rushed outside and saw them floating on the air, eyes shut, descending toward the grass. They were not far above my head, just above the line of trees, Iantha with her arms spread out like wings, and—my heart stopped in my chest—Coronis, hands on her swollen belly as if to shield it from the world, for she too was with child, further along than me, she must have known during her last visit and her face, look at her face. She landed on the ground and collapsed into a squat, opened her eyes. Her eye. For the other eye was blue and purple and swollen shut. Her nose had been broken, its shape distorted, bruises blooming all around it.

I ran to her. "Coronis!"

She pushed my arms away. "I'm fine," she snapped.

I turned to Iantha, who stood and brushed grass from the front of her robe.

"Good afternoon, sister," Iantha said. "We've returned as promised."

I studied her for answers to my questions. *You already know*, her expression seemed to say. She approached Coronis with a weary determination. "Come, sister, rise up."

"Curse it, Iantha, I am rising." She was on her feet, belly taut and round.

"Coronis," I said, "congratulations on the blessing of your child."

Coronis made a sound between a snort and a bark. "Thank you." She kept her stare out on the trees.

I didn't know what to say next, whether to mention her face. I glanced at Iantha, whose look seemed to warn me, *No*.

After all that talk of loneliness, I'd thought my sisters' arrival would bring immediate comfort, but instead I felt unsettled, as if Poseidon had shaken the earth and rearranged it beneath my feet. They had their own problems. They were not on my side. It was dangerous to succumb to believing they were on my side. And yet I felt the lure of it. I railed against the thought of hosting them, of even letting them cross the palace threshold, but it was far too late for that.

"Welcome, sisters." I forced a smile. "Will you please come in?"

I led them past the unfinished fresco, past Daphne with her rapturous contorted face, which they studied without comment as they passed. We entered the dining hall and I gestured for them to sit. Coronis ate hungrily, Iantha in birdlike bites. I took small pieces of bread—the only food I could bear—and ate them slowly, fearing my sisters might point out my lack of appetite, for now it seemed wrong to share my news. But if they noticed, they said nothing.

"Have you been well?" asked Iantha.

"I have," I said.

Iantha nodded curtly.

"I am glad to see you both," I added. "Coronis, are you all right?"

"Sister, tell me." Coronis glared at me openly now. "What in Hades do you think that means, 'all right'?"

I looked at her more closely. The bruises extended to her neck. I could see the marks of fingers where they had pressed, choked, threatened to steal her breath forever. "I'm sorry."

"You're not. You don't care."

"Of course I care. It pains me, Coronis—"

"To see me this way? To know it happened to me instead of you?"

"Yes."

"Liar."

"He's a monster," I said through gritted teeth.

"Ha! So I'm the one who landed with a monster." Her voice rippled with anger. "Perhaps the Oracle mixed up our names."

"And the child?" I said hopefully. "Are you glad of the child?"

Coronis looked down at her plate and did not reply.

"Let us speak of other things," said Iantha. "We must treasure the time we have. We do not know when we will be able to return, now that . . ." She trailed off. Glanced at Coronis.

"Yes, of course," I said. Obviously, after Coronis gave birth—even once she grew too heavy with child—the journey would be impossible. "Tell me, how is our mother?"

"Better." Iantha smiled. "Much calmer and in better health, with news of you."

"I'm glad." Warmth through my chest, a loosening of knots I hadn't known were there.

Iantha picked up a radish, took a crisp bite. "Tell us, Psyche, how is your husband?"

"He is well."

"Again he is not here?"

"No."

"He won't return today?"

"That's right."

"Ah. More business. And tell me," Iantha continued, "are you relieved when he is gone?"

It seemed a strange question, baiting. A test? I squinted at her, but her face showed only open curiosity. An innocent question. An invitation. I felt the pull of it, the yearning to confide. "In fact, I miss him."

"What part of him? His warm embrace? His golden curls? His voice?"

"All of that," I said, "but mostly, I miss . . ." I paused, searching for the right way to speak my mind. I could not say the whole of what I meant, that when Pteron was gone I missed the way our bodies spoke to each other, the way I came alive with her, how the universe seemed to distill down to the two of us, pressed close, breathing. I could not speak to them of lust, let alone lust for a woman. But I yearned to.

I yearned to be honest. To show them something real about my life, about what I'd learned of myself, who I'd become. I was a woman in love, a woman in lust, a woman-loved woman who'd seen past the edges of what women could be. I was pregnant with new life and with untold futures. I overflowed with incredible things to tell, with a vast inner world desperate to be seen. Perhaps I could share a little, even if a few drops, even if they landed at a slant. They were here now, my sisters, and might not be back for a long time. This was my chance. "Above all, I miss our conversations." I looked up at Iantha, expecting either empathy or envy, prepared for either. But instead, I was startled to see a glint of triumph. I turned to Coronis, took in her suddenly rapacious face.

Silence spread between us. Something was wrong. I felt unmoored, grasped the table as if to steady myself.

"What is it?" I finally said.

"The things you said you missed," said Iantha. "Including his golden curls."

"But last time," Coronis said, "you told us that his curls were dark."

I stared at them. Caught in my lie. Just when I'd attempted to share with them a shred of what was true. My chest tightened like a fist. What had I done?

"Sister," Iantha said, "who is your husband, really? Is he a monster after all? What are you hiding?"

I opened my mouth. No sound came out.

Coronis was watching me keenly now.

"Why have you lied to us?" Iantha continued. "We are your sisters."

She said it with a breeze of innocence, as if our being sisters meant a bond that could never be shaken or betrayed, as if they'd never once broken my trust or treated me cruelly. Deep in my mind, a voice scoffed at her declaration, but even as it did, another part of me gathered her words *we are your sisters* and the warm, confiding ring of them and wove them into a mantle in which to be wrapped and rocked, like a small beloved child. I felt weary of secrets, weary of pretense. Why indeed did I have to lie about my marriage? Why wasn't it possible to stand in its truth, stand in the light? *I built this palace*, Pteron had said, *for our freedom*. I wanted to be free. I didn't want to hide. Especially now, with new life growing in my belly, I wanted for my life to become whole. But what did that mean? I immediately heard what Pteron would say: *Is this not enough to be whole? Have I not given you enough?* And she had. *You have, Pteron. But I want to stop hiding from the light.*

"My husband . . ."

My sisters seemed to hold their breath. Waiting.

". . . only comes to me at night."

Confusion washed over their faces.

"What does that mean?" said Iantha.

"We've only been together in the dark. Without a lamp. That's why I don't know the color of"—I stopped myself from saying *her*—"the curls."

They stared at me. Eyes wide, absolutely still.

"You haven't seen him?" Coronis whispered, as if savoring the horror on her tongue. "Not once?"

I'd been tempted to confess the rest of it, to reveal my truths, that my husband was not a man, that she entered through the window and shape-shifted at will from woman to more-than-woman-yet-still-woman in a manner that defied the laws of gods and men, that I had forged a passionate bond with this woman I'd never seen in the light, that I craved her constantly and was bearing her child, but Coronis's face halted me. There was an edge to her, of bitter glee, that was not to be trusted, and if my first revelation had already made this arise, what would the next one do? I could not move my tongue to say it. I was torn between the urge to confess more to my sisters, to feel the sweet relief of being known, and the urge to shield my marriage—my treasured marriage—from their deeper motives. Careful, Psyche, I thought. I shut my mouth and shook my head.

"He *is* a monster, then." Coronis beamed with satisfaction.

Iantha's eyebrows rose. "You haven't seen him. He could be hideous."

"And he has you trapped here in his claws."

"No," I protested. "That's not it. There is . . ."

"What?" Iantha said. "In such a marriage—if you can call it a marriage!—there is what?"

I stared at her. She met my eyes and did not blink. All of a sudden I felt the crushing exhaustion of hiding, of carrying a forbidden truth. "Great love."

Iantha wiped her mouth delicately. When she was done, she exchanged a glance with Coronis, and once again I felt myself locked out of the channel of their silent exchange. I'd extended my compassion to Coronis, my honesty to Iantha—a piece of it—but their allegiances were not and would never be with me. In that moment I saw that it was too late. I'd lost them both.

"Let me tell you a story," said Iantha.

It had come from her head cook, who was known for rewarding the kitchen maids with a good tale around the fire after a hard day's work, which Iantha, for her own amusement, later pried from the servant girl who brought her bread and cheese in the morning. Where the cook had gotten the story, nobody knew; she was a woman who at once seemed ancient and ageless, with a stout voice and a face like finely creased parchment. In any case, Iantha continued, the story went like this: Once there was a humble shepherd who was minding his business, watching his flock, when suddenly an earthquake shook the land so powerfully it broke in two. The shepherd was shocked at what Poseidon had wrought, and thought of making the god an offering, which was what he really should have done, but instead he was soon distracted by curiosity and climbed down into the new fissure, thinking to himself, amazing, what a thrill, I never thought I'd have the chance to crawl into the earth while still alive, I wonder what I'll find. He was the kind of man who hankered for adventure, you know the type, always restless and rarely satisfied. And what do you think he found down there but an enormous hollow statue of a horse, and how did he know it was hollow? I know you're wondering that, Psyche, and don't look at me that way, Coronis, you've heard the tale before but you have got to admit, it gets better every time.

"I'll admit no such thing," Coronis said, examining her nails.

"You're fooling no one," Iantha said. "In any case, as I was saying. He knew the horse was hollow because there was a window cut into its body, and of course, being an extremely curious shepherd, he had to peer inside. There he saw a corpse, half-rotted, wearing nothing but a ring on its left hand. He took the ring and put it on. It didn't stink too much, and he was pleased. Then he climbed back out of the earth and hurried off to a meeting with all the other shepherds of the land, forgetting all about the corpse he'd stolen from. This shepherd meeting, as you can imagine, was very boring. It involved lots of details about flocks and this and that, which had to be dutifully gathered for the king. In his boredom, the curious shepherd started twisting his new ring this way and that on his finger. And wait, listen to this—when he turned the ring inside, gem toward his palm, the other shepherds started acting as if he wasn't there. He'd become invisible! Just picture his surprise. When he turned it back, they could see him again. It was the ring. The ring gave him the power to be invisible whenever he wished. So what do you think our good shepherd did? He used his new powers to sneak into the royal palace and right into the queen's chambers, can you imagine? He just strolled in and bedded her in the night, with his ring turned inward, so she couldn't see him approach, never saw his face until it was too late, it all happened in the dark—yes, aha, I see you're starting to catch on. Look at me, Psyche. There's nothing outside that window for you, you've seen all that before and it'll be there every day. This story is the thing you need, I'm telling you. This invisible lover of the queen, he used his powers to make her fall in love with him—"

"That's the part I don't understand," Coronis said. "Why would a queen find this invisible peasant so irresistible?"

I opened my mouth to laugh, but Iantha snapped, "Ask your sister."

I burned with fury, could barely contain it, but didn't know how to respond. What could I say? How could I tell them what Pteron was to me? How could I describe what she gave me and the way she was not invisible to me at all, the way darkness was not a shroud of secrecy but of protection for a love unblessed by the world?

Was that not the truth?

Or—?

If not, what was?

They knew nothing. They'd never understand.

This story of the ring had no connection to my life. And yet I felt an itch of fear.

"Psyche," said Iantha, with a sweetness I did not believe. "Are you all right?"

"Of course, I'm fine. So what happened to the shepherd?"

"Well," she went on, in that commanding voice she'd always used to remind us she was the eldest, to reset the rules of any game, "the shepherd. He'd won the queen's heart, with his deceitful, not-showing-his-face ways, and after that he used his invisibility power to kill the king. I don't know how, he must have snuck up behind him and then—pak. With the king dead, he took the throne for himself and became king, as men are wont to do when given the chance. And he was glad of it, but you know what, the kingdom was awash in sorrow because their new king was evil. The end." She waited for a moment for her words to imbue the air. "Psyche. Please. You see the moral?"

"No," I said through gritted teeth.

She sighed, as if dealing with a stubborn child. "Invisibility is a poison. It cloaks the actions of men in shadow. And men who can act in the shadows will do terrible things, simply because they can. Do not trust this man, Psyche. You cannot trust him, not until you look upon his face with your own eyes."

The rest of the visit blurred; I could scarcely hear my sisters over my mind's storm. I smiled politely but my hands shook as I passed the bowl of dates their way. The conversation shifted toward the mundane. Iantha pattered on about her servants, while Coronis sulked and watched me with an eagerness that seemed born of spite, wanting to find signs of weakness. Wasn't that it? Didn't they want to destroy what I had, as if the life I'd made were a ceramic pot they could smash against the wall? I felt sick, I felt numb, I wanted them gone. A terrible thing to think about your sisters, especially a sister who was battered and with child, but I wanted it all the same. I could not help Coronis, and Coronis did not want to help me. I couldn't trust her. I couldn't trust either of them. I rose to my feet. "You should go, before it gets dark."

Iantha looked out the window, hesitant, for sunlight still bathed the land. "We have a little time."

"Very little," I insisted.

Iantha studied me. She and Coronis had not said whether they intended to stay the night, and perhaps they'd thought I'd invite them to do so. But now that I'd told them my secret—one part of the secret—I could not risk their presence in the night, the possibility of their footsteps up the stairs to my bedroom door, let alone through it, when Pteron was here. It was not safe. Iantha must have made a similar calculation as I held her gaze and did not budge, made no motion to invite her to stay. It was rude, but I held my ground.

Finally, Iantha stood. "Let us go, Coronis."

I grabbed three silver plates from the table and pushed them at my sisters, against their protests, gifts for them and our mother, for even though last time they'd taken offense at the gifts, I knew there was equal risk of offense if I gave none. And in any case, let it be finished, let it be done. So what if it hurt them? It wasn't something I could stop. They followed me down the hall and past the unfinished Daphne-no-longer-a-nymph-not-yet-a-tree, out into the sunshine, into the grove, where they turned and faced me.

"Goodbye, sister," Iantha said tightly.

"Goodbye." I turned to Coronis. "Sister, I am glad for the coming birth of your child. Be safe and well."

"I'll try." To my shock, Coronis blinked back tears, and she seemed to me all at once like a frightened child who'd lost her way. I felt ashamed that just moments ago I'd seen her as an enemy. I closed the distance between us and embraced her; she tensed, then let her head fall to my shoulder. My robe grew damp with her tears.

"All right," Iantha said, "that's enough. Let's go."

Coronis stepped away, wiping the snot from her nose. I approached Iantha awkwardly and kissed her cheek. I didn't know what to say. I was still angry, yet I also felt a slash of pain, as I had no idea when or if I'd see them again. "Please send love to our mother."

Iantha nodded curtly, held the silver plates across her chest like a shield, and closed her eyes. Coronis closed her eyes as well, and soon enough the wind rose around them, swirling their robes, lifting them into the air. I watched their ascent into wingless flight until they finally became specks at the far end of the cliff and disappeared.

I went back inside. The house was quiet. There was nobody to stir the air or warm it. I felt profoundly alone. But how could I think that? Pteron would be back tonight; she always came, I was accompanied in this house. And more than that. I was accompanied in my body. Listen.

Descend. The fullness, a stirring, new life. Like a seed starting to sprout beneath the soil, long before breaking into air. I felt inward for that presence. Wanted so much to sense it. But whether I was connecting with the child growing inside me, or with some part of my own self, I could not tell. What's in my body, I thought fiercely, what *is* my body? And how can I still feel, even with my womb full, a loneliness that tears at my bones? Light streamed in through the windows, gilding the two empty chairs by the hearth. Such beautiful chairs, exquisitely carved, yet not once had they held the husband and wife of this palace, whether to hold court or simply sit with each other in the golden afternoon sun. Beauty, emptiness. Form without function. Where to go. What to do with myself. How to breathe.

I went to my unfinished fresco, sat on the stool before it. Stared at Daphne's leafy arms, the legs fusing into a trunk. I wanted to paint the chaos that came with transformation. I wanted to capture the last expression in her eyes before they disappeared, the purity of that moment of knowing herself in that tangle of victory and defeat. She would not be raped, but she would lose her body. She would be safe; she'd never be free again. What happened in her mind, in those last moments, before it turned green? What did it mean to her, to change? Did she ever find peace? She was transfigured, but not monstrous. Too many things were wrongly called monstrous in this world. What if monstrousness—this kind at least—was nothing more than the fierce uprising of the urge to be free? Was that why it felt so urgent to paint her, why every brushstroke felt insufficient for the task? Or was it the desire to turn back time to when Daphne's freedom still seemed possible, before Apollo cornered her and her face vanished into bark? I didn't know. So many barriers to freedom, too many. So many barriers to existence. It was a wonder any women or girls existed at all.

Daphne stood half-painted, half-transformed, hidden in the mists of what had not yet come to be.

Iantha's story stirred my mind and would not let me go. The ring, the shepherd, being seen and not seen. For him, invisibility led directly to deceit. That was not our story. Was it? Hiding, in our case, was not a cover for wrongdoing, an excuse to commit crimes, or if it was, our only crime was loving each other, claiming a marriage the world did not wish us to claim. Had we violated human law? Yes. Divine law? Yes. Would the forces of earth or heaven seek to shatter our marriage if the full truth were known? Surely, yes. But did that make what we were doing as terrible as what the shepherd did? We had not murdered anyone and did not want to flood a kingdom with sorrow. All we wanted was to live lives of our own making. This was something Iantha would never understand. She'd told that story as if to offer me wisdom, but in fact she'd wielded it as a weapon in battle. I could not trust her, I thought, and then just as quickly I heard her words in my head, *you cannot trust him, not until* and I throbbed with confusion, for whom could I trust? How to know? Trust seemed a fragile thing, a leaf in autumn, subject to the force of winds.

I had to trust Pteron.

I could not trust Iantha.

She did not understand my marriage, not just because she did not know its greatest secrets but because they were beyond her fathoming; if she'd known the whole of it, she would have battled against it even harder. Everything I knew about her shouted this to be true. I thought of Iantha's face as she told the story, worried for me and flecked with glee at my misfortune. Pteron had said my sisters might be bitter about my happiness, might seek ways to turn it against us. I hadn't believed her. I didn't want to believe her still.

I wanted more than anything to know what to believe.

I didn't want to think of Iantha's story anymore. It was not welcome in my mind, and anyway, what was its use? It was just an old tale devised to entertain people around a fire after a long day's work. It had no meaning, or if it did, it had nothing to do with Pteron and me.

Nothing.

Over and over, I told myself this.

And yet it haunted me.

"What's the matter?" Pteron asked me, at night in the dark.

"Nothing."

"It can't be nothing."

"It's only . . . that I missed you today."

"Mmmm."

"Did you miss me?"

"Of course. You know that. I eagerly await our nights together."

And yet you never visit me in the day, I thought, holding my tongue so as not to spark a fight. More and more often now, I held thoughts back to keep the peace.

"But there's something else on your mind. Isn't there, Psyche."

It was not a question, yet I felt her waiting for an answer. I longed to tell her that I was with child. I didn't know what held me back; I was waiting, but for what? For the unease in me to settle. For clarity. For a deeper understanding of where we were, who we could be together, what it would mean to bring a child into this household where one of the parents never appeared by light of lamp or sun.

But none of that came.

"Kiss me," I said.

16

She should have known. Of course she should have known. Some deep-sea part of her already knew, could feel the gathering forces of betrayal, but she pushed them down as far as they'd go. This was her refuge, this bed, this woman, this woman's arms. A secret place. A yes-place. A here-I-am-all-of-me place. She longed for it, longed to live in a world where it could be. She asked for no part of other gods' domains, not Apollo's chariot, or Ares's violence, or Poseidon's watery storms. She wanted only to inhabit her own realm as fully as she could. To embody desire. To be her whole self. Simple things yet out of reach, not because they were unnatural—for here she was, existing—but because the king of gods had decreed against it, because divine law had ruled against her very being. Olympus would never be home for her, nor would the mortal earth, so she'd set out to build a palace where she and her bride could belong. Their own palace. The palace of Eros, built of marble and spells, desire and dreams. A space for truth. A space for joy.

It was all she asked for.

Too much you know you're asking too much, look, no don't look, stop don't make me see—

17

Each day more leaves turned fire-colored and bent their heads toward inevitable descent. The sun blanketed the treetops with cool, thin light. The wind whispered of winter, biting with cold teeth. I walked the groves and tried to think. It was beautiful, our valley, but the cliff face was steep, and without flights on the wind, there was no scaling it. I started to feel myself enclosed in a deep ravine that, however enchanted, not only kept the world at bay but kept me from it as well.

Passion still filled my nights. I came to Pteron hungry and was sated every time. But I was restless. Words crowded my throat, unspoken. They clamored even as I surrendered to the tides of the body. *What are you thinking?* Pteron would ask, but I replied without ever giving a real answer.

I came to an almost-end with the fresco of Daphne. The forest around her teemed with life, its trees and creatures vivid, the huntresses steady with their bows. Daphne herself reigned at the center, one brushstroke away from complete. I could see exactly where the line was needed to flesh out her mouth and make the picture whole. But I couldn't bring myself to do it. I couldn't bear to finish. After months of labor, I left the painting one stroke from done, stealing glances at it whenever I moved through the hall, as if it might at any moment reveal its hidden meaning.

Over time, the nausea eased, replaced by the sharpest hunger I'd ever known. I sat at the banquet table and ate and ate. Every bite a wonder. *Grow,* I thought to the life inside me, *grow.* The pregnancy filled me with happiness, but also with fear. What kind of mother could I be, in this place? How were we to live?

One day I thought I felt a tremor in my belly, the jab of a limb. My daughter. Daughter? Son? I didn't know, but *daughter* was the word that soared through my mind as I cradled my belly, thrilled by the presence of this creature who was real, alive, growing in me.

It was afternoon. Golden light. I was sitting beneath my fig tree, spine against her trunk, eyes closed. I'd been coming to her this way more often lately, not making love, instead seeking wisdom or solace. Most of the time she answered only with the rustle of her wide-fingered leaves in the breeze, but once, just once, I thought I heard her send my own thought back to me, *Always it is better to be free.*

I thought of this now, resting against her as best I could.

Therein lay the trouble and the elixir.

I could not stay the same and still be free.

I stared up at the sky through the fig leaves, and the truth crashed into me with a force that made the grove around me spin.

I loved Pteron, but I wanted to defy her.

I craved her.

I would always crave her.

The craving of her was tattooed into my being.

But also, I had become a person alive to my own wanting, and I wanted many things. Knowledge. Sight. Things I had not yet begun to name.

I wanted to be my own person, and I wanted my whole being to be able to stand in the sun. I did not want to hide the thing we were together, to hide behind the image of a goodwife, for I was not that, I was more than that, I was beyond that entirely. I was as large inside as any man—as she, my beloved, had helped me learn to see. She'd exposed the lie of women's smallness. And yet it was also she who wanted to hide me away in the dark—why? She was afraid, that much was clear. Afraid of what? She wanted—what? Me to herself deep in the heart of the labyrinth, where we could each be Minotaurs without the risk of what our power might do. The truth of us could shake the world, mar its careful harmonies. But so what? I did not love the world as it was, the world in which a girl could be a thing and wives existed only to obey husbands' commands.

There were cages in the world worth destroying.

Surely it was hubris of the worst kind to imagine that the shape of the world would change just because we brought our passion into the light.

Absurd.

And yet. And yet. If it was not so, why this fear? Why such elaborate labyrinths if the Minotaur threatens nothing?

I was too large inside now to be ruled by fear.

I had other reasons, too. There was the child to think about, the spark inside me I kept listening to with every breath, with every step, at every quiver of my mind. She made me vast inside; she made me bold; she forced me to think into the future. I wanted to raise her—if indeed she was a girl—in a different world with fewer traps and cages. Perhaps the world could not be changed, but her home could be, or at least my bond with her could be. What I might be able to give her—and longed to give her—was a mother not ruled by fear. And a home where she could know the light, and know her family in the light, where her father—her female father? Also-mother? I couldn't fathom the right words, they were not enough to shape around our family, the family we were becoming, words for us did not exist—would be more than an absence and an occasional stroke of her hair in the absolute dark. How could that be enough?

Look what had become of me, daring to weigh the word *enough*!

And yet I was. I did.

And I wanted more.

To give my child more.

To know more.

To see more.

I wanted to see; I wanted to be large and full of vaulting futures; I wanted to be bold.

I wanted light.

That night, I left the lamp at the foot of the stairs, still burning, rather than snuffing it out at our bedroom door as I usually did. I tiptoed upward through the dark to the bedroom, where I waited for Eros with a soul torn in two, for I knew what I would do and was determined that it be done.

She arrived, we did not speak, I reached for her immediately. Her intensity rose to meet mine. I gave her my most savage hunger, and every time she began to talk I placed my mouth on hers and drank her words into my kiss. She seemed to take this as a sign that I'd resolved whatever had been plaguing me, that the future lay before us bright and smooth. She gave my body everything it asked for. My body asked and asked. She loved me with the force of a cyclone, with all the sweet brutality I craved, and afterward, I wrapped her in my arms and hummed her to sleep.

When her breathing finally shifted and I was sure of her slumber, I crept back downstairs for the lamp. I walked carefully, holding the flame steady, each step a rebellion as the walls caught shadows and seemed to whisper, *Are you sure? Is this you? Do you know what you're doing?* I had no answers. I reached the door. Stepped through before I could stop myself, before fear could take charge. Here, the room. The bed. Closer. Flame in hand, I leaned down.

There she was.

Right below me.

I could not breathe.

She lay in a pool of lamplight. Radiant.

I edged closer, to see, to breathe in all of her.

She glowed, my Pteron, with the aura of an incandescent sleep. Everything about her was exquisite, above all because I knew those shapes already, could recall them on my fingertips and skin: her hair—a rich brown—the line of her jaw, her limbs and hips, those hands that knew my secret places better than anyone in the world. She was my soul. Or so I thought. She was the shattering and the lighting of my soul. And she glowed in a manner that did not spring from the lamp but from her own being, which could mean only one thing: she was divine. I had known. I had not known. How could I have thought I did not know? Which goddess? Which goddess? My mind raced. I could not imagine, could not think. A goddess! She was my beloved and yet she was of a place beyond my mortal knowing, beyond the scope of what I could fathom with my human mind. The room whirled around me. I stared at her in silence for an infinity that stretched wide open and to which I would soon long with all my being to return.

Oil fell from the lamp onto her shoulder—and I know what the bards and gossips would come to say, how they'd forever tell that the oil dripped by accident, ruining my plans, because I was distracted by her overwhelming beauty, for according to their version I'd never intended to wake her or have my transgression revealed. I am not so sure. I already knew so much of her beauty and had been overwhelmed by it many times before. For that is the secret of beauty: it permeates a person, flows from them, in ways that transcend the human eye. It is not merely housed by visible form, as most people believe. I had bathed in Pteron's beauty every night, in her sound and shape, her scent, her grace, her emanations, her focus and her dreaming, the rove of her thoughts and the humid swim of her passion. Seeing her revealed her in a new way, yes, but because I'd known it all these many moons, it was more of an experience of completion than of shock, and for that reason it does not explain the spill of oil. I could not tell you exactly why the lamp tipped in my hand. An accident? Or did my body move faster than my mind, where the last shreds of caution lay? Could it be that my hand tipped ever so slightly because now that I held her with my eyes, I wanted to know her wholly, for her to wholly know me, for the bond we had to breathe out in the open, however steep the cost? My heat in that oil. Racing through the gap between us, to her skin. *No*, shouted my mind as it fell, for the mind can measure dangers to come even as the body leaps into the lightning storm. Drip. A hot liquid coin formed on her shoulder, and to my thrill and joy and horror she awoke.

She stared at me. Disbelief, pain, then a tangle of emotions. I could not breathe, faced with the intensity of her eyes, which even in this terrible moment were so beautiful that I felt a flash of anger at her for keeping them from me all this time—a flash that quickly sank under a flood of panic and shame.

She backed away from me. "What have you done?"

"Pteron, I—"

Her eyes darted around the room. "We've been seen."

"What? No, there's no one here but me."

"You've looked at me."

"Yes, I'm sorry, I just—"

"The shroud is broken. She'll know."

"Who will know?" What shroud? Perhaps she had another wife—the first thought that struck me. Strange, to hear fear in her voice, when she'd always been so brazen. "I'm sorry. I'll blow out the light."

"It's too late!"

I flinched at the harshness in her voice. What had I expected? Immediate forgiveness? I didn't know. But I had nothing with which to navigate this. I met her eyes, and for a moment it seemed I might find the tenderness I'd felt from her on so many nights. I wanted to ask, *Too late for what?* I wanted to ask a thousand things. I reached out to her. "Pteron—"

"How could you?" She thrust my hand away, sprang from the bed, the fleeting tenderness gone. She stood, naked and glorious, staring at me, breathing hard. I could do nothing but return her gaze. Finally, she strode across the room and tore back the tapestry through which she always appeared. The great cloth came loose immediately, for she was immensely strong; I'd known this in our bed, but now the sight of her muscular arms and the ease with which she tore the heavy cloth from its nails took my breath away. A tall arched window stood revealed. So that was where she came and went each night. I thought for an instant that Pegasus or a flying chariot might appear at the window to retrieve her, but no, I thought, she would not leave like that, we will talk, we will make love, we will find our way to the other side of whatever this moment has become—but then wings sprouted from her shoulder blades, blooming outward with the speed and grace of a hawk readying to soar, a great unfurling of golden feathers, for it had never been a winged creature that she'd ridden to come see me, she'd never had a chariot pull her through the sky, it was she who flew on her own wings and they were lush beyond compare. All that time her shoulder blades had held them, furled. It stabbed me, then, the realization of where I'd been, who I'd been with, what I'd had and lost.

"Please," I said, "stay—"

But already she'd leapt to the window and vanished into flight.

PART THREE

Heavens

18

She flew as if the night air were her only home, as if flight were the only solace in this world. Her wings pressed against the darkness, caught its currents and shifted them, sliced new wind into being. She had no thought for what her flight did to the air, how it shivered in her wake, arched its unseen curves, rippled as it held her aloft; if the air knew joy at her touch, she did not care; she soared with the brutal aim of a knife, as if to annihilate the pain. But she could not. Her wound was raw, fresh, hot oil now gone cold in the slash of night air. It burned. She burned. She was blinded by the sensation, closed her eyes in a vain attempt to see.

She could not see; there was no seeing; *how could she* and then the mind cut off and took to whirling. The air sustained her, offered a plushness over which she could glide, regal and eagle-like, with no need to beat her wings, but inside she was not regal, she was trounced, exposed, humiliated, stripped of all her grandeur for her fellow gods to see.

Or goddesses.

One goddess, in particular. Her mother.

She could not think now of her mother or she'd drop from the sky. Fly, she thought at herself, fly, Eros, you'd better stay up high and keep from tumbling to the human world in this pathetic state, that's the last thing you need, to fall into some sordid mortal valley when you're at your lowest, come on, push on, fly home—but what was home? And where? And here her thoughts snagged on too many thorns. She had her home in the divine realm and the home she'd made with Psyche, *for* Psyche, a palace sprung from her own imagination for the happiness of her bride and for the happiness she herself had hoped to find with her bride. Pain seared her shoulder. How could I have left her, she thought, and what is this shoulder-pain, is it the stab of having abandoned her or the stab of her betrayal? For it was she who ended things and there was nothing left for me to do but fly away, was there, not even if the great sweep of time into the future judges me for leaving the way I did, as it might, curse it, I might be cast as the wrongdoer in this story, at least in the parchments where mortal humans write their little tales spun from glimpses of the gods, not that I should care about what mortal humans write about us, but I do, we all do, even Zeus with his outrageously elaborate throne is captive to his own vanity and wants to be remembered by the human bards as mighty rather than those other things I've seen him be. But I can't help it, can I? Am I not divine? Did I not offer her my universe? And she betrays me. I had to leave. There was nothing else for me to do but disappear, leave her, because she'd left me first, ripped me open with the light of that lamp and ripped open also our beautiful world.

She beat her wings, one, two, launching waves of pain into the night. The air caught them, seemed to weep. Such grief. For she was a gift, that Psyche—but no. Throw that thought away, hurl it at the mountains. Psyche was a traitor. She'd had everything a bride could wish for, a palace, a constant feast, free days, romping nights, abject adoration—and none of that had been enough for her to honor a promise. She had torn the very fabric of safety. She had violated her beloved with that lamp. A rape of light—fly into the night, obliterate the thought, cut the darkness with the knife of your body, fly on. Eros's eyes had drifted open; she drank the stars, rose to approach them though they did not approach her back. She shut her eyes.

It had all been her idea.

She'd dreamed it all up, pursued this stupidity, so it was all her fault.

She'd set her own undoing into motion.

Why had she done it? Why had she let it matter?

Her shoulder shouted with pain, the wound from Psyche's lamp bleeding into the night, drops of blood mixed with lamp oil, a strange rain to perturb the shepherds' dreams.

She had wanted things that broke the delicate arrangements of heaven, that went against the laws of gods and men. She had wanted more and more, too much. Curse her for having wanted it. Curse her for not being the way a goddess was supposed to be.

Her strength sagged. The wound throbbed. Its rawness blossomed into the night, flesh melted back to the bone. With every bitter thought the skin peeled farther open—she had to stop—yet she could not help herself, could not hold back the rampage of her mind. It would heal, she knew, as all gods' injuries did, but even the gods were not immune to pain, and it was the soul's pain that made wounds like this one scream. But fly, Eros, she shouted in the great swirl of her mind, fly on, through this night of failure and defeat.

She could not escape the roil of her own thoughts.

She'd thought—what? That they could last forever?

Forever love with a mortal bride?

Eros! You're a fool!

Mortals died. Even at its best, with Psyche's full devotion, this bond would never have been more than a blink in the great expanse of eternity.

And yet it hadn't felt that way. There had been something end-less about Psyche. Not her time, not the years ahead of her, but the vastness of her mind. She seemed capable of encompassing anything: she embraced Eros, all of her, no matter how she arrived. No matter what hungers she revealed. No matter what shape she took. Her whole gender, body, lust—Psyche welcomed it all. It had been centuries since Eros had allowed herself to metamorphose in the presence of a lover. It had been forbidden. Psyche broke that. Freed her. Gave her witness, cherished Eros and hungered for her too, held her as she stretched the word *woman* into fresh abiding forms and held the great constellation of herself entire. It was more than she'd ever dared imagine possible. How Psyche's desire had met her own, how they'd lit each other up. Multivalent. Fluid. Bright as water leaping in the sun. Psyche came to know her better than anyone ever had, for in the dark Eros let herself be fully known, an elixir beyond compare. There had been no need of light. Light cut and broke the wondrous thing they had. Tore their sacred dark to shreds. That horrible moment in the bedroom. The stab of betrayal in her chest. How could she. The surge of rage again. How dare she. Why had she shattered their bliss? What would they be for each other now? Nothing, they had to be nothing to each other, everything was broken. What a shame. What a loss. It gutted her so hard she almost fell out of her flight, down to rocky crags. Nobody will ever look at me that way again, she thought, no one else can look upon the goddess Eros and see anything beyond their own desires. People want what I can give them, and so do the gods; aim your arrows, they say, shoot for me, all they're prepared to see when they gaze into my face is a mirror for what they want, not my own soul. Psyche listened for me, for the me underneath, and took joy in what she found. She made me hers. She was my life. She was my undoing. I thought I knew the risks before I leapt. But did I? I am Eros. I am a goddess. Mine are the cycles of the eternal stars. How could I blend souls with a mortal woman? It cannot be. And yet, what else should this be called? This ripping of my mind in two at losing her? How did you find such a woman, Eros, she thought to herself, beating her wings against the night, and what will you do now that she's lost?

Look at what you've lost.

It has no measure.

How we fit into each other!

Where I was root, she was soil, and I burrowed into her and found home.

Where I was river, she was riverbed, holding and shaping me at the same time.

Where I was cloud, she was sky, to dissolve in her a sweet annihilation.

Where I was flame, she was flame.

Together we could have burned down the world.

Yes, she thought, we could have.

How she longed to see the burning and the green shoots that would push up from the ash.

Instead, here she was, wounded, flying against the pain, soaring over mountains shrouded black with night and forests blurred to darkness, hailed by the stars, broken, shouting inside with grief and hurt and also fear, yes, she didn't want to admit it but the thought forced its way in: inside her was a sky-vast fear that made her wish this flight—for all its pain—would never end, for on landing she'd have to face the very thing from which she'd sought to protect herself when she conjured the palace and its valleys and the plush dark room in which she'd learned the secret face of joy, she'd have to step into the thing she'd risked when she defied orders to save a mortal girl from doom, the thing that terrified her more than any other force in the universe: her mother's wrath.

She glowered in the throne room, high on her dais, radiant with splendor and rage. Aphrodite. It would have been better to find her tearing her hair and gnashing her teeth; such fury, the kind that unleashed inner chaos, was easier for Eros to navigate than this, a contained force, dense, potent enough to light the sky, controlled enough to hit its target when least expected.

"Mother." The shake in her own voice disgusted her.

Aphrodite said nothing. Bright. Fearsome.

Eros stepped across the hall, toward the throne.

"Stop."

Eros froze.

"You are in the presence of a goddess." Chin held high. Hair in sumptuous braids that piled and curled around her head and cascaded down her shoulders, crown and mantle all at once. "On your knees."

She had never asked her own daughter to kneel before. They'd laughed about it, mocked Zeus's vanity in making his children follow such formalities. Not a single thing about this moment felt laughable. Eros was still many paces from her mother, across the vast hall. She fell to her knees and dropped her gaze to the floor. Intricate mosaic, blue and cream and turquoise, the dance of the sea. Silence sang. Silence shouted. The hall reeled in a storm of silence. She searched for something to say, though the words she'd planned withered, futile, insufficient.

Her mother spoke first. "She did that to you?"

Eros touched the wound on her shoulder—it stung—and nodded. She was still naked. Her mother had seen her naked thousands of times, but tonight she felt unbearably exposed.

"Hmm."

Eros waited. Pulled her wings in tight against her back but kept them present.

"For a girl like that, you betray your mother."

"I—"

"To think I trusted you."

The cold in her voice sent a shiver up Eros's spine. What could she say? That she was sorry? That she had not meant to? But she had meant to. She could say that she'd been wrong. But had she? The answer to that question seemed to writhe, a pit of snakes.

"How could you?"

"I'm sorry, Mother."

The next words boomed so loudly they almost burst her inner ear. "Are you? Are you? I don't know what you are!"

Eros crouched, ears covered, rocking on her haunches. Flooded by her mother's sound.

"Speak, child!"

She scarcely managed a whisper. "I don't . . ."

"Speak!"

"I don't know what I am either."

Aphrodite's metallic laugh shot through the hall, shook the marble columns. Eros braced her hands against the mosaic floor, as if to steady herself, as if the sea-patterns had begun to sway. There is nothing under me now, she thought, no ground to hold me, I am lost. Her mother laughed and laughed until the laugh became a scream that filled Eros's mind and chest and blotted out the world. "Get out of here. I don't want to see you."

Eros nodded and slunk backward out of the throne room, not knowing whether she was crushed or relieved or drowning in other sensations she could not name.

In her chambers, she curled up on the floor. Wings cupped around her, feathers soft against her skin. Bed to one side, chair and table to the other, a lamp she would not light. She'd always kept her room spare, knowing she could find any comforts she needed in the rest of the palace, taking refuge in simplicity. A balm to her now. Though not enough. She was home. She was not home. She might never feel at home anywhere again.

She would stay here, wait for her mother to calm.

She would stay and let her wound burn, froth, peel back to the bone.

She would not work—let gods and mortals go without the gifts her arrows gave them, let all beings love or hump or chase each other without her help, for she had lost her beloved, and now she'd lost her mother too. She had nothing to give. She was empty, bereft, a hull. She would stay in her room with her raw open wound, far from her angry mother, plunged into grief. Her mother did not come for her, nor summon her. Silence was met with silence. Never in her life had Eros been so alone. Her bond with her mother was gone. Breakable after all. How would she endure without the love of Aphrodite? How could she exist without a single being who could see her as she was? Too many thoughts. Too much disturbance. Torrents in her mind.

So she continued, through the day and deep into the night.

At night, she missed Psyche. Burned for her. Was she safe? Had she found her way? She'd been left with nothing, not even food on the table—and yes, Eros had been angry, had felt betrayed. But even so, she thought, she was my wife, my beloved, I was supposed to protect her and now she is loose in the wind. I don't care. I shouldn't care. Of course I care madly. And the temptation grew inside her to look, to open her inner seeing to Psyche's location. She shouldn't do it. How the universe might tremble if she did.

Dawn rose, fanned open into day.

She had to stay closed.

She kept her inner eye shut for a breath, another, and another.

But her resolve shook. Let me peer. Just once. A quick opening of the veils to the place that holds her, wherever it may be, and then I'll leave her to her mortal wanderings, as I'd already planned to do.

She opened her inner eye and reached for Psyche.

A great pile of mixed seeds. Psyche crouched before it, sorting. Determination in her face, and sadness, and emotions for which Eros had no name. The sight filled Eros with—what? Worry, and grief, and a quick stab of rueful glee, why not admit it, for the wound on her shoulder still throbbed. Well, Psyche, so you're suffering now, as I did at your hands after I gave you everything. How does it feel? But the thought vanished as quickly as it came. Her beloved. Her wife. So distant from her. Closed to her, to Eros—closed to the ecstasy and happiness they'd shared. That face, the same one she'd stroked so many times in the dark, learning its contours by heart. The same mouth that had spoken her most private name, *Pteron*, sung it, growled it, rubbed it into their skin like oil. Psyche, whom she loved. Psyche, whom she longed to protect. What was happening in that place? What was she doing with that ridiculous pile? One thing was clear: it was a test, and the test was impossible. Those thousands of tiny seeds could not be sorted with human hands. It was just the kind of task a vengeful deity would give a mortal to watch them sweat, to relish their pain.

Eros felt the room sway as she understood.

She spread her wings and flew to find her mother.

19

After she left—my Pteron who was Eros, the famed goddess of desire, as I'd known the moment her wings unfurled in the lamplight—I stayed at the window until it grew pale with dawn. I was not waiting for her return so much as confirming my sense that she was truly gone. I stared and stared into the sky. Black, then pink, then blue. No promises fell from the heavens, no lover flew back into sight; I'd been abandoned. The turmoil inside me had no language, no measure, no name. I went downstairs and found the palace changed, for the enchantment was over. The bathing tub held nothing but withered petals. The loom had disappeared. In the dining room, the food had rotted overnight, wreathing the banquet table with greedy flies. I fought them for a piece of moldy bread but spit it out before I could swallow it, as my pregnant body could not hold it down. If I stayed here, I would die. The thought pressed, a dull knife in the numbness of my mind. I lingered in the great hall for a long time, sitting in one of the ornate thrones, staring at my painting of Daphne. I could not think. I tried to think. Survive.

Am I meant to survive?

I fell asleep seated and woke from slithering dreams.

I looked around me at the great room, now a hostile space.

I left the palace carrying nothing but the clothes on my back and the amethyst necklace my mother had given me, draped against my chest. Perhaps, I thought, there were deeper reasons my mother had saved this necklace for me, the youngest child, the darkest one, the different one. The one most teased. Could she have meant it as a protection? An affirmation, unnamed? I'd never know. But I was grateful for it now. I stood in the valley and closed my eyes, as my sisters had done, though I already knew the magical wind would not come.

Nothing. No stir, no lift. No choice but to leave on foot.

I followed the stream down a thick ravine, straying farther from the palace than I had since I'd arrived. I searched the ravine's steep walls for places where my feet might find purchase and I might clamber out to the rest of the world. I didn't know what I was climbing toward, what I sought. A hold, perhaps, on the jagged rocks of existence. An understanding of darkness and light, what my hand had meant by carrying a lamp, tipping oil. I sought Pteron though I also did not. And anyway, she wouldn't speak to me, that much was clear. *The wind will connect us always,* she'd said, though now when I called her name into the wind there was no lift, no stir, no reply. Another broken promise. And if she came? What would I say to her? There was no returning to the marriage; it was over. But how could it be over? An avalanche of thoughts in me. I didn't want her back, I longed for her back, I sought the chance to beg for forgiveness and the chance to spit in her face.

I climbed for hours, on the verge of falling to my death. Sweat draped me. Hunger mauled at me from the inside. The cliff was unforgiving, impossibly daunting, and I might have given up entirely, hurled myself from the rock face and let it be done, if it hadn't been for the new life inside me.

But it was inside me, quickened, insistent, propelling me on my quest, urging me forward, *climb, Psyche, climb*.

By sundown I had reached the top of the ravine. A meadow spread out before me, with a few scattered trees. I was nowhere near the rock where I'd been tied by my father; I'd emerged on a different side to an unfamiliar landscape that seemed deserted, almost unearthly, no signs of human life. I roamed until I found an apple tree that clung to a few last withered, wormholed fruits. I picked them, ate and ate until my stomach could bear no more. Even the writhe of a worm in my mouth did not deter me. I made a bed of leaves. I'd face tomorrow when it came. For now, sleep. Nothing but sleep.

I woke abruptly in the dark. Alive with vigilance. Eyes wide open against the night.

I could not sleep, much as I needed to. There was too much to understand, too much at stake. I rose and began walking, groping the darkness before me, mapping my way with my fingertips, here a tree, here only air, keep walking.

I was here because I'd lost my marriage. But also, I was here because I'd chosen. Chosen what? Light. Expansion. Insistence on my voice. Was I allowed a voice? Before all that, I'd been shunned by my own people, cast out by my family, cursed by a goddess. As if a human being could be thrown away like a pile of goat droppings. I was not a pile of goat droppings. *So then what are you, Psyche?* I didn't know. Exhaustion crushed me. All I really wanted was a place, somewhere, somehow, in this world. With or without marriage, with or without a beloved; my daughter could be my beloved and maybe—maybe! what a thought—so could I. I longed for a scrap of space where I could hold my daughter, where we could be safe, left in peace to weave the fabric of our days. It didn't have to be a palace. A hovel would do. But could I have such a thing? And what would it take? What did the gods want from me?

My eyes had adjusted to the dark; in the starlight, I spied a clearing. I strode into it, resolute. Threw my head back. "Aphrodite!"

The stars seemed to flicker their warnings.

"Aphrodite!"

I took a deep breath. One more time. The old stories often told of spells that came in threes.

"Aphrodite!"

A rush of wind about me.

Up in the sky, a trembling, as if the wide black skirt of night split open to reveal the glow behind. Its brightness seared me.

You.

A voice, a radiance. Enfolding. Like nothing I'd ever heard or known.

So you're that girl.

"Great goddess."

What do you want?

"I wish for peace between us."

Ha!

Laughter spread thunderous across the sky, shook the ground beneath my feet.

You've got some nerve.

"I suppose I do."

And tell me, child, after all you've put me through, why should I give you peace?

I took a deep breath. She didn't need to give me peace. She owed me nothing and could torture me for her own amusement if she wished. This was the great goddess Aphrodite, whose temples had rippled with gifts before the suitors came for me. This was Pteron's mother, the one she'd shied from ever telling me about. The reason we'd been a secret. Of course. I could see it now, the hiding, the reason for fear. But this was no time for hiding. I understood what I needed to voice up to the black sky and I would do it, even if I trembled as I spoke.

"For your grandchild, who grows in my womb."

The light-fissure glimmered, pulsed, gleamed. The night seemed to rumble with a low, hypnotic sound. I stood, waited. Long moments passed.

Child.

I held my breath.

Let me get a look at you. Close your eyes.

I obeyed. A rush, a swooping. I felt the prickle of a presence, too close, too vast, snaking all around me, lithe and unbearably warm—and then it was gone.

When day comes, go to the temple at the top of this mountain. Sort what needs sorting. It will be the first of your three trials, and you had better thank me for my mercy.

"Thank you, great g—"

Stop it. Sleep.

A blast of air pushed me to the ground and into dreams.

When I woke, I saw immediately that my wanderings had brought me to the foothills of a mountain, a small building at its top. Aphrodite's instructions burned vividly in my mind, and I lost no time in climbing up the slope.

I would live.

I would face her trials.

I would show her whatever needed to be shown.

My heart was buoyant with hope, but hours later, when I finally entered the temple—a bare, abandoned place—the hope deflated. *Sort what needs sorting,* she'd said. At the center of the crumbling room stood a pile of seeds, various, intermingled, shoulder-high. To sort them all, kind with kind, would take a lifetime. It couldn't be done.

She was toying with me. Torturing me, after all.

She didn't want me to overcome the trials and win a place for myself in the world.

She wanted only to watch me suffer and fail.

Every inch of my being longed to scream, to collapse on the redolent dirt floor, to give up. Maybe I was as wretched as the Oracle had predicted. Maybe I should succumb, and simply rest on this cold floor, until the Fates finally claimed me as their own.

I knelt a moment, ready to fall.

But my body would not cower.

Life shouted in me, insistent.

I stared around me at the cavernous temple room. Light streaked in through the door. Flies lazed and hovered. It was a sacred space, was it not? Devoted to some god or goddess? What were sacred spaces if not portals to our fullest selves?

This trial might kill or conquer me, but I didn't have to surrender. I still had a choice. I could strive. Even if I died striving, it was better than dying in defeat.

I approached the pile and began. The sorting was slow, but it calmed my mind. Each seed in the cup of my hand, a prayer. Anything could be a prayer if you held it so. Millet. Lentil. Curved barley, tiny poppy seed, firm brown wheat. This harvest. Such bounty. Born from the abundance of the earth.

After an hour, I'd barely made a dent, but I saw to whom my prayers should go.

20

Eros found her mother bathing, the three Graces fawning over her, washing her feet and hair. Aphrodite lay in the fragrant water, allowing herself to be worshipped. It never ceased to surprise Eros, how the three Graces, each a formidable immortal force in her own right, waited on Aphrodite with such pure reverence, as though simply being close to her beauty were gift enough. Nor could she fathom how her mother could keep from melting into pleasure under their hands. To her astonishment, her mother sought lovemaking only from males. Even though Aglaea rubbed her mistress's foot with a gratitude bordering on ecstasy, and Thalia brushed her fingers gracefully through Aphrodite's loose, wet hair, such elegant hands, well did Eros recall those afternoons over the centuries when she'd learned what those hands could do, and as for Euphrosyne, standing there with the soap, her mouth alone could surely bring any woman to her knees—but no, none of that now, this was not the time. *Focus, Eros!*

Aphrodite did not look up as her daughter alighted before her.

"Mother!"

"What now?"

"What have you done to Psyche?"

"What do you care?"

"That's not—"

"Oh, child." Aphrodite snorted like a horse. "You're being pathetic."

"I don't care about her. Not anymore."

"You've always been a bad liar."

"I'm not lying—"

"I could have protected you better all this time if you'd just learned how to lie."

Eros held herself very still. She had learned to lie, with her whole mind, with her whole body. Or to hide. Was there a difference between the two? She thought of the palace she'd made, its bedroom. Round walls. Plush dark. Endless curves, no corners. She'd shrouded her marriage to keep it free. Hiding was freedom, or so she'd thought. Was it still true? She didn't know. Her pain was true. Her shoulder, seared with light. "You gave her that task, didn't you, Mother? The seeds?"

"It's good, don't you think?"

"It's impossible."

"Not for a god."

"She's not a god!"

"What a shock!" Aphrodite said theatrically, eyes wide.

"Mother, please."

"Please, what? What do you want from me? You had to have known I'd find you out sometime. Tell me, what did you think I'd do?"

"Nothing." In truth, she had not thought so far ahead; she saw now that in her passion she'd indulged a dream—a baseless dream—of keeping her palace secret forever.

"You thought I'd do *nothing*?"

"No. I did not. But perhaps I hoped you'd be gentler with her."

Her mother laughed, dipped her head back, and let her hair undulate beneath the water like hungry kelp. "Oh, Eros, you have been many things, as I of all beings should know, but you have never been a fool."

"Any revenge you take should be on me. I'm the one who betrayed you. It was my scheme, not Psyche's."

"But you are my daughter."

"What does that mean?"

"I have to tell you?"

Unspoken between them swam the rest of that thought, *and we have always been united, it has always been us against the rest of the gods, defending each other in the face of Olympus, their rules and slights and jostling for power, their ploys to confine us.* She felt the plea beneath her mother's words. But her own hurt insisted on being heard. "There is no worse suffering you could inflict on me than this."

"Good!" Aphrodite made no attempt to hide the triumph in her voice. Her eyes flashed. Euphrosyne bent to caress her with the soap, studiously not looking at Eros, though Eros felt the heat of her attention, the flicker of delights once shared and now recalled. She would not react, would not be pulled in, but the spark fortified her for the fight ahead.

"Mother, please, I beg you. Do not do this. Give her some reprieve."

Aphrodite studied her for a long time. "Well, since you seem so keen, you may be surprised to hear that this was all your little wife's idea."

"What? How can that be?"

"She came to me."

Eros felt the marrow of her bones grow cold. "She was here? In the palace?"

Aphrodite sighed. "No. But she called out to me and I was bored, maybe even a little curious about this girl who'd twisted you into knots, and who I thought was dead—child, she was supposed to be dead! So I went to see. She was standing alone in the dark, poor thing. Unkempt, underfed. You really abandoned her just like that, didn't you?"

Eros said nothing.

"And you call that love?"

Confusion snared her. What was love, to a god? What was devotion? Certainly not what Psyche had done. "I call a lot of things love and so do you."

"So does Zeus. Seems to me that in your secret rooms, you acted a bit like him."

A spike of anger. Zeus? She was nothing like Zeus. As if Eros had had the power to build a life for herself! As if she'd been anything but tender and respectful with her beloved! There was no comparison! How could her mother—

"She was brave, you know." Aphrodite seemed amused. "The way she spoke to me. She asked to make peace—can you imagine?"

"And you refused her?"

"No. I said I'd give her trials, to prove her worth. You see, I can be reasonable." Aphrodite examined her toes, lifted idly from the water. "And I like to be entertained."

Eros fought back the urge to leap at her mother, teeth bared, aimed at her throat. As if that could protect her wife. *The wife you abandoned,* a voice inside her crowed. *Maybe you should tear your own damn throat.* She felt a fierce urge to protect Psyche, futile and too late. She also wondered about what lay beneath her mother's words. Her blithe tone. If all she'd wanted was to destroy Psyche, she could have found more brutal or immediate ways. There might have been no trials. Perhaps there was a chance at mercy. "Mother—"

But Aphrodite raised an arm and froze. Her lips curled, as if she'd tasted something sour.

"What? What's the matter?"

"She's done it."

"Psyche?"

"Who else?"

"How?"

"Ants came to help her."

"Ants!"

Eros reached out her mind to see, and there they were, droves of them, tiny and determined, scurrying with seeds on their backs, sorting them efficiently into piles. Psyche on her knees, letting them run across her open hands, weeping with weariness or triumph or relief. That face. Beloved face. Eros's breath caught in her lungs.

Aphrodite glared at her daughter. "Apparently, even though you abandoned her, she has friends. I'd better go see."

"What are you going to—"

"Stay out of it. Back to your room!"

"Let me go with y—"

A blast shot her off the ground. She saw white, nothing but white, bright-blinding. Spin. Break. Burst. She fell through space, fell through time, she was nowhere. She opened her eyes.

Back in her room, alone. The door glowed, tampered with, enchantment-bound. She grasped the doorknob, tried to push: she was locked in. Her mother had sealed the door. She was a prisoner in her own home.

Nights passed. Worlds passed. Time stretched and melted; nights and days wheeled into each other with thick slowness, with blinding speed. Eros could not go anywhere, could not fly, not to a field or a forest or the sea. She hovered outside of time. She had no need of sleep, nor food or drink. She railed. She spun. Even her sight could not reach Psyche. She searched: nothing. Her mother had thought of that too, had thought of everything, had shrouded Psyche, wherever she was, from divine sight. What trial was she enduring now? Was she still human, or had she been converted into some creature as punishment, like Arachne and so many other unfortunate mortals who'd defied the gods? She had no way of knowing, nor of helping, doing anything to change the course of fate. Her wound burned. Pain flared along her shoulder, spread to the rest of her. All that striving to build a palace, to make it beautiful, to create a reality where she could be whole, and where had it landed her? In a cage of her mother's making. Never had she felt so powerless.

What if that's how Psyche felt, subjected to your rules?

A thought alive with thorns.

It wasn't the same. Her rules had been meant to liberate. To forge a space of wonder.

A cage full of wonder is still a cage.

But how else to be safe when you—are like this—

She couldn't bear the weight of her own thoughts.

She dove inward, toward the depths. The inner universe. Primordial, vast. A bottomless sea. And then she was not so much diving but falling, down, wetly down. Surrounded. Foam. Life. Whorls, salt, memories. Suspended in the depths of her own mind, she felt again the quivering vitality of her youth, the balm of sun on her bare skin, the way her laugh could quake the leaves on their branches, the ripening of her powers, learning to shoot, the unspeakable beauty of learning to shoot, the ecstasy of this arrow cast, and that one; she saw it all again; her gold-tipped arrows strewn along the deep like the treasures of shipwrecks, silent testimonies to the ways she'd shifted fate. Lead-tipped arrows, too. The twin forces of her work. There had been so many arrows. Many of them she'd cast at the behest of her mother, or of some other god, and others she'd shot for her own reasons, out of mercy, kindness, or curiosity, bringing good into the world, for the force she embodied was good, it sparked new life, it brought gifts to bodies and to spirits and connected beings to each other, though sometimes—look at it, don't look—it brought harsh things too, and her shots had not always been kind, for arrows could be launched for other reasons, including—don't say it—no—revenge; yes, once, just once, out of revenge.

She did not want to think of it, did not wish to remember. It had been her own worst moment. Centuries since she'd allowed her mind to graze the memory, for she'd chosen to sink it deep, far from her waking days. But it was here. Here. She fell into the memory, forced to relive it, forced to see. How she'd thought she was alone, standing on that hill, shooting arrows at a distant tree, practicing, perfecting her aim, relishing the vigor of the day; she was young then, just beginning to shoot, long before Zeus had brought down his rules. She reveled in the practice of her archery, in her own embodiment, the existence she'd been given. A warm breeze kissed her bare arms. Birdsong clamored. Spring buds trembled, poised to blossom. Apollo had been watching from the sky. She didn't see him descend to the nearest hill, didn't see him watching her with a mocking expression on his face, until he called out. *Eros,* he said, *what do you think you're doing? You think you can shoot? You think you're so special because you've been given the power to ignite passion?* Her hands froze on her bow, drawn taut. She turned toward his voice, arrow still aimed away from him, at a nearby tree. He shone. He smirked. Scorn in his face, and also, beneath the surface, something nebulous and unsettled. *I don't think I can shoot,* Eros said. *I simply do it. Ha!* Apollo scoffed. *You're no warrior. Your bow work is so clumsy I'm surprised you ever hit your targets. You wish you were a god, but you're a goddess. You're not like us. You should stick to a torch for setting hearts on fire, and leave the arrows to the real males.* And then he flicked his eyes down her frame.

She hadn't realized the form she'd taken, hadn't realized her phallus hung against her left thigh beneath her silken gown; she'd been so focused on her shooting that she hadn't paid attention to the shift. That was how it was for her, in those early days, when she was alone and had no need of pretense: her body fluid and free, the shape of her as mutable and natural as breath. All her parts, in harmony with each other, affirming their own particular song. But now Apollo had seen, and the look on his face flooded her with a hot shame, followed by an even hotter rage.

She would show him. She'd fight back. She could not let him be the herald of her humiliation, for if she did, he'd never stop, nor would the other gods. *Apollo,* she said, *mark my words: you think you can vanquish everyone, but my arrows will vanquish you.* With that, she flew away, leaving his scornful laughter in her wake.

That was the day revenge was born, a blade in her heart. After that she lay in wait, seeking her chance to spin Apollo's fate and prove her power over him. She found it soon enough. A gold-tipped arrow to his chest. A lead-tipped arrow for Daphne. His overflowing lust for her, her revulsion and urge to flee. And there it was, the source of her enduring shame, what hounded her even now, centuries later, whenever she saw laurel trees dotting the land: that she, Eros, in her vengeance against Apollo, had destroyed Daphne's life. Yes, Eros had won; she'd gotten what she wanted. Apollo had finally been forced to admit Eros's power, and her mastery of arrows, and had even shut up about her female phallus, but the victory was hollow, for though Daphne had avoided rape, she could only continue to exist as a tree, a caged freedom, not truly freedom at all. Many nymphs across the land berated Eros when she came to them to romp and love and play, *Eros,* they said, *how could you? You killed our sister's spirit, you used her as a tool in your battle with another god. Do we mean so little to you?* For Daphne had been loved. Her sisters grieved, wept, placed their offerings under laurel trees. For a few human generations, Eros was shut out of their world. Eventually, they seemed to forgive her, or at least they spoke of it no more, and Eros returned to her favored status among the nymphs. She went to them gratefully—to their dances, to their arms—and pushed the memory of what she'd done away, into the depths of her.

Now, as she plumbed her own mind, locked in her room, she could not escape it. What she'd done out of despair, out of shame. *But what if,* another voice hummed, surrounding her in the deep. *What if what?* she thought. She hovered in the sea of memory. Sank in. Back on the hill she stood, young, fluid, and there was Apollo, opening his mouth to insult her. The moment it began. What if. She could make. Another choice. She stared at Apollo, his bare muscular chest, his smirk. The face of someone mocking, repulsed, threatened. Threatened? Afraid? Was it that all along? The moment loomed like a great portal, and she inside it, holding it differently, refusing his shame. Seeing him. Seeing herself. Whole. Steady. With nothing to defend or hide or prove. She could have made another choice. True strength lay not in conquering others, but in wholeness, the clarity to refuse other people's shame. If only she could have done that. Could do it. Here. Facing Apollo. *What if*—she opened her mouth to speak and out poured seawater, full of shuddering fish.

Eros.

A voice cut through the thickness. Not Apollo. A female voice. Perhaps the start of another fever-dream.

Eros!

She opened her eyes. It was no dream; someone stood in her dim room, the room where she'd been locked in by her mother. Psyche—no. No mortal could have slipped past the enchantments. This had to be a goddess, one powerful enough to supersede Aphrodite's spell. Rich wavy hair silhouetted against the dark. The figure raised her hand and a lamp appeared in her palm, already lit. She was lovely. She was always lovely, her beauty as formidable as her heart.

"Good, you're awake."

"Demeter—"

"Greetings, Eros."

"I salute you, goddess. How did you get through the door?"

"No matter. The enchantment is still sealed. Much as I have chosen to help you, I'd still like to avoid your mother's wrath."

Eros sat up. A thrill coursed through her. "You're going to help me?"

"I already have. Eros, don't fight with your mother. You must find your way back to each other. We've all come to rely on the harmony between you two, and between the forces you oversee."

"The force I oversee is not harmonious. You know that more than anyone."

Demeter flinched in the dim light. Eros had not meant for the words to sting. But there they were, the wounds, just below the surface, still raw after endless time. How could it be that goddesses could be wounded so deeply, in such lasting ways? But Demeter had known many devastations, perhaps more than any other deity. Her way was gentle, for she ruled over agriculture, over the grains in their fields and grapes on their vines. It was she who brought abundance to the earth and to farmers' harvests and who therefore made life possible. All that bounty and life-giving, yet over and over she'd been violated. Zeus had betrayed her by promising her daughter in marriage to Hades without her knowledge or permission. Hades had betrayed her when he stole her daughter to the underworld and kept her there by force without telling anyone where she was, sending Demeter into a grief that shriveled crops and spread famine across the land, so it was told, and even then, Zeus knew where her daughter was and did not say. Another violation. How she fought. It was not only grief that made Demeter destroy the harvests of the world. Eros had always known it was something else, had seen it shine in Demeter's eyes: rebellion. Maternal rage. She would find her daughter if it meant decimating all of Zeus's world. Her fury lashed across Olympus, strangled the earth below, shot frigid cold across both land and heaven that had never been felt before. She triumphed eventually, at least to the point of learning where her daughter was and seeing her again, but then, in the midst of her battles, as she fought for her beloved daughter's life, Poseidon decided to pursue her against her will. She was flayed by grief, a tempting target. What do you do when your sister is beside herself with pain? Rape her. Rape her in the form of a horse. She bore his child. Three Olympian gods, three violations. Zeus. Hades. Poseidon. They were all her brothers. They should have protected her, stood by her as she nourished the plants that would nourish the land. Instead, she'd had to fight for her existence, an existence that still took place among them, in their midst. She could never extricate herself fully from the brothers who'd hurt her. She was forever enmeshed. Eros had always wanted to ask Demeter about how she'd done it, how she'd kept her heart intact, her inner force radiant and loving despite it all, but she'd never dared.

"I do know that. But it would be worse without you here. You are the force that melts away the violence. That turns desire into something welcome, a honey, a gold-tipped joy."

Eros squirmed. Pushed down the remnants of her fever-dream. "I try to."

"And you want your own joys. Right? That's why you lied to your mother."

"Yes."

"You love her? This mortal girl?"

"It's more than that. I'm lost to her."

"I see." Demeter leaned forward, eyes keen. "Then fight for both of them. Your mother and your bride. Stand up for everything you want."

"But Psyche betrayed me. She broke a promise when she lit that lamp."

"And? You broke a promise, too. To your mother. You want forgiveness, then give it, too."

"What if I cannot?" The rage surged inside her again, streaked with pain. How could Psyche have punctured the safety of their haven? Why hadn't all her luxury and adoration been enough?

"Oh, Eros. Come on. If there's one thing I've learned from what I've been through, it is this: you cannot let your wounds lead. Doing so will eat you. It blinds you to even the most obvious things, including your own power."

Eros gulped the cold air. She could not speak. Daphne ran through her mind, unbidden, arms riotous with leaves.

"Anyway, I thought it was quite bold of her. She wanted to see you.

She wanted you entire. Can you blame her for that? Can you blame her for wanting to have some power in your shared home?"

"She had power," Eros said, her mind full of Psyche's glory in the dark.

"Did she?"

"Oh, yes—"

"The same amount as you?"

"I—she—is a human. There is no comparison. Her strength is different from mine."

"Who set the rules?"

"I did."

"Why you?"

Because I built the palace, Eros thought, *because I'm the goddess*—though suddenly she heard how these reasons might sound. She stopped herself. A pit yawned open inside her; she could start to glimpse the way those rules might have felt constraining to her bride no matter how much she'd intended them as a gift, and it was a terrible thing to see. "Neither of us could live in the open! We had no choice but to exist in a separate place, where we could be together away from prying eyes. I was the one who could create that for us, so I did."

"And were your rules always kind?"

Of course! They were to protect us! But Eros found herself looking away, toward the floor. "They were needed."

"Impose too many rules, and any palace becomes a prison. Most wives live that way, imprisoned, like Persephone—" Demeter's breath caught. She seemed to blink back tears. It would always be with her, Eros thought, the grief for her daughter, for grief was inextricably bound to love. "That's marriage, most of the time."

"Not my marriage. It was the opposite of a prison." *That was the whole point!* A wild shout inside her.

"Which is?"

"A freedom place."

"To turn marriage into a freedom place—that is a bold dream."

"Yes."

"And perhaps you realized it, for a time. But only in one chamber. What if you could have more?" Demeter reached for Eros's hand. "What if your freedom place could be larger than one room?"

Eros felt sick at the pit of her being. "Not possible."

Demeter stroked Eros's hand with her thumb, as if to smooth away dirt, and said nothing.

"That's never been possible for those who are like Psyche and me. That's why we were hiding."

"Well, now the lamp is lit. That's over. So what are you going to do in the light?"

"I—"

"Your young wife, she hasn't wasted any time."

"You've seen her?"

"I've done more than that."

Eros strained to think. "You said . . . you helped. Did you help her?"

"Yes. She called out to me, and pleaded. I didn't show myself to her, but I took care of it. She's very smart, your girl, to pray to me of all the gods when faced with a trial of seeds."

Eros thought of that temple room where she'd seen Psyche, kneeling at the pile of mixed seeds. Grains. The realm of Demeter, she who makes the grains grow. Of course: it would be within Demeter's powers to sort such a pile, to send creatures who hewed to the minuscule, to efficient work, to seeds so small they went unnoticed even though they contained the future. "You sent the ants."

Demeter smiled. The radiance of her smile cleansed the room.

Eros could not help but marvel at Psyche. That she'd been sharp enough to think of it, in the thick of danger. To sense which deity to call, without having met them, without knowing their temperament beyond the stories that circulated in villages and towns. To cling to her own knowing and survival when all seemed lost. How brilliant, her bride. "How can I thank you?"

"You'll have your chance. I want you to remember this favor I've done for you, and to keep me in your favor in return. Should I ever have more children, I want you to intervene on their behalf, so they can find real loves. So they can know the delights of the flesh and spirit that you've known with your own bride."

No more Persephones, Eros thought. "Yes. I promise."

"And one more thing."

"Yes?"

"I want you to do the same for me. Not now. But when I'm ready. And not with a god—don't you ever stab a god with lust for me. I'd like to find a love among the mortals, like you did."

Eros smiled. "Consider it done."

"A male one, for me. Find me a kind man. They exist, you know."

"I do. We'll find him."

"You won't forget?"

"I won't."

"Good. I'll tell you one more thing, then go. The way your mother loves you—do not take it for granted. She loves you the way Gaia loves her daughters. The way I love mine. Ferociously and without end. Fight for it. Fight for yourself and your bride and fight for her, too."

"I will," Eros said, but her words fell into the darkness left behind as Demeter and her lamp disappeared.

Eros was still sealed in her room. The enchantment held fast.

She kept her eyes open to avoid the falling inward, the sea-dreams.

Under her gaze, time danced and folded and unfurled. She watched it move. She listened to her wounded shoulder, the hum of her thoughts, the hungers of her body and its music. Listened for the mesh of all her songs.

21

Days passed before I faced another trial. After the seeds were sorted—the droves of ants a benediction, my tears of relief watering tidy new piles—Aphrodite did not come to me. No congratulations, no hint of next steps. I'd have to wait. I wandered the landscape, which continued to be empty, devoid of people, no buildings in sight. I grew used to foraging for berries and fruit that could stave off hunger, along with the occasional squirrel I killed with a stone and ate charred over a fire or raw, freshly skinned. Unsightly fare but my body demanded it, demanded flesh for me to eat at any cost, to keep my daughter hurtling toward life.

Finally, it came the way it had before: in the depths of the night, from a brilliant fissure in the sky. This time, the voice descended to stir me from sleep. Instructions, crisply given: a day's travel north there roamed a flock of vicious sheep, whose bite had enough venom to kill three hale men and whose fleece was pure gold. Droves of mortals had died trying to steal their fleece; none had achieved it. I was to harvest a thick fistful and present it to her. That was my second trial.

I traveled north the next day. My sandals were worn through, and one of my feet bled from its sole, leaving dark red dots along the earth. I ached and throbbed, but I kept walking. No surrender, no turning back.

I heard them before I saw them, aggressive bleats filling the air. I'd known sheep on my father's land and hadn't thought of them as dangerous, but the sound of this flock shook me. It filled my ears, drowned my thoughts, threatened to shatter my mind.

I kept approaching despite my fear.

At last they came into view: enormous sheep, forty or more, towering almost as tall as me. Sharp teeth, biting, fighting with each other, fleece gleaming golden in the sun. One tore a lizard's head clean off for no other reason than to watch the red spray. There was no shepherd with these monsters, nothing contained them. Their venom terrified me. One snap of the jaws and I was done. But how could I complete my trial without risking their bite? A rush of despair, followed by a wave of something else, warm and lucid, covering me. *Breathe.* I took a breath. I was too close. I was not safe. Could they smell me? Quickly, I climbed a nearby tree, downwind, and watched them for a long time.

My foot grew numb, pinned beneath my weight, as I balanced on a thick branch against the tree trunk.

Below me, the sheep frothed and churned like a restless sea.

I felt like an animal, crouched protectively, awake to the wild.

Inside me was a wildness, too.

The bleating poured and poured into my ears.

How will I live through this?

How does any creature live?

What is alive keeps going. Keeps listening. Watching. Taking the next breath and the next.

We see another day through the grit of our teeth, the flash of daring, the strength of claws, yes. But when our strength is overcome, then what? Time to shift. To draw on other parts of ourselves. Stealth. Sight. Steadiness. The power to go quiet and hear shadows.

I went quiet, and I watched. The sheep fought and bucked and tumbled. Around them, trees held steadfast. Shadows lengthened, hummed. I listened closer—and then a voice rose from the grass, from the earth below, or perhaps from the depths of my own being. *See the unseen.* At first, I didn't understand. But as twilight lowered its dusty shroud, I finally saw it. The sheep were so violent, they often snagged on surrounding branches, leaving imperceptibly thin wisps of fleece in their wake. Just a hair here, another there, caught in shadows. Unseen. Slight and weightless in the gathering dark.

I thought of the sheep enclosure where I'd once spent my days, how animal traces had flecked the fence, ground, edges.

The sheep finally began to slow. Even the most vicious mortal creatures will at some point lose their steam. The trick was to outlast them. I could do that. I stayed where I was. I waited and waited until the sheep collapsed, one by one, into sleep. It took a long time for the last one to finally go still. When it did, I lowered myself carefully to the ground and tiptoed around the grove, retracing their steps, recalling their brute dance, threading my hands along the dark nooks and snags where their fleece had shed. I had to be extremely quiet, but I'd honed that skill since my earliest days of life, and it served me now. I searched with my fingertips. Here. Here. Wisps of fleece, adorning the blackness. My hands tore on thorns but I kept on. How many strands to please a goddess? How many strands to get free? Gather, gather, do not stop. Gather as your hands bleed. Gather the whispers of your future, insist yourself into the days to come.

*   *   *

At last, I had a thick fistful. It was almost but not yet dawn. I walked until I found a hillside, bereft of trees. I climbed the slope and stood at a high point. Held my fist toward the sky, bearing the golden, blood-flecked fleece. "For you, Aphrodite," I called out, ready for her to seize the prize, hoping she'd thunder down the third and final trial.

22

Eros had a long time to roll Demeter's words through her mind before Aphrodite finally appeared. Resplendent. This time with her hair loose around her, billowing and full. At the sight of her mother, something deep inside Eros leapt awake. As a child, she'd buried herself in that hair, gotten blissfully lost in it and found herself again, wrapped in the supple richness of her mother, the strands her playthings, her wonder, her home. How had she ever thought she could trick such a formidable goddess? How had the world ever breathed without her? A bleak place it must have been, the world before Aphrodite, without Aphrodite. A world that should never exist again.

"Get up, Eros. The floor is no place for you."

She had been on the floor? Without knowing. She rose, slowly, to her knees.

"Oh stop it—you don't have to do that. I was angry. I still am, but save the kneeling for pleasuring your little wife, if you should ever see her again."

"So she's still alive?"

"Yes."

"You'll let her live?" Eros was standing now, palms open, full of hope.

"I didn't say that. We're not done yet. I know you're angry, child. I know you've suffered. I suppose I've extracted a decent dose of revenge."

"Does that mean you forgive me?"

"It means I might one day."

Eros felt a wash of relief. A signal of peace between them, peace to come, reassurance enough to mend a rip inside her. They would find their way back to each other, however long that way might be. "And Psyche? Did you send her on another trial?"

"Yes. And she won it. She's no slouch, your girl."

"Thank you."

"That compliment wasn't directed at you."

Eros felt her hands curl shut. She took a deep breath. "I know, I know, I betrayed you, and I abandoned my beloved. I'm a monster or a fool."

"Or both?"

"Or both. But tell me. What did you make her do?"

Aphrodite reached up and stroked her own hair, which shone in the dim light. "I sent her to the gold-fleeced sheep, the vicious ones."

"You what? They are savage."

"I know."

"And she got their fleece?"

"She did."

"The first human ever to do so?"

"I told you. No slouch."

"How?"

"By her wits."

Eros wished she could have seen how Psyche did it, how she'd bested those brutes—she couldn't wait to ask her all about it! A catch in her throat. She was stabbed by longing to be with Psyche, to hear her voice, hold her, revel in her stories, bask in her pleasure. *What have I done?* "No god helped her, then."

"Not with the sheep. I do think someone interfered with the first trial, sent the ants." Aphrodite wrinkled her nose. "I don't know who."

Eros said nothing and kept her face as blank as she could. She would hold Demeter's secret for eternity. "No more trials, then? We are done?"

Aphrodite cocked her head, studied her daughter. Her exquisite face unreadable. "We are not. There is a third."

"No."

"There must always be a third."

"Why? Because other gods said so? Because the trials for other humans came in threes? Who cares about that? You are the great Aphrodite, you have the power to forge anything you wish."

Aphrodite walked toward the table, stroked the unlit lamp. "Nobody has that kind of power, daughter."

"Or all of us do."

"We do not."

"Well, we should—at least when it comes to forging things for ourselves."

Aphrodite looked up in surprise, and Eros too felt startled at her own boldness. But the days in this room—and the months with her bride—had changed her, made her less cautious and more true. She could not or did not want to stop. It was too hard-earned, too keen, this vision inside her. She pressed on, into perilous ideas that had spent these long nights churning in her mind. "What if everyone has the right to exist? What if power not bestowed on us is still ours to claim?"

"From where? You think it's so easy. That is not how power works." Aphrodite's fingers returned to the lamp, traced curves along it. "Nobody holds it all, not even Zeus. We are part of a vast web of divine forces that holds us all in place. Really, Eros, we discussed this centuries ago, don't you remember?"

"I do."

"Good. That kind of simplemindedness is for mortals. I raised you better."

"You're right. I do know better—or, perhaps, I have known better. But right now, today, I wonder. About that webbing."

"What about it?"

"It's the webbing that holds the power?"

"In a way."

Something in her rose and brightened, like a flame. "Then there's only one choice."

Aphrodite nodded, relieved. She had picked up the lamp now, cupped it in her hands. "That's right, daughter, we must accept—"

"No, that's not it." Eros longed to shape words around long-simmering thoughts, to transform the hazy mass of them into something that could be transmitted, spoken, known. "Just the opposite."

Aphrodite frowned.

"To have our own power, to finally be free, we have to slash the web itself."

Open shock on her mother's face. "What are you saying? The web can't be slashed. It is the source of power, it is power itself."

"No. Not all of it. We exist in an Olympian web, but there was power in the universe before the Olympians were born. There was Gaia, the Mother Earth herself, who birthed the Titans—"

"And then helped take them down." Aphrodite's voice bristled with warning.

Here it was. The part of the story that was not always named. The wound at the root of Aphrodite's birth and Eros's own. The wound at the root of the known world. The Titans—with Kronos in the lead—had taken down their own father and slashed off his phallus, thrown it to the sea, to dissolve and froth for centuries and ultimately give rise to the two of them, Aphrodite and Eros. It had been fecund, that wound. It had torn the sky, changed the cosmos, fomented battles and her mother's birth, followed by her own. But why had Kronos done it? Where did he get the impetus to cut down his father, Ouranos, the sky? From his mother, Gaia. It all happened because Gaia wanted it so. She was the one who whispered the plan into Kronos's ear. When she saw that the father of her children would not love all those children equally, she moved to have him defeated, broken, shorn. And much later, when her son Kronos did not free her other children and began to devour his own—swallowing all power into himself, obliterating others—she plotted against him too. She helped the Olympians topple him. At the root of all the revolutions, a mother's rage.

Eros spread her palms wide open. "Yes. Gaia took down the Titans and the sky before that. Because they imprisoned or consumed her children. Because she wanted all her children to be free."

Aphrodite's face went taut. "There were monsters among her children. Remember Typhoeus? How he almost destroyed Olympus?"

"How could I forget?" It thrilled Eros to be speaking this way with her mother, visiting memories, probing the depths. They were not yet attuned—she had not been forgiven—but the chance to talk with such abandon was a gift. "We swam away from him, two fish in the river. It was beautiful."

"It was terrifying. We were fleeing for our lives. Monsters must be quelled."

"But how do we know which beings are monsters?" A shard of memory, her young self standing before Zeus's throne as he threatened her, called her *an aberration*. She would not push the memory away; she would keep it in hand no matter how it cut her. For it was time for her to face herself, to know herself whole. "Who decides?"

Aphrodite put the lamp down. She formed a mist around them, a foam of secrecy, so that no other gods would hear them. Lowered her voice to a whisper. "Daughter, these are dangerous words. You wish for Gaia to rule the universe? You wish to see the Olympians overthrown?"

"I wish for all beings to be free," Eros said, and meant it with every fiber of her being, for it was not just for herself, had never just been for herself, the great experiment, her daring creation, the palace, the shielded place, the freedom place that Demeter had dared imagine spreading into more than one room.

"That's not possible."

"Why not?"

"Eros, you do not understand this world. You think because you help the humans play at pleasure—"

"It's more than play, Mother. It's the quick of life. You know that."

"Fine. I do." She seemed to study a spot on the wall for secrets. "But Gaia's time is over; history can't be undone. The web of power can't simply be taken down like the laundry mortals hang in the wind. And even if it could, can you imagine what would happen?"

"Yes, I can."

"Chaos."

"No."

"Then what?"

She saw it with such fierce clarity that her body filled with the vision, became it. Perhaps she'd been wrong, about the lighting of the lamp. Perhaps Psyche's act had not only hurt Eros, but also catalyzed the opening of a portal into new understanding, a new realm of being, in which she, Eros, the goddess of desire, could harness her power and dive through revelations in as yet uncharted ways. "The weaving of new webs."

Aphrodite paused, eyes wide. Her hands rose, fluttered as if searching for something invisible she'd lost. "Chaos would come first. Or perhaps the Titans would return to power. Do you think Zeus defeated them so easily? Do you think the world was better under their reign?"

"Who knows?"

"Eros! This is not a joke."

She held her mother's gaze. Brazen, but also tender. "I know."

"Then be serious."

"Of course I don't want the Titans to return to power. They'd be no better than Zeus. I'm not talking about turning back time, but moving forward."

"Into what?"

"New forms."

"And what would happen to us?"

Eros heard the genuine fear in her mother's voice. She spoke gently. "We'd be free. All gods and mortals would be free."

"You and I, we're free now."

"No, Mother, we're not."

Aphrodite sighed and sank onto Eros's bed. "You're hard to argue with."

"Thank you, great goddess."

"Stop that. You've always been a trickster." She patted the place beside her as invitation. "There's always been a part of you happy to stir the waters just to watch mud rise."

Eros sat down next to her mother, basked in her glow. "Mud is wonderful. I love mud. It's a shame the way it's seen as—"

"Yes, child, I know, I've heard you say it all before. But sometimes, there's a reason we don't want a cloth to get soiled, or a jug to crack, or a storm to devastate the land. Order has its place and meaning, too."

"I can't believe this. You sound like Hera." She'd meant it as an insult, and it worked. Aphrodite winced, stung.

"I am the furthest thing from Hera."

"Maybe you're not. Maybe the opposite of Hera is me." Eros smoothed her blanket with one hand, felt the delicate embroidery beneath. She was thinking aloud now, wide awake, startled by her own thoughts, awash in them. "So what if the order of things gets shaken? Storms already devastate the land. Too much order devastates the soul. Especially when it's the wrong order for that soul, imposed by the wrong god. Why can't the shape of things arise from within instead of being forced on us?"

"My love." Aphrodite leaned close. Her hair fell forward, over her shoulder, and she did not move it away. Eros caught the scent of her, jasmine and seashells and the first hints of spring. "Now you're speaking of yourself. The way your body is, your desire, your—way. You want a world where you can be unruly and immense."

"I am immense. And unruly. That's always true no matter what the laws have to say." Her hand was close to her mother's now, two or three stitches of embroidery away. "I want a world where I can be myself."

"Which you have."

"You of all people know that's not true."

They stared at each other for a long time.

"I'm sorry," Aphrodite said. "I do."

"I'm not an aberration, Mother. It's not only me. Did you know? I've looked into so many human souls, measured their desire. There are many like me. The current way of things is crushing for them."

"And suddenly you care about the crushing of human souls?"

"Don't pretend I'm the only one. You care too."

Aphrodite raised her chin defiantly, but she seemed amused. "Even so. No more talk of changing the web of power."

"Why not?"

"It's impossible. There would be war among the gods, more terrible than anything we've seen in our lives, with no guarantees of who'd come out on top."

"What if there's no such thing as on t—"

"I'm not finished. You're so worried about the suffering of mortals, but many mortals would suffer if the order of things changed, too."

"Which ones?"

"Does it matter?"

"Yes."

"You're impossible."

"Yet here I am."

Aphrodite let her hand shift slightly, so that their smallest fingers touched. "Would it help tame you, pray tell, if you were granted a wife of your choosing?"

It would not tame her; she was beyond taming now; yet Eros felt a surge in her chest.

It was one thing to have married Psyche in defiance, and in secrecy. To do so with the knowledge of the divine realm would be another matter, a force that would push open space where it had not existed before. "Is that a real offer?"

"I'm not sure yet. It's all very complicated. There is still the third trial. And Zeus. And, perhaps most complicated of all, there is the baby."

"What baby?"

"You cannot be serious."

The light in the room brightened, thickened, grew strong enough to slash Eros's heart. "Psyche—"

"Is with child. Yes. You really didn't know?"

The dam broke, her throat flooded with light, she could not speak.

"How could you not have noticed?" Aphrodite made no attempt to hide her amazement. "Perhaps because you've never been with child. Or you simply weren't listening for it, given that your body is . . . its own way. I don't know. Which brings me to the thing I need to ask you: When you went to your little wife, did you change all the way into a man, the way Zeus mandated you to do? Or did you defy him, grow your spear and keep the rest?"

Eros opened her mouth but still no words formed on her tongue.

"Hmm, yes, I see. You wild child. Well, congratulations. You're the first goddess ever to impregnate a mortal woman." Aphrodite smiled at Eros for the first time since this whole journey had begun. "Sometimes I think this is why Zeus tried to cage you. What he was so frightened of all along."

Eros was still reeling, doused in sun. "I don't understand."

"That a child could be produced without a father, violating divine law. That a woman's seed could grow in a woman's belly, two females making a life. No male to claim the baby and command its fate. Maybe that's why he insisted you be all of this or all of that, what makes the in-between so dangerous to him." Aphrodite raised an eyebrow. "Or maybe he just hated the thought of a woman on his terrain."

"I don't want his terrain, only my own."

"I know that. I do."

"I don't have a father either, except Hephaestus."

"Hmpf, Hephaestus."

"Don't mock him, Mother. He is good." She thought of him at the forge, hammering metal into elegant shapes, all muscle and devotion, shaping beauty, shaping gifts. Using his physical strength to build, never to harm. "I've learned a great deal from him about being male. About masculine love."

"That so?"

"Not that way. Stop it. What I mean to say is, I was conceived without a father. So what does that make me? A violation?"

Aphrodite shrugged. "Maybe to some."

"And to you?"

"To me?" Aphrodite fell quiet. Her hand covered her daughter's, held it tight. When she spoke again, her voice was tender. "You, a violation of divine law? Of course not. You're its renewal."

Warmth through her chest. She let it fill her. "And my baby? Psyche and my baby? Mother—" Eros fell to her knees beside the bed and let the tears stream down her face. "Please forgive me. Allow us a place with you, together."

Aphrodite's face changed, shifted, finally broke. "Oh, daughter, I'm trying to stay angry at you, but I cannot. You have always been with me. There is no me without you."

"And no me without you," Eros said.

"But the girl—I don't know."

Eros took both her mother's hands in hers, gazed up into her radiant face. "She is not your enemy. She was never your rival even when the men of earth were too stupid to know it. You are Aphrodite, the great goddess of beauty; she was just a scared girl."

"She's a woman now."

"A scared woman, then."

Aphrodite had not clasped her daughter's hands back, nor had she pulled away. "Or a brave one. Or both. I'd rather not admit it, but I can't deny that her success in the first two trials has taken me by surprise."

"And still you won't tell me where you sent her. Mother, I want her with me. With us. I love her, I am hers."

Aphrodite made a pained sound, and Eros knew the roots of that pain went deep. Aphrodite did not have, with Hephaestus, a marriage that bound two souls. She'd had plenty of lovers, as many as she wished, but none were constant companions. Of those, she had only one. Her daughter, her firstborn, a faithful soul-deep bond that had been her joy and solace until this rupture had blasted them apart. All at once Eros could see how her own marital happiness could feel, to her mother, like a loss.

"I'm yours too, Mother. I am always yours. You and me until the end of all worlds."

"I never thought you'd betray me." Aphrodite bent forward, face behind a glistening cape of hair. "You. You among them all."

"I know. I am sorry."

"I cannot bear existence without you."

"Then don't. Accept me back."

Aphrodite held very still. Eros thought of her in fish form, that day they fled Typhoeus the storm-monster: the shimmer of her, the liquid dance. How clearly it had still been her in that long, slippery body. How elegantly she'd swerved among the stones. The euphoric glint of sun on her scales, shattering its rays with bright abandon. Her mother, forever a gatherer of light. Her mother, forever grace. The two of them a circle, swimming, swimming, forging their own current in defiance.

Finally her mother raised her head and stood. Her eyes were damp, but they shone clear. Their gazes met and Eros felt their return to each other, the bliss of their bond, a blend of energies whose luminosity overflowed and spilled out to the heavens and to earth. Down below, mortals going about their days would feel the radiance showering on them, take delight, receive the blessing without knowing its source.

Eros had one more urgent question. "Where did you send her? Where is Psyche?"

Aphrodite turned away, toward the window. "Oh, child."

"You must tell me. Mother, please."

"Promise not to be angry."

Her tone sent a chill through Eros. She was still on her knees, and didn't dare rise. Her mother was silent for what seemed like an endless time. When she finally spoke, she kept her eyes on the window, as if speaking to the orchard below.

"I sent her to retrieve a box of beauty. I thought it might be fitting. Persephone's beauty. Forgive me for it, and we'll be even."

Eros's mind spun. It was the cusp of winter. "But that's not possible— it would mean—"

"That's right, child. She's in the underworld."

PART FOUR

Earth

23

She wanted me dead. That much was clear. Why else would she send me on a mission like this? I stood at the mouth of a cave, for I'd heard tales about caves containing portals to the underworld, though those same tales asserted that no living mortal would ever find the way through. Only the dead could enter, could cross the River Styx and get past Cerberus, the great three-headed dog who guarded the gates.

Aphrodite had sent me here to die, or to fail.

But if she'd thought that would make me surrender, she'd miscalculated.

For I was already supposed to be dead.

I'd been abandoned twice now. First by my village and family, tied to that rock, thrown away like a jug beyond mending. Then by my husband, who'd professed eternal love only to desert me, leaving nothing but a stain of bloodied oil. Her reasons had been more complicated, knotted in ways I was still continuing to trace for understanding.

But no matter the reason, being left for dead is no small thing. It changes you. It can bring terror but can also strip it away. At the edge of the accepted world there breathes another way of being. I had lost so much and yet I carried so much inside me. I'd survived thus far and that very knowledge made me bold. I was awake to the moment, to the cave's mouth as sun deepened to twilight all around me. Listening, though for what, I didn't know. For a sign, a hint, an instinct. Until, in the last dim light, I saw a patch of wildflowers at the foot of a laurel tree. Miraculous this late in the season, at the start of winter. Violets, tender and plush. I thought of what I knew of Persephone's story, or at least, the human versions of the story of this goddess I'd been sent to find: how she'd been picking wildflowers with her friends, gathering them into a basket, when Hades swooped down and grabbed her by force. A kidnap. A rape. A maiden interrupted in her play, lilies and violets scattered to the ground, petals crushed against a chest that thrummed with terror. Had the violets been a special love? Was it true, what they said, that as the carriage knifed down into the underworld, the young goddess had wept not only over her fate, but also over her lost flowers?

I picked the violets and made a wild bouquet. I cradled it against my chest as I settled down at the opening to the cave.

Night fell.

Sleek creatures cawed and howled in the hidden forest.

I sat in the cold, eyes wide open, gazing into veils and veils of black.

It was almost dawn when it came to me. Why it took so long, I'll never know. What disappears takes time to rekindle. What's declared dead takes time to find its wings. It came from a deeply buried place, like a single ember left under heaps of ash. The song. My mother's song. The one she'd hummed over me during my bridal bath, from the old ways, before the Greeks arrived, when corpses had no need of coins under their tongues to pay the ferryman to the underworld, for our ancestors—what had she said, pull up the words from memory's grave—*flew. We used to fly there, with the help of Vanth.* Vanth. I had nothing to lose. I opened my mouth. I sang the melody, first wordlessly, and then, because I did not know the original words, I sang the only word I knew, Vanth, Vanth, curving over the lilt and sweep of that old tune. The world grew pale around me, tinged with cool early light. I sang for a time that seemed forever, my heart a flung-open door in my chest from which the sound arose. Vanth, Vanth, come to me, help me, your daughter, your lost yet breathing daughter, hear my call, I know despite what the Greek men say that you're not dead, that you'll never be dead, that my bones remember you, help me go, help me descend, help me fly.

A whir around me

Sweep of wings

Unbelievably tall, breasts bared, eyes blazing, torch in hand

Into my eyes she looked, and down into my soul, seeing everything with a boundlessness that

I could not breathe and

Meeting her gaze I fell—

She caught me

On her back her wings spread and I clung to her, rested my face against her lush white feathers and

We flew

24

How long we flew, I do not know.

Down, down. Into a darkness ignited by her torch.

We flew over the great River Styx, the long, dark plain of it. Black water, smooth and wide, wider than I'd known a river could be. Its surface calm, yet rippling with the hints of slippery secrets below. It both entranced and terrified me. At the other shore, a tunnel opened its wide mouth and we dove into it. By the low light of torches lit in iron brackets on the walls, we flew on. Cerberus appeared in the distance, his hulking body large as a house, his three heads keeping guard, ears pricked, fangs bared, three snouts sniffing for intruders. We flew right toward him. Scents of old meat, wet dirt, pine. His middle head rose to catch us in his jaws as we passed, rattling its chain—I held my breath—but Vanth flew too high for him, he could not reach us, sharp teeth gnashing the air at my heels. Flecks of foam shot from his jaws and stung my skin, but did not stop us. He barked at us, a trio of overlapping voices, hounding our escape as we flew through the iron gates behind him and into the narrower tunnel beyond.

From that tunnel, corridors. Wastelands. Yawning spaces packed with disembodied souls. I felt more than heard them. Heard more than saw them. The sound of what? Hunger. Vast hunger that could not be filled. I moved through them, soared through a thousand ravenous dead dreams. *Forgive me,* I whispered into their midst, *I can't do more, I'm only passing through.*

It took all night. An instant. A century. I aged, flying, or was renewed. Time twisted out of shape, lost its meaning. My soul pulled at the edges of my body, threatened to spill out like water from a cup. *I am supposed to be dead.* But I was not dead. I felt the dead around me, an endless lake, and I was not-them. The woman left twice to die, who did not die. Guarded by Vanth, resting against the warmth of her, I said and said it, under my breath, insisting it into being: *alive, alive, alive.*

At last, a vaulting cavern, its roof resembling a curved black sky. A palace loomed at its center, huge and austere. Nothing grew from the ground. No trees, no flowers, not a single blade of grass. Vanth descended, crouched. I knew she meant for me to step off her back, and I did not want to—every fiber of my being railed against it—but where else was I to go? I had called her to help me, to bring me here. I'd asked for this. And how could I repay her? I had nothing. Almost nothing. I took off my mother's amethyst necklace, let go of Vanth, and after one last nuzzle in her feathers I set foot on the black soil. I held up the necklace, and she took it immediately between her teeth. "Thank you, Great Spirit," I said, but she was already gone.

The gates of the palace were closed, but not locked. They swung open at my touch. I walked through them and into the hall before me. This was no labyrinth: the long passage led directly to a great room, visible in the distance. I saw two thrones, one containing a female figure that had to be exactly who I was looking for. Persephone.

Keep breathing, I told myself. One foot. Next foot. Don't touch the walls, don't fall and let your hands touch the floor, don't touch anything. This place is not for you.

"Who's there?" Persephone called out, her voice a music.

"My name is—"

"Not now. Come closer, let me see you."

I obeyed. Down the long hall I walked, feeling her eyes on me.

At last I arrived in the great room. It was dim, vast, empty. The air hung dense and heavy; I had to concentrate to breathe. There were no windows, no breezes to let in from beyond these walls. The space held nothing but a banquet table at one end, laden with food, and a platform, which held the two thrones, one empty and enormous, riddled with emeralds and skulls. The throne of Hades. Beside it sat Persephone, her throne resplendent too, though it bore no bones, only gems and metal finely wrought into shapes that swirled and slashed behind her. She was beautiful, her long black hair a mantle, matching her silken black robe. She held herself regally, and I felt a rush of fear that quickly dissolved in the flood of something else. Not pity, exactly, for I was still new to encounters with the divine and could not fathom pitying a goddess. Compassion, perhaps. And shock at the weariness in her eyes. Even so, in the face of her splendor I became keenly aware of the dirt on my robe, my matted hair, the raggedness that came from weeks of sleeping on forest floors. I'd been surviving on foraged berries and fruit, the occasional squirrel or bird. I'd become a feral woman, homeless and frayed, with no choice but to let her see me as I was. I kneeled and lowered my head.

"Great goddess Persephone. It is my honor to be in your presence."

"Hmf."

I held the violets toward her. "These are for you."

"For me?"

"Yes."

She did not rise. A swirl of wind unclasped my fingers from the stems and carried the flowers up to her. She caught them, stared into them with wonder and other emotions I could not decipher. Memories, perhaps, undrowned from the depths of time. A passion for violets. Petals destroyed. Her gaze filled with a hunger so intense I averted my eyes.

"Where did you find these? So close to winter?"

"At the mouth of a cave."

"The earth must love you. Or my mother, perhaps. Did she send you?"

"No." I thought of the prayers I'd sent up to Demeter, never knowing whether they'd be answered, hearing nothing. The exhaustion of my trials rose up, threatened to drown me. *Stop. Concentrate. You're not done yet.*

"Then who sent you?"

"Aphrodite."

"Why?"

"To ask for a small box of your beauty."

She laughed, a harsh bark of a sound. "Mine? For her? And she sent you, a living mortal?"

"Yes."

"You shouldn't be here. This trip could kill you."

"I know."

"What did you do to enrage her?"

"I—"

"Let me guess." She leaned back against her throne, hands landing on the armrests like delicate birds. "I don't receive a lot of guests down here, you know. And you're an unusual one. You can't just rush away. Hungry?"

She gestured toward the banquet table, and her face was innocent and inviting, but I'd heard the stories, I knew the rules: a bite of food in the underworld tethers you to it, traps you there, had trapped the very goddess who sat before me. "No, thank you."

"Suit yourself. Let's see. You're a pretty one. Perhaps you challenged her, declared yourself more beautiful?"

"No."

"Insulted one of the Graces?"

"No."

"Insulted her husband Hephaestus—no, wait, she wouldn't care about that. Her daughter Eros?"

I hesitated. "Not exactly?"

"Then what?"

I took in a breath. Thick air, pungent with earth and mystery. "First, other people—men—declared me more beautiful than her. It was not me who said it, I never wished it so. And then I was blamed for a curse and forced to marry a monster, only the monster was—" I broke off.

"Was what? You can't stop now."

"Was Eros."

Persephone gazed at me for a long time. Face keen, engrossed by the story. "You. You married Eros?"

"I didn't know who she was."

"I see. And Aphrodite hated you already."

"Yes."

"Let me guess. Eros did it without her mother's blessing."

"Yes."

"Ah! I guessed right!" She looked around, pleased with herself, as if accepting the accolades of a nonexistent audience. "That Eros. She's always been unruly. I used to relish watching her when I was little, as she practiced her shots or strutted around Olympus. Of all the goddesses, she seemed the least afraid of the gods. As I grew older, we got along quite well. Though I wanted to avoid her arrows. I thought it would keep me free." Persephone fell silent and her face became unreadable. "Where is she now?"

"I don't know. She forsook me and left."

"Why?"

"I broke her rules."

"Only she gets to break rules, is that it?"

Persephone seemed amused, and relief streaked through me at her commiseration. I would have liked to tell the whole story right then and there, confess it all, about the lamp and why I lit it, the marriage nights, what we created together before it shattered, what the rules of our palace had constrained and also what they'd brought into being. I'd chafed against those rules, I'd wanted more; but before that, I'd known bliss in that dark room, and love, truth, the most exquisite power. I didn't know, then, who Eros was, and had no understanding of the divine realm. Now that I'd faced Aphrodite and her trials, I glimpsed more of what Eros had been up against. She'd flouted fearsome laws to build our palace. She'd hidden it so we could exist. She'd intended it as a space for us to be together and free—she'd tried to tell me this, though only partially and in ways I could not fully understand. Still. She had been paying a cost not yet visible to me, the cost of existing when worlds don't want you to, worlds both human and divine. What if, in breaking the agreement, I'd broken something inside her? Who in our story was the betrayed one? The abandoned? Spin the prism and new light refracts. It was too much to think about right now. I took a deep breath, kept my mouth shut. Persephone had asked a question, but it seemed dangerous to venture an answer.

Nor did it seem that Persephone sought one. "So do you love her?"

I searched inside, through the turmoil, beneath it. "I do." The reality of it settling in, like a rock at my core. I could not help but love her.

"You were forced into a marriage, but you love who you're with. Lucky girl."

"I—well. I'm not with her now. She's cast me off."

"Ah. Right." She studied me, and for a moment I glimpsed the bond we might have had if we had met in another time, as girls together, how we might have lain in meadows and shared secrets as the sun rose high, picked all the wildflowers we wished with nobody to crush their petals, or ours. What a friendship we might have had, I thought, in that impossible other life. Persephone seemed to wade through thick thoughts of her own. She sighed. Cupped her hands before her. "Well, perhaps this will help."

She closed her hands, opened them. A box sat on her palm, no longer than her smallest finger.

"Come closer."

I approached gingerly.

"Here's a box of my beauty. Just a wisp of it. Why Aphrodite would want such a thing I'll never know. She has more than she'll ever need, but I don't mind. Too much beauty is a burden. It endangers us. It always will, unless the worlds change. But I think you know that. Take this to Aphrodite and don't forget I helped you."

"Yes, great goddess. Thank you."

"You brought me flowers. You carried them to this place where they don't grow. I won't forget that either. Go on, take the box."

She reached her hands toward me. I took the box from her. It was light, as if made of feathers. Persephone looked no less beautiful than before.

"Now go. You shouldn't be here."

She blew in my face, and her breath became a wind that swallowed me whole.

Swirling. Swirl-black. I reeled through darkness.

A tornado of air spiraled forward, long and taut, and I hurled through its center, the eye of the storm.

Forward, forward. As if I were moving through the body of an ethereal spear. As if I had become the spear, my head breaking the way open, cutting a path through ghosts and rock and utter dark.

Breathe, was all I could think to myself as I clung to the box, to my body. *Breathe, Psyche, breathe.*

Finally I landed. Soil beneath my hands and knees. Grass. Damp. Air in my lungs, the air of the living world. I took gulping breaths. Opened my eyes. I was on a cliff, a place I'd never seen before. Around me scattered oak trees raised their branches against the crystalline sky. Before me, below the cliff, lay a sight I'd tried to imagine all my life yet for whose beauty I could never have prepared.

The sea.

The wide and sparkling sea.

I stared at it, with hungry eyes. As if the sight of it could feed me. As if that yawning blue could fill my soul. As if my great-grandmother's eyes were somewhere inside me and I could somehow return the sea to her, satisfy old yearnings, older than my own existence. As if I could swallow the sea with my gaze so the new life growing inside me could have it too. Exhaustion fell on me. I'd completed the third and hardest trial. I held the box that Aphrodite had requested. Beauty sealed into a small container in my hands. But what was beauty? Look at the sea, gorgeous and complete. Its presence did not rob beauty from the grass, oaks, sky, dirt, rocks, anything else around me. Aphrodite ruled over beauty, it was her realm, she must understand it better than I ever could with my mortal mind. Yet still, I chafed. The box prickled my palm. I didn't want it, didn't want to keep it nor to hand it over to the goddess who'd punished a girl for being beautiful—but no, I thought, that hadn't been the reason, look closer, see it, hold it clear: she punished you for drawing the attentions of men. Persephone had drawn male attention and look where it got her. Melia had drawn it too, and look what happened. The story of beauty was enmeshed with the story of something else, a brutal force that kept too many chained. I wanted no part of it anymore. After all these trials, everything I'd done to have my chance to confront goddesses and claim a space on this earth for myself and my child, I'd lost the willingness to collude. This box I held, Persephone's box, was meant for Aphrodite's hands, for me to give it to her, but I would not do it. Even the quickened life in my belly was not enough of a reason to obey, for what if the baby was a girl? What language of beauty would reign in the world she entered? Were we to be boxed or kept in sheep enclosures or raped or used to the end of time? Or was there room to weave another story, on the loom of desires born in darkness? What would it take to untie beauty from the brutal force, to slash that rope? No more, I thought. No more, at least, from me.

I moved to the edge of the cliff. Just below me, waves rose and fell against stalwart rocks. A mesmerizing dance, supple, vital. It stole from no one, caged no one, sang beauty with no limits and no end. I felt strong, feet rooted to the ground.

"Aphrodite!" I called out. "I have what you asked for! But it isn't for you."

I opened the box and held it out to the waves. A shudder, a flow, a glittering burst on the water's surface as the contents of the box reached the sea. I threw the box to the water and watched it float and bob like a tiny boat without passengers, holding only dreams.

"Well?" I shouted into the wind. "Great goddess, are you going to kill me? Or will you finally let me be?"

"What a way to speak to your mother-in-law," said a voice behind me.

It wasn't Aphrodite.

My breath caught.

I spun around.

There she stood, a few paces away, wings folding behind her, for she'd just landed from flight.

Eros, in full light of the sun.

25

I stared at her. Stone in my throat. This sight I'd longed for, tried to con-
jure, railed against in restless dreams, her face, her form, as exquisite as
I'd remembered, more so, almost hard to bear. I wanted to drink her with
my eyes. I wanted to hurl her from the cliff to the sea.

"You came," I said.

"I did. I'm here."

"Took you long enough." The words escaped my mouth before I
could stop them. For a moment I felt exposed, vulnerable, a wounded
child.

"I know. I'm sorry. I was wrong to leave you the way I did."

I couldn't speak. Too much surged in me, demanding space. We held
each other's gaze, and I wanted to pull my anger out of the great tangle
of emotions and wrap it all around me like armor, but there was so much
else, too, including my fear of her anger, that rage with which she flew
away: I searched her face and could not find it.

"You look well, beloved," she said.

A spike of pain in me at the word *beloved*. "I do not." I knew what

I looked like, the filth, my hair matted in rough braids, my starved and ragged state, and yet I felt no shame. I was tall inside; I was larger now. I felt the wounded child in me sink into a warm embrace. "You abandoned me. I could have died."

"But you survived."

"Disappointed?"

A storm of emotions clouded her face, inscrutable. "How can you say that?"

"You didn't protect me." My own anger pulsed up to meet her words, extinguished only by the wave of sorrow that rushed in, close behind. "You promised."

"You are right. I should have." Shame tinged her every word. Eros had folded her wings behind her, a golden frame. Her left shoulder bristled red and raw, visible beside the strap of her white gown, a wound healing over, generating new skin. Had I done that, with the oil? But how could it be? How could such a small spill cause such a great wound? Looking at her now, she seemed magnificent, and yet so small. Suddenly I could see everything inside her: regret, grief, fear, anger, hope, a burning sadness, beyond measure or control. "I am here to ask two things of you. And the first is your forgiveness."

I didn't know what to feel. I felt a thousand things. I wondered how she'd known to find me here. So much mystery to the ways of the gods. And yet they could be fragile, hurt, petulant, all these other traits we humans thought of as our own. I hovered at the precipice of my truths. I saw the empty window again, the night she left, slowly filling with pale light. I saw the banquet table of our palace, swarming with flies. I saw the red spots my bleeding foot left on the earth. "Do you know about the trials?"

"I do. Oh, Psyche. They were too cruel, I tried to tell my mother, tried to stop her, but it was too late."

I fought back tears. "What else do you know?"

Eros opened her hands. "I know you are the flame that lights my soul."

That wasn't what I'd meant; her words spun me.

"That I wish for us to return to each other," she went on. "For the chance to love you again."

She stepped toward me. She was closer now, close enough to touch me, but she did not. My whole body cried out for her, for those hands I'd felt on me, in me, so many times, yet only now could see in broad daylight. They were elegant, limber, muscular. It took all my strength to resist leaning forward, into her open palms. But I did resist. "How can I trust you?"

She studied me quietly. Her warmth did not flag. "Could we sit together? Talk?"

"I don't know." Within me, turbulence. The pull toward Eros, the pull toward my dignity. I swam in the crosscurrents, struggled not to drown. I stared out at the sea, tried to fill myself with blue. "I'm waiting for Aphrodite."

"She's not coming. She's leaving this conversation to me."

"But the box—"

"—that you just threw into the sea? You really want to explain that in her presence?" A smile danced behind her eyes, and oh—how I wished to be close to her.

"I am not afraid of her. I will fight for what I believe."

"You don't have to fight, not anymore." Eros smiled in full now, and it lit up the air. "You've prevailed, Psyche. Please. Come rest with me."

I looked at her for a long time. All those months she'd kept her face from me, and now I was determined to see. I wanted to know her with my eyes. She must have felt the intensity of my stare, for she turned away, curls falling over her face.

"No," I said. "Let me look at you."

She did as I asked.

I looked.

A gorgeous face, chiseled, strong.

Great beauty in every feature, but it was her eyes I sought above all.

Eyes wide open, falling into them an ecstasy as keen as any other we'd shared.

I fell into her eyes but also did not fall. I stood on my own feet and met her. She was a glory, infinite inside, but so was I.

I nodded. "Let us talk."

We walked until we found a good place to sit, on the earth, in the shade of a majestic oak tree. We spoke for hours. Listened. Filled each other's cups with the stories of us. All those nights we'd spent together in the dark, naked and enmeshed, and yet so many stories still waited to be told. I had never considered some of the things she recounted. She held my hand and stroked it with her thumb as she spoke. I tried to fathom her words, but they kept stretching my imagination in new ways. The youth of a goddess, the rising into the self for an immortal being, how fraught with pain it could be. I pictured her, Eros, the way she described herself, rebellious and free, her body changing naturally at will. A secret self, vast, unsanctioned. The rage of Zeus, her mother negotiating on her behalf—that same mother who had hounded me and tried to destroy my life, now cast as a kind protector, a part of the story I struggled to absorb—and the deal of the Nine that had broken her spirit, closed her to sensual love for one hundred years, *Until there was you, Psyche.* One hundred years! I could barely imagine such a sweep of time. *But there is more, beloved. I want you to see all of me, even the worst thing.*

And then she reached far back in time, through the fog of human myth, and confessed about Daphne. Her story with Daphne. What she'd done to her to take revenge on Apollo. *Because I was wounded, because I was afraid, because I let his shame define me, because you see, Psyche, my love, my sun, there has not been a place for me anywhere on earth nor in the heavens, not as all of me. I've had to fight to exist.* The tale a boulder on my chest. For Daphne had also wanted simply to exist, and I said as much, I could not help it. *I know,* said Eros. *I did a terrible thing. I wish I could erase it.* Then do it, I said. *I can't, Psyche, that's not how power works, not even for a goddess.* I thought of Daphne, her dreams, her innocence. I tried to picture her, twisted halfway into laurel bark the way I'd rendered her on the palace wall. She'd been so unsettled by that painting, Pteron, for reasons I hadn't been able to understand, not then. There had been no laurel trees in our valley, and only now did I see that she must have planned it that way, used her divine powers to keep out what shamed her, what she could not bear to see.

I was silent for a long time, and Eros did not rush me. Birdsong rose around us, sharpened. When I finally spoke again, I found myself talking about Persephone, how she too was a woman trapped, and what it was like to meet her, the violets I'd picked for her and how I'd flown into the underworld. *You flew?* Eros said. *Tell me.* And I spoke, then, not only of Vanth, but of the lost language, the lost gods, my mother's roots, which also were mine. Eros clasped both of my hands now, in a state of pure attention. I spoke and spoke, and as I did the farm rose up before me, the women's room, my childhood bedroom, the river, the path down to the copse where terror had been born. I swayed a little, felt the breeze in my hair. The terror. Melia. I had thought I'd never speak of it, that words should never touch it, but now, in the wake of Eros's confessions, the memory choked me. So I told it. How Melia had been forced by my suitors, using my name. I could not tell it without seeing it unfurl before my eyes. *Oh my love,* said Eros, *you don't blame yourself, do you?* Sobs erupted from my chest, and that was when she took me in her arms, held me as I shook and wailed. I closed my eyes. Body, her body, as I'd felt it so many times in the dark. Her body a respite. Her body a haven. I let her cradle me. When I finally calmed, she held me for a long time as we gazed out at the glittering sea.

"I want to know you," Eros whispered. "All of you. And for you to know all of me."

"Is that ever possible?"

"What do you think?"

"Eros, you're a goddess! Why ask me?"

"Because you know things, Psyche. You are wise. Your thoughts are nectar to me."

I felt her words as a balm, and remembered how she'd always done this, affirmed the worth of my thoughts. Yet she'd also often withheld her own. "You kept too many secrets from me."

"I know. I'm sorry. But you kept quite a big secret from me, too."

"You mean the light? I—"

"No," she said softly. "I mean the baby."

I was stunned. I met her eyes. Thrill and wonder and tenderness vaster than the sky. There was so much I wanted to say, about how it had been to carry our child, what I felt of her, the way she was at that very instant kicking at my body from the inside, insisting on life. Eros touched my belly, and I almost fell into our shared joy.

But then she said, "You should have told me."

I bristled at her words and brushed her hand away. "You're the one who started all the hiding."

"I told you: I had to do that. At the time, the marriage couldn't exist otherwise."

I was struck by those words, *at the time*, wondering what they could mean. But first I had other questions. "Not even for a goddess?"

"No."

"What's the point of all that power, then, if you can't use it?"

Eros looked at me for a long time before replying. "You're right. It was a mistake to conceal so much from you—I see that now, and I'm sorry for it. But I saw no other way for us to be together. I risked everything to make a place for us, to keep us safe."

"I thought the gods were always safe. That only mortals could experience real danger."

"There are gods, and there are gods. Bending rules, the ones we bent—that's never safe."

It was still new to me, the story of her struggles, the reality of how some cages could apply to women and goddesses alike. "How were we supposed to raise a child in that circumstance? With one mother and no father except some shadow in the dark?"

"A father who's a woman."

"The problem was the dark."

"The dark was meant to protect us from a hostile world." She sighed. "Anyway, the hiding is all over now. You lit the lamp."

"You forgive me for that?"

"I already have. I'm even grateful."

"Grateful! How can that be?"

"When old ways shatter, new paths can open. Which brings me back to my question. Can you forgive me?"

I looked out at the sea. It seemed endless, stretching all the way to the lip of the sky, but according to the tales of men, it ended at the shores of other lands, including my father's homeland, islands, faraway Troy, places lapped at by the same constant waves. I felt an ache I couldn't define. I wanted the whole sea inside me, wanted to float in its enormous body, wanted both at once. "You said you came here to ask me two things."

"Yes."

"What's the second one?"

She pulled back slightly, disoriented by my refusal to answer. "Well. The dark is gone now. Olympus knows, my mother knows—everybody knows."

Everybody. I tried to imagine it, a crowd of gods talking about me, our love, our nights. "And yet I won't be killed?"

"No."

"Turned into an insect or a beast?"

"No. In fact, they want to celebrate our marriage."

The ground seemed to spin beneath me. "Who?"

"Zeus. My mother. The Olympians. It's all been arranged."

I stared at her, searching for a sign that this was a joke, that of course it was impossible, but her face remained serious. "Your *mother*?"

"She spoke to Zeus herself. Declared our case to him for us. The wedding feast is being prepared right now on Mount Olympus. Everyone will be there—Zeus, Hera, Apollo, the Graces, my stepfather Hephaestus, Artemis, the lot of them. You'll meet them all at once, poor thing."

"When?"

"As soon as we arrive." She squinted at me with a mix of shyness and triumph. "The only thing missing is for you to accept. Psyche. My love. The second question: Will you come with me to Mount Olympus and be married before all the gods?"

The sky pierced me with its blue; I could not bear it. As if I'd lost my skin, become porous, become a cloud. "I—I don't know."

Her mouth fell open. "You what?"

"I need to think it over."

"What is there to think over? I'm offering—"

"Stop, Eros. Give me some time. Don't follow me."

I stood. She stared at me with shock and wounded pride. I left her, walking toward the windblown cliffs to be alone.

I roved the cliffs for a long time. Wind swirled about me, beckoning. I pulled my braids loose and gave my matted hair to the wind, so it could dance, so I could dance, so I could feel. Listen to the wind. Listen to the sea. Wave after wave declaring itself in whispered foam. How constant it was, how sure of itself. I wanted to walk into those tongues of water that caressed the rocks below. I wanted to splash myself with seawater, let it wash me clean. I wanted to glide across the sea in a ship like the ones the Greeks had used to come to the land where I was born, only not to take the homes of others, simply to stand on deck with nothing but sea below me, the depth beneath the hull. Would it feel like liquid earth beneath my feet? I wanted to know the sea; I wanted to know myself; each of those knowings seemed a dive into great depths, mysterious, boundless, thrilling. I stared up at the sky, home of the gods. Site of the wedding I'd been offered. So much longing in me. I longed for her. I longed for life. But something else brewed in me, too, an understanding. I had a choice to make, a real one. I could say no. I could refuse her and survive. I could live on my own somewhere on this earth or even below it, for Persephone might well take me as a sister-friend, one of the many paths I could venture down to find my way if I chose to. My life was mine and I could shape its direction. I hadn't known this about myself before. I had been through so much—abandonment, trials, loss and fear, blood and hunger—but I wouldn't trade what I'd endured for anything. For now I understood my strength. Eros was right, I had prevailed, and I had that now.

I leaned into the wind, its wild breath in my hair.

I had that now.

Power.

A power that was always mine to claim.

As I walked back toward Eros, she appeared small beneath the oak tree, though she was not small and well I knew it. She was formidable, radiant, my beloved. I saw now that in the weeks of my trials, she'd gone through inner trials of her own. We could forge something new together, perhaps, rooted in our new selves. She stood as I approached. Waited for me with open palms and folded wings.

I reached her and smiled. "Yes."

"Yes?"

"To both your questions."

"Ah, Psyche! I'm so—"

"But I have a request."

"I'm listening."

"Can my mother come?"

"To Olympus? It's not usually—"

"For her daughter's wedding."

"I see." She tilted her head, thinking. "I suppose it can be arranged."

"Thank you."

She held my gaze. Opened her arms. I stepped into her embrace and there it was again, her scent, her welcome, her desire and my own. "Beloved," she murmured. I felt her hands in my hair, like the first time she'd ever touched me, when everything began. Desire rose in me, unbidden.

"Now I can tell you about the wedding gift."

"Which is?"

"Zeus has agreed for you to become immortal."

I raised my face to hers. Pressed into her chest to steady myself. "That cannot be."

"It is. The cup is ready. Drink from it and we can stay together forever. We'll live in Olympus, in full light of the sun."

"What about your palace?"

"Psyche. It's our palace. It was never mine, always ours."

"You made it."

"For us. For you."

"Our palace," I said, savoring the words, wondering what it would mean to let them sink into my tongue. My mind raced. Could this moment be real? What is real? What is the world? Immortality, a realm I couldn't fathom. To join it seemed a transgression, another one to overlay the various transgressions that had already woven through my life's loom. To live among the gods, on Mount Olympus, might for many human beings sound like a dream, but I could see, along its edges, the flapping hints of a nightmare. The palace where I'd come to love Eros seemed, from this perspective, even more of a refuge. "So can we live there?"

"Sometimes. Olympus will also be our home."

"I've never heard of such a thing happening."

"It's rare. You're one of the few mortals to ever be invited to live there. Heracles was, but he was a son of Zeus."

"I suppose I should be honored."

"Yes."

"But it sounds . . ." Thoughts pulsed in me, more than I could put into words. Some kind of discomfort deep below the surface, as if my mind were a river running between shores where it didn't belong. ". . . alarming."

"It won't be." She grinned. "Not always."

"Are you telling me the whole truth?"

Eros laughed. "All right, perhaps not. Olympus is—well. A complex place. As is earth. But we'll be respected, I promise. I won't let it be any other way."

I wondered whether she had the power to uphold that promise. She was, after all, one deity among many, and she'd just been telling me of her own struggles to be safe among the gods. If her powers had limits when it came to protecting herself, where would that leave me as her plucked-from-the-mortal-world bride? But still. She was divine. And perhaps more importantly, she seemed determined to defend me at any cost. I studied her face. Resolute. Bathed in love. A face I'd learned through touch. "I have a lot of questions."

"Really? Tell me."

"I've heard your mother has many lovers, even though she's married."

She raised an eyebrow. "And?"

"Is that how you'll be, too?"

"Does it matter?"

I thought hard, deeply. "I don't know. You are Eros, goddess of desire. It may be in your nature to roam."

Eros smiled.

"And yet I'd hate it if you did so and expected me to stay chained. Men do that, but I don't want to be that kind of wife."

"Listen to you! So bold!"

"I am serious. To be honest, I'm not sure I want to be a wife at all—I want to be with you, that's not what I mean. I'm talking about the word itself."

"The word 'wife'?"

"And 'husband.'"

"Yes. I understand," said Eros. "They're too small, I can't fit all of myself into either of them."

"Neither can I."

We stared at each other, gilded in sun, alive with ideas.

"So do we make new words?" I said. "Or make the old ones larger to fit more of ourselves?"

"Which do you want to do?"

"Neither. Both. You told me once that words have power, that I can make them belong to me. I want to do that, to be wife and not-wife, husband and not-husband, to take the word 'marriage' and stretch it in ways that would shock the old gossips and the bards."

She was gazing at me with a kind of awe. "We'll do all that and more."

"Can we?"

"We can and we will. I can't wait to see what we invent along the way. Tell me more about this matter of roaming. What you want. Other women?" A trace of worry in her voice. "Or . . . men?"

"I didn't say that. What I want is—" I searched for the right word. "Fairness."

She stared as if seeing something in my face for the first time.

"And who knows? Eternity is long."

Eros laughed. "Hmm. That it is." She cocked her head, held my gaze. "All right. So either we both roam or we're both in chains. Is that the idea, my love?"

"Something like that." I felt a thrill, a swell of pride, at having asked for my own terms to my life. As if my life were mine to weave. An open loom. The stool before it mine alone.

"Fine then. I understand. We can have that kind of marriage."

"Can it still be called a marriage?"

"If we say so. They're our words now."

A glow inside, deep in my bones.

"So, beloved. What else?"

"The child. We'll raise her to be free?"

"A girl?"

"I don't know. It's what springs to my tongue, I don't know why. Her, or him, or whoever emerges. Will have powers. Yes? Will be a deity?"

"It seems likely."

"So she'll be free."

"To the extent that any god is free."

"Hmm." I thought of Persephone, trapped on her throne. "I want more for her than that."

"More!"

"I want her to be truly free. Not just her—all girls."

"You want big things."

"Always."

"I love that about you." She smiled again, with more radiance. "I want that too. We can dream it. We can hope it."

"We're going to do more than hope."

She was stroking me now, her hands leaving trails of fire along my skin. "Psyche, my Psyche, your mind is a wonder. How I've missed you."

I wanted to succumb to her, those hands, but there was more speaking to be done. "I mean it. I want our child to be free, and I plan to teach

her—or him, or—to cultivate good things wherever she goes." I thought
of the box I'd just thrown to the sea, the way it caught the light as it spun
over the waves. "Every woman's path is cursed as long as the laws are bent
on our diminishment. The laws of men, the laws of gods. They curse us,
and I want to break them all."

"I understand. Me too."

"Really?" This startled me, filled me with happiness. "Good. No more
Melias, ever again."

Eros placed her hand at the small of my back, where it brought solace,
but also woke a deep lust. "That was a horror. But alas, there will be many
Melias."

"I cannot bear that."

"The world churns on regardless of what can and can't be borne."

"But violence? It has to churn on?"

Her hand ran slowly along my back, poured light into my being.
"Have you seen the world?"

"Pteron."

"Oh, when you call me that—"

I stilled her arm, gently. I wanted her, but there would be time enough
for that, years of it, centuries. "Promise me you'll try."

"Try what?"

"To keep fighting. To protect me—"

"Of course. I'll always—"

"And other mortal girls, and people like me, people like us."

It was still nebulous, what I was asking for, on whose behalf I was
asking. It would be centuries before I fully grasped what I was seeking,
what I already sensed in that moment would be my purpose in the godly
sphere. I would be the guardian of the soul. The truths of souls. Like
mine. Like yours. I wanted to reshape the world in hopes there would
be a future time, a future place, in which you could exist, you to whom
I've been telling this story, my kin, my faraway descendant, my beloved

instigator of songs and pleasures and truths not yet named or welcomed by the laws of god and man. You who refract the sunlight in new ways through the secret prisms of your joy. You who might see a flash of yourself in my story with Eros. You who were born perfect yet outside the rules of whatever temples oversee your times. You whose desire shatters the cage. You, born hundreds or thousands of years from this moment by the sea. You who might have loved me if you could have known me, whom I already love even though I cannot see your face, for I feel your beauty in the timeless, boundless dark. You are exquisite, completely yourself. Beloved. Friend. Utterly free. I dream that your freedom might inscribe new triumphs into the souls of those who came hundreds or thousands of years before, in a glowing slash through time, because we, the old ones, envisioned the dance of you, willed it to flourish, fevered with passion for a world where you could be. I wonder whether I'm part of the cycle in ways I'll never know. Whether hundreds or even thousands of years before my birth, a young woman dreamed of my existence, longed for me to come into the world. Whether that longing helped give rise to me and to my winding, transgressive human path. And whether that longing is twined into mine, now, for you. I want so much to believe you will exist. I want so much to reach across time for you. I will do it: I'll never stop trying.

Eros had been silent a long time. Finally, she said, "Yes, my love. I will fight for that. I promise you."

I nodded. There was more I longed to say but it stayed in me, shining, embers beyond speech.

"It's my fight too," Eros said.

I reached for her face. Cradled it in my palm. "Yes, my Pteron. It is."

She closed her eyes and leaned into my touch. Her face broke open—with pleasure? pain? something else?—and it was a new gift, to watch it happen in the light. When she opened her eyes, a tear slunk down her cheek. She blinked, took my other hand. There was so much more we each could say, but there would be time enough, all the time in the cosmos. "Shall we? Your cup awaits, and wedding flowers, and a whole pantheon of divine congratulations—a party in the heavens, all for you."

I squeezed her hand. "Except that it's for *you*."

"For us. From this moment forward, always Us."

I smiled. "All right then. For us." It had been broken, the Us we'd been before. We would never return to it again. Instead, we were reassembling the pieces in a new way, like a mosaic made from a shattered plate, or if we were fortunate, like shattered water, which returns to a unity as seamless as before. New paths. New shapes. Stronger, perhaps, for having made wounds in each other, begun to heal. Stronger for having touched the wounds, seen ourselves, let ourselves be seen, said yes again. Perhaps. I didn't know. All I knew was that before me lay a road full of the unknown, chosen by me, not thrust on me by Oracles or fathers or husbands in the dark, but decided on with eyes wide open on a sun-drenched afternoon. I would go to Olympus. I'd affirm my marriage and become immortal. I'd have my baby and devote myself to what I wanted to create for the world. I choose you, I thought, looking right at Eros. I choose myself. I choose passion and also truth. I'd heard so many stories about Olympus, how time stretched there and compressed, how a moment could open endlessly, just as it can in earthly life. What would it be like, to meet the gods? To look into their eyes, to take their hands if they outstretched them, to join them in their world? To meet so many of them in one day—I felt dizzied, yet ready, standing here, feet rooted on the earth. Whoever I was destined to become by the end of this day, and the ones that followed, I wanted to experience fully who I was in the now, in this hard-earned and wide-flung now, to tattoo this moment into me so I could carry it into whatever came next.

"Just one more moment alone," I said. "Before we go."

I leaned into her; she embraced me; her wings fanned and reached and enfolded us both. In the feathered nest of her, I was home. Later the legends would tell it that after our wedding, after I drank from Zeus's cup, after other cups had been raised in our honor and the heavens recognized me as a bride, after the trumpets and dance and wine and gifts and song, we would have everything. But what I will tell you is that everything was already there, inside us, between us, around us in that last moment before we stepped into the clamor of the gods. For an infinite moment we held each other and the world held still. Together we stood. Together we breathed. Together we dreamed of futures aching to be born.

ACKNOWLEDGMENTS

I'm grateful to so many who helped this book come into the world.

Vast thanks to the phenomenal, brilliant Michelle Brower and the whole fabulous team at Trellis Literary Management, including Natalie Edwards, Allison Malecha, and Khalid McCalla, for believing in this book and working miracles. Thanks also to incomparable editor Michelle Herrera Mulligan for taking the leap, for championing this book, and for stellar and insightful contributions that helped it become its best self. Thanks also to everyone at Atria Books and Simon & Schuster, including Wendy Sheanin, Lisa Sciambra, Hannah Moushabeck, and Erica Siudzinski for the hard work and incredibly warm welcome.

I'm thankful to my colleagues and extraordinary graduate students at San Francisco State University for providing a steady fount of intellectual and creative exchange. Thanks also to Baldwin Center for the Arts, the Center for Oral History Research at Columbia University, and the Emerson Collective for the kind support of a Baldwin-Emerson Fellowship.

I'm indebted to many scholars, from classicists and historians to queer and trans theorists, whose work was indispensable to my extensive research. In the latter category, I'm especially grateful for Jack Halberstam's *Female Masculinity* and Jen Manion's *Female Husbands: A Trans History*, each of which blazed intellectual trails with regard to transmasculine, nonbinary, genderqueer, and butch ways of being and knowing throughout time.

I'm unendingly grateful to my circles of community, from literary friendships and chosen family to all the beautiful amalgamations in between—all the people who provided insightful feedback on early drafts; engaged in essential, thought-expanding conversation; offered me their loving company, a harbor in life's storms; or otherwise shared their support and immense generosity. Thanks especially to Lupita Aquino, Alex Cohen, Angie Cruz, Aya de Leon, Marcelo de León, Ceci De Robertis, Jaquira Díaz, Cristina García, Lars Horn, Chip Livingston, Shanna Lo Presti, Madeline Miller, Beth Nguyen, Achy Obejas, Lilliam Rivera, Margaret Benson Thompson, Jacqueline Woodson, and many more. A particular thanks to Blue Sirius, for deep wells of inspiration.

Thank you to my relatives in the U.S., Uruguay, Argentina, Italy, and France, scattered by migration yet always connected by love and by the stories our lives have woven.

Infinite thanks to my children, Rafael and Luciana, who inspire me and light up my soul every single day, and who fuel me to keep working for a brighter future for their whole generation and those to come.

To all people who contribute—in ways great and small—to the huge, crucial, utterly unfinished project of creating a world where all are safe and free, thank you. I see you, I'm with you, let's keep going no matter what. To those who form part of queer and trans communities: thank you. How wondrous that you're here. That we're here. This book is yours as well.

Gracias a todas, a todos, a todes.

Amor y ánimo siempre.

ABOUT THE AUTHOR

A writer of Uruguayan origins, **Caro De Robertis** is the author of *The President and the Frog*, a finalist for the PEN/Faulkner Award and the PEN/Jean Stein Book Award; *Cantoras*, winner of a Stonewall Book Award and a Reading Women Award, a finalist for the Kirkus Prize and a Lambda Literary Award, and a New York Times Editors' Choice; *The Gods of Tango*, winner of a Stonewall Book Award; *Perla*; and the international bestseller *The Invisible Mountain*, which received Italy's Rhegium Julii Prize.

De Robertis's books have been translated into seventeen languages and the author has received numerous other honors, including a fellowship from the National Endowment for the Arts. In 2023, they became the first openly nonbinary person to receive the John Dos Passos Prize for Literature. In 2022, they were an inaugural Baldwin-Emerson Fellow, gathering oral histories of queer and trans BIPOC elders in collaboration with Baldwin for the Arts and the Center for Oral History at Columbia University. De Robertis is also an award-winning literary translator, and a professor at San Francisco State University. They live in Oakland, California, with their two children.